TAKE-OUT

AND OTHER TALES OF
CULINARY
CRIME

TAKE-OUT

AND OTHER TALES OF CULINARY CRIME

ROB HART

Copyright © 2019 by Rob Hart
Cover and jacket design by 2Faced Design
Interior design and formatting by: E.M. Tippetts Book Design

ISBN 978-1-943818-42-6
eISBN: 978-1-947993-52-5

Library of Congress Control Number: 2018964753

First trade paperback edition January 2019 by Polis Books, LLC
221 River St., 9th Fl. #9070
Hoboken, NJ 07030

www.PolisBooks.com

POLIS BOOKS

Table of Contents

To my grandmother

"I've long believed that good food, good eating, is all about risk. Whether we're talking about unpasteurized Stilton, raw oysters, or working for organized crime associates, food, for me, has always been an adventure."

—Anthony Bourdain

INTRODUCTION

SOMEONE ELSE NOTICED before I did.

Over the course of several months, I wrote and published short stories involving a bagel maker, warring food trucks, and a restaurant scam. So a friend asked when my collection of food noir stories was coming out. At which point, I was working on a story about a bouncer at a pastry shop.

It's not surprising I'd fall into a theme with writing about food. I like to eat.

But it's more than that, too.

I was born and raised in New York City, which is a pretty good food town, and a place where people will spend hours arguing over where to find the best slice of pizza.

I was raised by a grandmother who demonstrated her love for her family every night around the dinner table, sharply at 6

1

p.m. She instilled that in me. When she passed away, I took over Christmas dinner. It's something I look forward to with a great deal of pride and nostalgia. And a bit of sadness, because my lasagna will never be as good as hers.

Also, my dad is a New York City firefighter, and if you know firefighters, you know they can cook. Eat dinner at a firehouse in New York and you'll count it among the best meals of your life, and not just for the camaraderie. I asked him, once, about why that was. He said it was because you never knew when you were having your last meal.

That, to my mind, speaks better than anything else could to the gravity of a good meal.

Food is the thing that binds all of us, across continents and cultures. No matter where you go, there are signature dishes and traditions of hospitality. Sharing a meal is as much about emotional sustenance as it is about the physical.

We build childhood memories around food.

We plan trips and events around eating.

Which makes food a fantastic storytelling device, especially within the confines of crime and noir fiction. They're intersections where passions collide. And not all of these stories are strictly fiction. Those warring food trucks? Inspired by a story in the *New York Times*. The bakery bouncer? I got the idea walking past the velvet rope at Big Gay Ice Cream in the East Village.

These stories represent five years of writing and, I say, with humility, some of my best work. Two of these stories were shortlisted for *Best American Mystery Stories*, and one made the final cut. Another was nominated for a Derringer Award. Still another, the first time I read it in public, was accepted for publication on the spot by a magazine editor.

I hope you'll indulge me: while many of these stories are very specifically about food, I did play a little fast and loose with the rules. Some of these stories take place in restaurants or bars—sharing drinks counts as a tradition of hospitality—or the food element is secondary to the narrative. One story is about hunger. In another story, the food reference is a punch line.

Many of these stories have been changed a bit from their original publication, but I remain deeply indebted to the editors who first put them out. Two of these stories are brand new. One of them is my favorite thing I've written, but I'm not going to say which.

And for the record, the best pizza in New York is at Denino's on Staten Island.

HOW TO MAKE THE PERFECT NEW YORK BAGEL

THE METAL BOWL is cold when I remove it from the back of the refrigerator. Plastic wrap clings to the surface like skin. It peels back easy, the dough cratered underneath. There's a subtle sour smell coming off it. I put the bowl on the counter, give it a tap on the side. It wobbles but doesn't fall.

A perfectly fermented sponge is the best part of this process. Nailing that first step, it never loses its shine.

I scrape the sticky wad of starter dough into the industrial mixer, measure out the rest of the ingredients: high-gluten flour, yeast, salt, didactic malt. Not even eyeballing it because I can feel the exact moment the correct amount has sifted out of the old plastic jug my father used for this step.

The bell over the door of the shop dings. I set the mixer to its lowest speed, the whirring sound of the motor bouncing off the green tile in the small kitchen. A voice simmered for years in the restaurants of South Brooklyn calls out, "Mikey Bagels. What's on the menu today?"

"Same as always," I call back. "Plain or salt."

Paulie shifts his not-insignificant girth onto the worn stool in the corner, nestled between the dead ATM machine and the cooler that's barely keeping bottles of soda and water at room temperature. He says, "You know what I like? Those everything bagels. When are you going to start making me some everything bagels?"

"I make the bagels my father made. Plain and salt. Putting anything but salt on a bagel, it's like a sin. How many times do we have to do this?"

Paulie pulls a mostly-smoked cigar from his pocket, jams the chewed end in his mouth. "Mikey Bagels, Mikey Bagels. What am I going to do with you?"

"You're the only person calls me that, you know?"

"What, Mikey Bagels? Your name is Mikey, you make the bagels. What else am I supposed to call you?"

"It's a funny nickname for a Polish Jew, isn't it?"

Paulie laughs, the cigar nearly tumbling from his mouth. He holds it between two stubby fingers and points it at me. "We're practically blood. How much do the Italians and the Jews have in common, huh?" He ticks off on his fingers. "Secret family recipes. Devotion to our religion. Guilt related to our religion. Rhetorical questions. I could go on."

"You're funny, Paulie."

"How long until we get some bagels, huh?"

"Got some almost ready."

Paulie nods, fans open a copy of the *New York Post* and disappears behind the thin pages of newsprint. I head to the back, stop the mixer, put the dough onto a tray, and cover it with plastic wrap so it can proof. Then I pull the finished batch of bagels from the oven.

Warm and crisp and deep, deep brown. True, hand-rolled bagels that make your jaw hurt to eat. Not those semi-raw pillows turned out by machines that pass for bagels today.

The hot bagels go on the rack to cool and I cut a long strip of dough to roll into a new batch. It's dark in the kitchen, most of the bulbs blown, but it's not worth the money to replace them: I could do this with my eyes closed and half-asleep.

Wrap the dough around my fist, tear it off with my thumb, seal it on the cutting board by rolling it with the heel of my palm. My father's voice whispers in my ears, walking me through the process, even now.

The bones in my hand creak against each other, the pain jolting through my thumb and up my arm like mild electric shocks. Carpal tunnel or arthritis or the march of time. Whatever it is, not pleasant.

But it's all about the hand roll. You don't roll a bagel by hand, it's not a bagel.

After, each one goes on a cutting board dusted with a yellow field of semolina. I pause occasionally to look at them and that makes the pain worth it. Nobody makes them like this anymore. Nobody.

Paulie shuffles into the kitchen and pulls a salt bagel from the rack, passes it from hand to hand because it's still too hot to handle. He asks, "Where's my schmeer?"

"Go schmeer yourself, Paulie."

"You lazy bastard..."

He disappears to the front. I make it to the final bagel when Paulie appears behind me.

"Don't be mad," he says.

"Paulie, how could I ever be mad at you?"

"I wasn't spying, just…" He holds a piece of paper in his hand, staring down at it like it's in a foreign language he's trying to decipher.

The water in the dented kettle is at a boil. I turn the knob down a little. "I wasn't trying to hide it."

"What does this mean?"

"It means someone took a truck, filled it with money, and backed it up to the house of the guy who owns this building."

"You've been here forever. Aren't you, like, grandfathered in or something?"

"Not if I can't pay my rent. All they have to do is triple it. Which they did. I can barely afford it where it is right now."

"You make the best bagels on the Lower East Side. Probably in the whole damn city anymore." Paulie shakes his head, looks at the floor like he lost a member of his family.

I dunk a rolled bagel into the water, let it disappear halfway below the surface before dropping it the rest of the way. It bounces around, buoyed by the roiling water. I count off in my head, thirty seconds on each side.

"There's got to be a way to fight this," Paulie says. "Talk to the community board or something. Get the people involved, you know what I mean?"

I pluck bagels from the boiling water with a wired ladle, fashioned by my father from who knows what, dip them into the pot of ice water next to the stove. "You know how many bagels I throw out at the end of the night now? The community would rather go to Starbucks. Get a pastry and a fancy coffee."

"There's gotta be a way. There's gotta. We can't abide this, Mikey. What about those two knuckleheads who come in here sometimes? Billy and Richie. Word is they're hooked up. Maybe

8

they can go knock some heads in..."

I transfer the last of the bagels, fish them out of the ice water one by one, and place them facedown in a tray full of sea salt. When they're all in place, I turn to Paulie. "Whose head are they going to knock in? It's a bank doing this. Who do you fight? Go find the guy who runs the bank. Where does he live? Some castle in the sky? Who even knows. I'm seventy-three years old and my hands hurt."

Paulie's face goes dark. "You remember how we met?"

"Of course I remember."

"After what you pulled you should have been dead and gone. But you were a fighter, and we respected that. The balls you had." He shakes his head. "What happened, huh?"

He doesn't wait for me to answer, just turns and leaves. The bell dings over the doorway, the sound of it echoing off the kitchen tile.

I pull the bagel boards from where they're submerged in the sink—more artifacts of my father, redwood planks a little shorter than a baseball bat, with a burlap runner to keep the bagels from sticking. Soaked until saturated so they won't catch fire in the oven. I place the bagels on the burlap, spacing them an inch apart.

The whole time, I'm glancing over my shoulder, at the letter that Paulie left on the counter. The letter had been folded in threes to fit in the envelope, and the two ends stick into the air like an accusation.

THE FIRST TIME the door dinged and Paulie came through it, he was forty years younger and a hundred pounds lighter and wearing a suit, the crease in his pants sharp as a razor. This is back when the made men wore proper suits, not track suits.

Back when my hands didn't hurt so bad.

He was with another guy, the two of them preening like they owned the block. Which they didn't. Their boss did.

I was behind the counter, placing bagels behind the display case. Paulie came up and put his hand on the top of it, the thick gold ring on his pinkie clicking against the glass. The two of them radiating menace like heat, trying to hide it behind the veneer of their smiles.

Paulie said, "A dozen of your finest, if you will." As I piled them into a paper bag, he asked, "What's your name?"

"Michał."

"Your pops used to own this place?"

"Died last month. It's mine now."

"I'm sorry for your loss." He paused, letting the platitude sink in. "You like it? Keeping up the family business?"

"I like it fine, sure."

Paulie nodded, clicking his ring against the glass, looking around the place like he was interested in the décor. I counted out a dozen bagels, tossed in a thirteenth, and placed the bag down like it might burst. Paulie slid a few bucks across the counter and accepted his change.

"Thanks, Mikey," he said. "Mikey Bagels, I think I'll call you. What do you think about that?"

I shrugged. "It's not my name, but it's fine."

Paulie pursed his lips, handed the bag to his partner. "Look, something else. Does the name Manny Calabrese mean anything to you?" He didn't wait for me to answer. "Manny, he's the guy runs things around here, you know what I mean? He's a good guy to be friends with. You know how it is. Dangerous neighborhood. But if Manny is looking out for you, no one's going to touch you."

"Are you shaking me down?"

Paulie's face split into a smile that showed off every single one of his teeth, put his hands in the air. "Nothing like that, no. Think of it like a partnership. We work together."

The other guy was rooting around in the bag of bagels. Paulie reached over and pulled one out, took a bite. His eyes went wide. With a stuffed mouth he said, "This is great. Perfect New York fuckin' bagel right here."

"Same recipe my father used. He was a founding member of the Bagel Bakers Local 338."

Paulie huffed. "What's that?"

"The bagel-makers, when they emigrated here from Poland, they founded the union. Used to be you couldn't make bagels if you weren't a member. The meetings were held in Yiddish so no one would know the recipes. You know what they used to do when they found out someone was making bagels who wasn't a member?"

Paulie swallowed the portion in his mouth, shrugged.

"Same thing you guys are thinking of doing to me if I don't get in on your little protection racket."

The two of them froze, like they'd never heard a threat in their life. And I'd never made one, either. My heart was racing so fast I was worried I'd pass out. Then Paulie said, "Sounds like quite the racket they had there. Quite the racket. But I never heard of this union. What happened to it?"

"Bagels get rolled by machine now. Nothing is sacred."

"So they're not around anymore. That's a good thing to know." Paulie shook his head. "Mikey Bagels, Mikey Bagels. I like you. You seem like a smart guy. I'll tell you what. I'm going to tell Manny Calabrese you were too busy to talk, but that you seemed like a friendly guy and I wasn't worried. So I'll come back in a few days and we'll talk again. Get this all straightened out. Give you a little time to consider...how things could go."

He raised his hand up like he was offering a handshake, then turned it into a fist, brought it down hard, the pinkie ring smacking against the glass, spider-webbing it. He used his elbow to finish the job, sending shards of glass to rain down on the fresh bagels, and I was more worried about them than the case.

Paulie brushed off his elbow, said, "I know you'll make the right call here."

The two of them stepped to the door. I felt a surge of fear like bile coming up my throat, choked it down. I called after them, "I'm not afraid of you or your boss." The door closed behind them and I raised my voice, hoping they would hear. "So do what you have to and I'm not going anywhere."

I stood there a long time after they left.

TWO DOZEN BAGELS go in the trash at the end of the day. They sound like rocks hitting the bottom of the can. The fatal flaw of authentic bagels: in a few hours they turn into concrete. The homeless shelter around the corner won't even take them.

I prep some more sponges to go into the refrigerator and proof overnight, dumping the ingredients into metal bowls, mixing them with my fingers until they hit the right consistency. A little sticky, a little tacky. I cover the bowls in plastic wrap and place them in the back, where the cool air circulates better, wipe down the kitchen, the semolina and high-gluten flour disappearing into a wet dishrag.

Once the stainless steel sparkles, I turn off the lights and stand in the dark. Try to remember the first job my father gave me. Official Bagel Inspector, I think he called it. I would stand on my tiptoes, peering over the lip of the table, watching my father roll the bagels with thick-muscled hands and place them on the cutting board.

The memory is there, just beyond the reach of my fingertips. The way my father smelled, the heat in the air, the line of people wrapped around the block.

It teeters on the horizon, but then it slips over and it's gone.

I pull down the gate of the store and it rumbles like thunder crashes. I twist and clamp the heavy padlock. Look up at the sign, the red paint in the cursive script cracked and faded to a dingy pink.

Sal's Bagels.

Sal, shortened from Salomon, because in America they like names that are short and not so obviously Jewish, my father said.

I step into the stairwell next door, to climb up to my apartment above the store. Something else that'll disappear along with the business. Halfway up, I stop and decide I'm too anxious. I walk outside, make a left, and walk through the neighborhood I don't recognize anymore. Something to make me tired, but also, something else to be depressed about.

Tommy the butcher, he used to be on the corner, the front window of his store crammed with hanging tubes of maroon cured meat. It's a bank now. I pass the vegetarian bistro that used to be a hardware store. Every morning they would pull shelves onto the sidewalk. This is back when you could trust people to pick up a coil of wire or some screws and then come inside to pay.

Some of the bars have the same name, but it's only nostalgic if you don't know the original owners, all of whom are long gone. When I went to those bars, you would go in and ask for a beer, that's it, and if you asked for anything else, you were asked to leave. Now college students huddle outside, smoking cigarettes, looking at this place like it was a playground or an amusement park.

13

The city looks different. Smells different. Cleaner, like it's been scrubbed with antiseptic. The things I remember are gone, and I feel an empty space in my chest. Something vital is missing and I can't breathe as well without it.

I stop outside the bakery around the corner. The lights are still on, glowing yellow through the huge front windows. There's a long line of people at the marble counter, and a sign in the window advertising jalapeo bagels and sweet potato bagels and chocolate bagels.

Nothing is sacred.

The cold wind bites my neck. I bunch up my shoulders and shiver, head back to my apartment. Climb the stairs, drop my keys on the kitchen table, and strip off my work shirt. I pull a bottle of vodka from the top of the refrigerator. The light on the answering machine is blinking red. I press it and sit.

"Mister Joselewicz. This is Mister Chapin. We spoke last week. I tried to call you at the store today but nobody answered and I couldn't leave a message and…well, I was hoping to stop by tomorrow so we can talk about the future of the building. I'll come by around opening." A pause. "Be well, and I look forward to meeting with you."

I sit at the kitchen table and stare at the machine. I dig the fingertips of my left hand into the soft web of skin between the fingers on my right hand, try to rub away the pain. I consider the vodka but don't open it. There's no real solution inside the bottle.

My head dips forward, yanked at by the gravity of sleep. My thoughts drift to Paulie, what he said about busting heads. Like it could be that easy. That was a different time. Different time, different values.

WHEN PAULIE RETURNED, he didn't return alone. The bell above the door dinged and I looked up from the remains of the display case. Only the metal trim was left—I had cleared out all the glass but hadn't gotten around to replacing it.

I didn't need to be introduced to know it was Manny Calabrese. He wasn't a huge guy. A little stocky, and not tall, but he seemed to tower over everyone around him.

He stood at the counter for a moment, sizing me up, before saying, "I heard you make a good bagel. I would like to try one, please."

I nodded, pulled out a plain one, asked, "Schmeer?"

Manny nodded. "Of course."

I placed my palm on the top, cutting through the bagel sideways, crumbs flying across the cutting board. Manny said, "I knew your father. Do you know that?"

"He never mentioned you."

"We weren't close. Your father never played ball. I gave him a pass because of that damn union. Those Yids were some tough bastards. But they don't count for much no more, and I'm tired of looking at this store, thinking about all the wasted income."

I put the bagel on the counter, cream cheese curling out of the sides. Manny picked it up, regarded it like a piece of art, and took a bite. He nodded, chewed, swallowed. "You make them like your dad made them. That's good. If you want to keep making them, it's going to be a hundred a week. That's less than anyone else in this neighborhood, and only because you make good bagels. I think that's more than generous, don't you?"

The way he said it, like it was an act of charity, rage blossomed in my chest like a red-petaled flower. I told him, "A hundred a week is the difference between me eating and not eating. No deal. I'll give you a dozen free bagels a week. Best I can do."

Manny took another bite, chewed it carefully, like there might be something sharp hidden inside. When he finished, he turned his head without taking his eyes off me. "Paulie, Rick. Go in the back, look for the most expensive thing you can find. Smash it up."

The two men smiled at each other, clenched their fists, made their way around to the side of the counter. Invading the space that only me, my mother, my father, and the health inspector had been allowed into. No one else, ever.

I took a step back. Manny said, "Normally, I'd have them break one of your hands, but then you can't make the bagels. I'm not a bad guy, is what I want you to know."

Rick was first, not concerned with me, looking toward the back, his eyes searching for something to destroy. Sitting on the counter was a bagel board. Without thinking, I picked it up and swung it with both hands, caught him across the jaw, sent him sprawling to the floor, taking down the coffee maker with him. It shattered on the white tile floor.

Paulie stopped. He and Manny looked at Rick, groaning, holding his jaw. I held the board up, pointed it in Paulie's face, but I was looking at Manny. "My father escaped the *Geheime Staatspolizei* to come to this country. He fought to make a better life for us. I will not let you take what he built."

Manny's lip curled into the facsimile of a smile. He said, "Okay, kid, if that's how it's going to be." He could have been furious or he could have been amused and I wouldn't have known the difference. He didn't take his eyes off me but he turned slightly, to speak to his men. "Paulie. Rick. Out."

Rick used the counter to pull himself to his feet. There was blood smeared across his chin and his jaw looked distended. Paulie got underneath him and led him through the door. Manny nodded. "If that's the way it's going to be."

He left, too, a dark cloud in his wake.

For the next four days, every time I left the shop, I expected to catch something heavy across the back of my skull. Every time the bell over the door dinged, my heart paused and waited. There wasn't much to do. The cops were in Manny's pocket. I could have gotten a gun, but that was a temporary solution.

When Rick and Paulie came back on the fifth day, I was sure that was it. Rick's jaw was still red and swollen, and there was a thin piece of dull metal wrapped around the back of his head to hold it in place.

Rick looked at Paulie, who lingered by the beverage cooler.

Paulie said, "Manny told you to do it, so do it."

Rick walked to the counter with a look in his eyes that could have melted glass. My hand went to the bagel board sitting next to the register. It wasn't a fair fight but that didn't mean I would go down easy. He mumbled something through his wired jaw.

I asked, "What?"

He sighed. Spoke louder, each word carefully enunciated through clamped teeth. "The bagels, please."

THE FIRST BATCH should have been in the oven already but I got in late after stopping at the grocery store to pick up plastic containers of poppy seeds, sesame seeds, roasted minced garlic.

I pour equal parts from the three containers in a sheet pan, follow it with some sea salt. I pluck the bagels from their ice bath, let them drip dry, and place them facedown in the mix, then facedown on the bagel boards. I ignore the pain reverberating through my hands. As I put them in the oven, I feel like I'm doing something wrong, looking over my shoulder, expecting my father to scold me. The kitchen fills with the thick smell of toasted seeds.

The bell dings as I put the first batch onto the cooling rack. I head to the front, hoping to see Paulie. Instead I find Chapin, the kid from the bank, his hair slicked and parted, his fingernails buffed and shined. Wearing a suit with razor-sharp creases. He smiles a plastic doll smile but doesn't offer me his hand.

"Mister Joselewicz," he says.

I watch his hands clasped in front of him, tell him, "You know, no one ever gets that right. My last name. You must have been practicing."

The smile on Chapin's face dims a little. "So, have you thought about what we discussed?"

I place my hands on the counter and my finger brushes against the bagel board. The one I stopped using to make bagels after it got blood on it. I keep it next to the register, as a reminder or a memento or because I can't bear to part with something my father made, I don't know.

The door chimes again. Paulie lumbers in, says, "Mikey Bagels, what have you got for me today?"

"Check the back."

Paulie looks Chapin up and down, then heads into the kitchen. Chapin opens his mouth to speak but is drowned out as Paulie hoots and hollers. He comes out of the kitchen holding up one of the bagels. "You made me my everything!"

I shrug. "You're a good friend, Paulie. I just wanted to say thanks before this son of a bitch shuts me down."

Paulie says, "This the prick from the bank?"

Chapin says, "Sir, I..."

Paulie puts a stubby finger in his face. "No, shut up. You're a prick. This guy has been in business since before you were a cell in your dad's balls. And you think you can come in here and take him out. Bullshit? This guy, his family, they've dealt with tougher than

18

little shits like you."

"But..."

"But nothing. You ought to be ashamed of yourself. Destroying neighborhoods. Destroying history. I got nothing but respect for this man." Paulie puts his arm around me, pulls me close. As his fingers clasp my shoulder, I feel a rush of warmth. The pain in my hands disappears. Paulie's voice rises, face reddens. "You know how me and this man met?"

Exasperated, like he's talking to a child, Chapin asks, "How?"

"Like this." Paulie takes the bagel board and swings it, smacking Chapin across the jaw.

Chapin collapses into a pile on the ground, trying to yell, the sound coming out garbled and thick. He grips his face and blood seeps out between his fingers. He stumbles toward the door and bangs into it before sliding out.

I know I shouldn't, but I laugh. Then Paulie laughs. And then the two of us are bent over, holding each other up, laughing into each other shoulders.

When we're calm enough that we can breathe, I tell him, "You know this can't end well for us, right?"

"I still know a few of the bulls in this neighborhood. Anyway, we're old men now. What can they do that someone else hasn't already tried?" Paulie takes a bite of his bagel. Through a wad of chewed dough he says, "This is a damn good bagel. Look at you, mister traditional, changing things up."

"Maybe I'll get a new sign, too. What about that?"

Paulie swallows. "That ain't such a bad idea. The thing needs a little touching up."

"What do you think about Michał's Bagels?"

"You know it should be Mikey Bagels, right?" He laughs. "It's fine, it's your business. But I thought you were ready to close up yesterday?"

I pat Paulie on his shoulder, step into the kitchen, pull one of the everything bagels off the rack. I join Paulie back out front, take a bite, and the bagel isn't bad. Maybe even a little nice to try something new.

FOODIES

THE KNOCK AT the side door reveals a young couple. They stand in the white glow of the streetlights, shuffling in their shiny shoes, gazing at the sidewalk. Standing apart, as if to hide from each other, their faces draped in shadow.

"The password," I say.

The boy mumbles something at me and I tell him to speak louder.

"Red dragon," he says.

I open the door all the way and they dive past me, the boy's shoulder brushing against my chest. Seeking refuge from the expanse of the street, fidgeting like mice chased into a corner.

This is not uncommon. Everyone has a line. For most people, that line is the back door of my restaurant, and it takes courage to cross.

FOODIES

The door safely closed, the couple is suddenly an inch shorter. Their shoulders were that tense. I get a better look at them in the soft amber light.

The boy is blond and squarely handsome, freshly shaved. He looks like the type who mentions the name of his college within moment of meeting new people. The girl is brunette, hair-straightened. Pretty in a way that would fade into the background of a pleasant group photo.

They're dressed neatly. Collars and buttons and smooth fabrics. Comfortable in this kind of clothing. They're not married, but from the way his outstretched hand hovers near her, he's considering it.

This dance happens three or four times a night in the dim, quiet storage room in the back of my restaurant. Hidden from the cacophony of the front, where scrubbed couples share complicated plates of charcuterie, aged from the meat of pig and cow and lamb and duck.

What happens back here is a more exclusive experience, advertised only by word of mouth. Much of that, I imagine, delivered in the form of hushed, tentative whispers.

New York's restaurant scene is surmountable only to the smartest, the most talented, the most willing. This is a city where a week's salary will buy you a meal at Per Se and a handful of crumbled bills will buy you a meal at a filthy stall in Chinatown, and you'd be hard-pressed to pick a favorite between the two.

To sustain, to thrive, you need something to set you apart.

There are four options, as I see them.

One, you can appeal to the base human desire for sugar, salt, and fat. Wrap it in a veneer of nostalgia and call it "comfort" or "rustic."

Two, you can try molecular gastronomy. Invest in an anti-griddle and immersion circulators and maltodextrin. Embrace the

22

science.

Three, you can come up with a stunt concept. Like burritos, but the burrito wraps are made of bacon. People line up three blocks deep for that sort of nonsense.

The fourth option, the one that I've chosen, is to appeal to that demographic that calls a meal a "journey" without a dash of sarcasm. The people whose Instagram accounts are an endless parade of carefully prepared, poorly-lit plates.

The couple before me, they hover, unsure of where to stand. As for their visit here tonight, I believe the girl to be the instigator. She's looking deeper into the restaurant, curious, while the boy is looking at the exit. This is verified when the girl says, "I heard we have to sign something?"

"Some things I don't believe should be put into writing," I tell her.

That established, I turn up my palm and smile. They can't see me smile because they still won't look at me. But the boy sees my hand. He pulls a wad of bills out of his back pocket and places it on the flat plain of my fingers. The wad is folded over once and secured with a purple rubber band. I flip through and find it's all there. Without another word I move through the narrow hallway toward the black door in the back. They follow.

When they get this far, they always follow.

From the shelf next to the black door I take a small plastic bin, which, normally I would use to store clean silverware. I hold it toward them and say, "We do not allow phones inside the dining room."

They hesitate.

"They will be kept safely and returned to you immediately after dinner," I say. "While we encourage and expect you to share this experience with your more adventurous friends, I'm afraid it's a social media free zone."

"Aren't you afraid of the wrong people finding out?" the girl asks, her voice growing more confident. "Like, we could just tell anyone. We could tell the cops."

"You understand what you are here for tonight, yes?"

The girl nods.

"And you understand the implication of that, yes?"

The girl nods again. Slower this time.

"Then no, I am not worried."

There's just enough of an edge to the statement that they acquiesce, the boy pulling a shiny smartphone from his pocket and placing it carefully on the bottom of the bin. The girl takes a battered flip phone from her purse and tosses it on top. The boy winces. I place the bin back on the shelf, up high and out of reach, to give the illusion of safety.

I open the door to a small wood-paneled room, barely bigger than the one table and two seats in the middle. Atop the table is a skinny candle in a silver candlestick. Bach's cello suites play low on hidden speakers.

Points for ambiance.

On the white-clothed table are two plates. Each plate is set with a silver fork, a silver knife, a folded white cloth napkin, and an empty wineglass. Everything carefully buffed and set with gloves to prevent even the whiff of a fingerprint.

Piled atop each plate is a wrinkled nest of red cured meat, streaked with thick bolts of white fat. Next to the meat is an orange dollop of chipotle mayo, two slices of crusty bread, and three cornichons. The plate is wide and curved, the food arranged like a painting.

The couple lingers by the door. I stand aside, hold out my arm. Welcome them. Smile, even though they still won't look at me.

"Please," I say. "Be seated."

They settle into their seats and I produce a cork on a silver platter. The boy looks at me, unsure what to do, so I place it down and tilt out a taste of box wine poured into a bottle of 2003 Latour Bordeaux. He swirls it, takes a sip, and nods.

The drinks poured, the guests settled, they finally look up at me. Their eyes quivering.

"You are about to join a very elite club of diners," I tell them. "After this you will be different. Embrace it. Do not concern yourself with what society thinks. Society is behind the curve for people like us. You are pioneers."

The girl stares at the pile of red meat on her plate, her hands folded in her lap. She asks, "Who…?"

"Do you really want to know the answer to that?"

She shakes her head.

No one ever does.

And no one wants an audience for this. I bow, deeply, and take my exit.

Close the door and head back to the kitchen.

Pull the wad of bills out of my pocket and count it off.

Another successful transaction.

I check my watch. Figure on fifteen minutes. Wonder what I'll find. Some people vomit. Others sit there and leave the meat untouched. Some practically lick the plate clean. Only one person so far has asked for seconds.

Regardless of the outcome, all of them have a story to tell.

In this town, experience is currency. Changing a person, giving them a story, therein lies the secret the longevity. Everyone is desperate for an inside angle on this unknowable city. To appear as though they've mastered something that could never be tamed.

This is the sweet spot in which people like me can thrive. The people who are willing to embrace the risqué.

I pull the wad of bills out of my pocket and count it off. Then I pick up the phone, and place an order for another ten pounds of jamón ibérico.

It's expensive, at ninety dollars per pound. But you can sell it for a five hundred percent markup when you can trick yuppie foodies into believing they're eating human charcuterie.

Only the strong survive the astronomic rent of the Meatpacking District.

THE GAS CHAMBER

THE WHISTLE WENT off and Eddy fell in step with the single-file line marching into the dining hall. His stomach gnawed on itself. Between processing and a ferryboat running behind schedule, he missed breakfast.

As he passed the long row of empty cells, their occupants shuffling somewhere ahead of him, he reached out and drummed his fingers on the metal bars. Hunger, at least, was a problem with a solution.

The dining hall made him think of his high school cafeteria back in Utah. White paint peeling, thick columns holding up the ceiling. The whole thing like it was poured and chiseled from one giant slab of concrete.

Instead of long tables with benches like he expected, the place was filled with four-top tables, many of which were already taken by inmates, sitting in plastic chairs and hunched over metal

27

trays. The low murmur of hushed conversations and harsh metal clacking of silverware permeated the room.

There were three guards strolling the gaps between the tables, eyes swinging like searchlights. That was a little different from high school, too.

Eddy watched as the inmates accepted trays of food through a gap in the bars, from a counter that fronted the kitchen. He figured on something that only vaguely resembled food, flopped onto his plate with indifference, but when he caught sight of the menu board, he risked a brief smile.

Split Pea Soup
Roast Pork Shoulder
Mashed Potatoes
Stewed Corn
Bread & Coffee

Eddy accepted a tray of food and a lukewarm cup of black coffee from a hatchet-faced man behind the counter. The food looked better than any meal he'd had recently. He took it and wended through the dining hall, looking for an empty seat.

There weren't any in sight. Within seconds his heart was racing. A man standing alone in a place like this probably looked a little like a target. Every second he was on his feet, he was drawing attention to himself.

He came across a table with three men and an empty seat. He paused and thought about asking if he could sit, but didn't want that to be perceived as a sign of weakness. He pulled out the seat and sat, hoping he hadn't just made a mistake.

His skin was hot with anger and regret. This was his fault. He knew it was his fault. All he had to say was no. Instead, he said yes.

It was a mistake he'd repay for the next ten years.

The man directly across from him, his face a topographical map of scars, slate gray hair slicked flat to his skull, raised an eyebrow.

"Here we go," he said, his voice like a handful of gravel in a tin cup. "We needed a fourth man."

Eddy glanced at the other two men, faces down, shoveling food into their mouths. He looked at the man across from him. "For what?"

The man's eyes darted around the dining hall, focusing on the guards, who were all far enough away they couldn't hear. "If we're going to get the hell out of here. I'm Milton, by the way."

Milton jerked a thumb at the nervous-looking man to his left, with a shaved head and glasses and sweat collecting at the base of his neck. "That's Abner."

He turned the thumb and pointed it to his right, to a towheaded blond who looked like a linebacker gone to seed. "And this is Franklin."

"I'm Eddy."

Abner looked up. "Would you like to hear something interesting?"

Milton rolled his eyes but Eddy said, "Sure."

"In Russia, prisons are called gulags," Abner said, pushing his glasses up his nose and toward his eyes. "They're not very nice. People try to escape all the time. When they do, they bring an extra person along. Someone they can eat if they run out of food. They call that person the cow. The cow doesn't know he's a cow, but he is all the same. If they start a fire, it would give away their location. They eat the cow's kidneys and blood because you can eat those without cooking them."

"Jesus," Franklin said. "Kidneys and blood? You gotta say that

29

kind of stuff while we're eating?"

Eddy suddenly didn't feel welcome. He went to stand, looking around for another free seat. "I can find a different place to sit…"

Milton put his hand up and motioned for Eddy to stay where he was.

"Abner thinks he's being funny," Milton said. "His kind of funny isn't most people's kind of funny. Abner, we're not in the middle of the Russian wilderness. You can see San Francisco from the windows. We just have to get across the water. Believe me, that's going to be the easy part."

"It's not so easy," Abner said. "Lots of people have tried. No one's ever done it."

"We'll get to that part when we get to that part," Milton said. He turned to Eddy. "First day in?"

Eddy nodded.

"Welcome to the gas chamber," Milton said. "Eat quick. We only get twenty minutes. Move fast enough, you can get seconds. But your plate needs to be clear at the end, no matter what. You leave food on your plate, maybe they give you a warning this time, being it's your first day. Next time, they start revoking privileges."

"Thanks. No one's really explained…"

Milton raised an eyebrow. "I said you have to eat quick."

Eddy nodded and tucked in. The soup was a touch bland but the pork shoulder was perfectly cooked, falling apart before he even put his knife to it, and the mashed potatoes were among the best he ever had. He cleared half his plate before he realized the food was singeing the roof of his mouth. He was so hungry he didn't care. He paused to catch his breath and looked at the other men, who were eating with equal fervor.

"Why do you call it the gas chamber?" Eddy asked.

Franklin nodded toward a small box near the ceiling, painted white to blend into the wall. "Tear gas canister. We misbehave, guards turn 'em on."

Eddy looked around the room and saw seven he could count from his vantage point. He took a big bite of corn. Perfectly buttery and salty.

"This food is pretty boss," Eddy said. "Not what I expected."

"They got a thing about the food here," Franklin said. "They figure if it's good, we won't cause trouble or try to escape."

"Little do they know..." Milton said, laughing.

Franklin rolled his eyes. "Okay. You obviously want to tell us. What's this plan of yours?"

Milton looked around again, to make sure no one was listening. "It's well established that digging instruments are hard to come by, correct?" He glanced at Eddy. "At the end of the meal, the guards check to make sure all your silverware is accounted for." He stuck a finger in the air. "So don't go dropping anything."

"You think a spoon is going to get you out of this place," Franklin said. "You're a kook, Milton."

"No, I am not a kook," Milton said. "I've got it all mapped out. Just need something to dig with. And I figured out how we get a spoon or two. It'll take a little time, but, you know, time is the one thing all of us have."

Everyone paused and looked at Milton, who was smiling like he couldn't possibly stop smiling.

"We bribe one of the lifers," Milton said.

Franklin huffed. "That's your plan? First you invite this stranger into the crew, like we can even trust him. Then you tell us the way to get this done is getting even more people involved?"

Milton stuck a finger in the air, again. "First, there are plenty of guys here with nothing to lose. Chances are whoever does it for us ends up on D block for a bit, but we can make it worth his while."

He put up a second finger. "Second, you got, what, eight years left?" He turned to Abner. "You got seven. That I know. I got seven, too." Milton looked at Eddy. "How many you got, kid?"

"Ten," Eddy said.

Milton winced. "Ten years on the rock. You're in the prime of your life. You don't want to spend the prime of your life here, do you?"

"Does anyone want to be here at all?" Eddy asked.

"It's not that bad," said Abner.

"Shut up," said Milton, drawing out the word so it sounded more like "shaht." "The point is…"

Abner made a low whistling sound, like a bird being strangled. Milton fell silent, putting his head down and cramming food into his mouth. Eddy looked up and saw an Easter Island statue in a guard's uniform pass the table.

"Gentlemen," the statue said, in a way that made it sound like he didn't think they were gentlemen.

Milton looked up and smiled. With a mouth full of food he said, "How are you today, sir?"

"Missing the days when you goons weren't allowed to talk in the cafeteria," the guard said. "Just the sound of silverware for twenty minutes. Music to my ears."

The guard wandered away, eyeballing another table.

Abner leaned toward Eddy. "That's Kowalski. He says that every day."

"So this theoretical and charitable lifer," Franklin said. "What's the chance he keeps his mouth shut when the guards turn the screws?" He threw a hard glance at Eddy. "What's the chance our new friend doesn't go right to a guard as soon as we're done eating? Maybe he thinks he'll get a little reward."

"I don't…" Eddy started.

Milton spoke over him. "Anyone here for life is going to know better than to rat." He looked directly at Eddy. "No one here is stupid enough to rat."

Eddy nodded and kept eating.

"It's like, there was this one guy," Milton said, leaning forward, dropping his voice. "Dimed a couple of fellas who were making pruno down in the bakery. Booze supply runs out and people are clawing at the walls. It wasn't pretty. You know what they did to him?" He whistled. "That wasn't pretty, either. Face looked like the inside of a pot of chili. I get nightmares about it sometimes."

Eddy tried to swallow the food in his mouth but couldn't stop thinking about chili.

"It's too bad you don't have a pen and paper," Milton said, giving Eddy a hard stare. "This is a lot of important stuff. The kind of things you don't want to forget. You get me?"

Eddy nodded, scraping at the remnants of food on his tray. How clean was clean enough the guards wouldn't give him trouble?

He had a lot of questions.

So many he didn't know where to start with them. But it was nice there were people to show him the ropes. He'd spent the last few days forgetting how to cry. Maybe this wouldn't be so bad. Hell, maybe there was a chance to get out sooner.

"I'm just saying," Milton said. "It's good to have friends in here. If you feel like you owe me anything, I'm around."

"I got it," Eddy said. "And I appreciate it."

"Do you?"

The question was sharp and it made Eddy's mouth run dry. He swallowed, pushing the wad of food down his throat, and nodded.

"I do," he said.

"Good," Milton said. "Looks like we're all about done here. I'll get a guard to come over so we can get the hell out of here. We can show you around a bit, Eddy. With any luck, you won't get to know this place too well."

Milton put his hand in the air and stood, Franklin and Abner standing along with him. As Abner stood, his elbow bumped his cup of coffee onto Eddy. The cup was mostly empty, but as the liquid splashed his gray pants, Eddy jumped.

"Sorry about that," Abner said, reaching down to blot at the streaks of coffee with a napkin. Eddy pushed his hand away.

"No harm," Eddy said.

Kowalski stopped in front of the table and surveyed the four of them.

"You ladies done playing grab-ass?" he asked Abner and Eddy.

"Just an accident," Abner said.

"An accident," Eddy repeated.

Kowalski nodded and looked down at the table, mumbling to himself. When he got to Eddy's tray, he stopped. "Where's your spoon, inmate?"

"It was...just here."

Eddy looked around the empty trays and small piles of silverware. He was sure he left it right on top—positive he did that—but there was only the fork and knife. He looked up at Milton. The way Milton was smiling made his heart climb into his throat and expand until he couldn't breathe.

"I ask again, where's the spoon, inmate?"

Milton raised an eyebrow, the corner of his lip curling up, and mouthed the word: "Chili."

"I...must not have taken one?"

"Right," the guard said, putting a massive hand on Eddy's shoulder. "Let's go have a talk. See if we can't jog your memory."

As the guard led Eddy away, he heard one of his lunch companions softly calling after him: "Moooo."

CREAMPUFF

PEOPLE CALLED HIM "Creampuff."

No one knows if it was a nickname thought up by the staff, or if he actually called himself that. That's just what people called him. It could have been like when you call a big guy "Tiny." Cognitive dissonance. Here's this big black guy, and he answered to Creampuff like it was John or Paul.

There were a lot of things people didn't know about Creampuff, but here is what is known: he was huge, like a recurring childhood nightmare. People say he was nearly seven feet tall, but that's just the way truth gets warped by word of mouth. He was more like six-three, which is still pretty big. He had gauges in his ears wide enough you could fit your thumb in, and a thick beard like a jumble of cables that reached down to his sternum. And always he was wearing a gray wool skullcap, even in the summer.

He had one tattoo. A series of black lines running parallel down his left forearm. It started with five lines. The last time anyone saw him, when the morning shift found his body in a thick pool of blood, throat cut ear to ear, there were seven lines. No one knew what they stood for. Nearly everyone had a theory. Most of those theories had to do with how many people he had killed.

Which is a little heavy, and not really based on anything. Creampuff was only a bouncer.

Granted, he was a special kind of bouncer, with a skill set tailored for these strange, modern times. He was required to deal with a hugely diverse range of people—zombie tourists to rich yuppie jerks to bridge-and-tunnel trolls to the most dangerous animal in New York City: moms pushing baby carriages.

Creampuff was a bakery bouncer.

The kind of job that didn't exist ten years ago and suddenly is in such demand, colleges should teach a course on it.

You know what a canelé is? It's this little pastry that originated in Bordeaux, in the southwest of France. It gets cooked in a copper mold, which forms a deep bronze crust on the outside. Inside is light custard flavored with vanilla and rum. They're the perfect little mouthful, barely bigger than one bite, and you can get them in a lot of places in New York, but only a few places actually do them right.

Patiserie in the East Village is one of those places turning out perfect canelés, going back to the 1940s, when the store first opened. But as with any business that isn't a bank or a real estate agency, one day, they found themselves struggling to meet their rent. Their canelés, being a thing of legend, did good business, but still, were barely keeping them afloat. It's hard to keep the lights on when your star product sells for three dollars a pop.

So the owners of Patiserie brought on a hotshot pastry chef—a kid with half his head shaved and cooking utensils tattooed up and down his forearms—to put a new spin on the menu.

And this new chef considers the canelé.

It's classic, but as a canvas, a little blank. He tinkers with it for a few weeks, and eventually figures out a way to get rum-infused ice cream on the inside.

Think about that. Instead of a warm custard, it was still-cold ice cream. To properly caramelize the crust of a canelé, you've got to hit it with a ton of heat. Plus, introducing alcohol into the mix screws with the melting point of the ice cream. All that, and there was still cold, perfectly-unmelted ice cream on the inside. This thing was a marvel of modern kitchen engineering.

Word spread, and within a week of it hitting the menu, the chef was on *Good Morning America,* the plastic-faced anchors making a show of begging him for the secret to his cooking process, which of course, he wouldn't reveal. They did come up with a new name for this treat: the creamelé.

So that goes viral, and the next morning, there's a line down the block and around the corner. Everyone wants a creamelé.

Suddenly, all the employees who are supposed to be cooking and baking are working crowd control. That's no way to run a business. Especially since three people needed to be assigned to the creamelés, which were made in a back room with blacked-out windows, which no one but the chef and his helpers were allowed inside.

Enter Creampuff.

Nobody knows where he came from. He just showed up one day, arms crossed over his chest, his eyes cold and unmoving like blocks of chipped ice. Some people thought he was the embodiment of order, attracted by the gravity of chaos, here to bring order to an entropic universe. Truth is, it was probably a job posting on

Craigslist.

Patiserie only had the capacity to make two hundred creamelés a day, and you could only buy one at a time. There was no calling ahead to reserve them. You had to wait in the line. And they were a ten-foot treat, meaning you had to eat them within ten feet of the bakery. Wait too long, and the ice cream would melt.

Every single day, people who wanted ice cream for breakfast would line up as early as 4 a.m., when the first shift of bakers would arrive.

Doors opened at 7 a.m.

By 9 a.m., that day's allotment of creamelés was gone.

So you've got a line to control. There are people running outside the bakery to eat their creamelé. And then, there are all the people trying to game the system and get in without waiting in line.

This is what Creampuff faced every single day—because he worked seven days a week. But he had a system.

If you were there for a creamelé, you got in the creamelé line. Five people were allowed inside the store at a time, and only five people. One person in, and one person out. Even if you were with a group of people, even if you were with your husband or wife, you got split up to go inside. Creampuff only made an exception when parents had their kids with them—not that kids could have a creamelé, because there was alcohol in it.

In front of the store, on the sidewalk, there was a sign on a pedestal explaining how the line worked. Plus a lengthy explanation on Patiserie's website. Not that it helped much. Because people in New York think they are the center of their own little universe, a lot of Creampuff's job consisted of dealing with people who didn't want to wait.

There were the richie riches who would stride up to him and

wave a bill under his nose. Usually a twenty, sometimes a hundred. Creampuff would take it, stick it in a pouch on his belt that read "Donations for Charity," and cross his arms.

No one ever asked for their money back.

Two celebrities and the chief of staff for the mayor walked to the front of the line like it wasn't even there. Creampuff surely had no idea who they were, but it wouldn't have mattered. Even after they pitched a fit, invoking the don't-you-know-who-I-am? protocol, Creampuff shrugged, put his hand up, and waved them toward the back.

Pregnant mom pushing a stroller, arguing she couldn't wait because her precious little darling had toddler yoga in fifteen minutes?

Back of the line.

Tourist on his last day in New York City, and he'll never be visiting again, and this is his last chance to try a creamelé?

Back of the line.

A man diagnosed with cancer, a week to live, and a creamelé was his final wish?

Creampuff offered to let him cut if he presented a doctor's note. The guy never came back.

The line was sacrosanct to Creampuff. The way he figured it, the people who dragged themselves out of bed in the middle of the night to wait for a pastry—they were crazy. They had some gaping chasm inside their souls that they tried to fill with food, and honestly, the whole thing was a little sad.

But they made the effort. Creampuff had to at least respect that much, and not let anyone who didn't make that effort cut in front of them. In a city where chaos is the accepted norm, a line has to mean something.

Creampuff had a memory for faces, too. More than once a

line-cutter would come back, a day or a week or a month later, and when they finally made it to the front, Creampuff would shake his head. He didn't even have to say anything. They knew what they had done. And each one of them shuffled off, cradling their shame.

Same thing with the non-creamelé line. The store had a separate line that led to another counter for people who didn't want a creamelé. Some people thought they were being clever, sneaking around to that side. They also found themselves blacklisted.

This is the new face of New York City. Living here used to be a game of survival. Now it's about conning your way into frozen treats. Creampuff was a product of the way things used to be. He rarely spoke. When he did, he never raised his voice. The only time he ever smiled was when there was a child waiting with a parent, and for a fleeting moment, he would soften. For the most part, he would nod, or shrug, or point toward the back of the line. And people listened. The kind of people who on a different day you'd expect to be a problem, they fell in lockstep.

Creampuff carried with him that aura of not-to-be-fucked-with. He was one of the people this city couldn't chew up and spit out.

It got to be where Creampuff became part of the creamelé story, like a member of the Royal Guard in front of Buckingham Palace. People would want to take pictures with him. They would tell him jokes to try to get him to laugh. Girls would flirt with him to try to make him blush, but he never did.

One guy said with a name like Creampuff he must be a homo. That was the only time anyone can remember Creampuff laying a hand on someone. He grabbed the guy by the back of the neck, pulled him close, whispered something into his ear, and the guy took off at a full sprint, blanched white as a field of snow.

It was around this time, that Creampuff's legend was growing, that the first break-in happened.

Rival bakers had been trying to replicate the creamelé without success. Either the crust would be soggy, or the ice cream would melt, or they would burst during the cooking process. It was one of the most sought-after recipes in the city, and some people even offered to buy it, but the owners of Patiserie wouldn't entertain offers.

They had gone from just another bakery to one of the hottest destinations in New York City. The prime minister of Mozambique queued up on three separate occasions until he was finally able to get a creamelé. Why sell off the keys to that kingdom?

The morning of the first break-in, Creampuff arrived to find that the front door had been pried open. The register hadn't been touched, but the door to the creamelé kitchen was ajar. Luckily, the chef always brought the custom bake pieces home with him, so all the perpetrator found were a few standard ovens and raw ingredients—nothing that couldn't have been guessed at already.

This is when Creampuff began sleeping in the store.

No one asked him to. Just one day there was a cot. Once the evening shift had been cleared out, he would show up, lock the front door, and disappear into the back. People began to speculate, about whether he had a place to go, or even had a home. He only seemed to own a few shirts, a few pairs of pants. He never spoke of life outside the bakery, and no one ever came by who seemed to know him.

For a while, with Creampuff living in the bakery, things were calm. Business continued to boom. The owners made so much money they were able to buy the building the store was housed in, ensuring that future generations of the family would be secure. They even thought of expanding to another storefront, in the West Village. The creamelés were the star attraction, and the chef was their most valuable player, but still, Creampuff was given a share of the credit, for maintaining order and appearances.

For being part of the story.

Then came the day they found his body.

No money had been taken. The creamelé room hadn't been touched. There was just his body, sprawled out on the white tile, blood cutting geometric trails through the grout.

There were some theories about who had done it. Maybe one of the rival bakeries, in a robbery gone bad. There was also a multinational dessert corporation that waved a seven figure check in front of the owners, and were told to bug off. A corporation certainly would seem capable of murder in the pursuit of profit.

Some wondered if it was revenge. Someone who wanted a creamelé and didn't get it, come back to make Creampuff pay for the slight. Or something else from his life catching up with him. Rumors began to circulate that he was in witness protection, and the fame achieved by the bakery had blown his cover.

How else to explain the savagery of a murder like that, in a town where people have forgotten what it means to be savage?

After the crime scene had been processed, the owners learned that Creampuff's body had been unclaimed. Having paid him in cash, there was no address for him on file. He had become another anonymous death in an anonymous city.

So the owners and the employees put together a collection for the funeral. The costs were eventually completely covered by an anonymous donation. Some person of means who had stood in that line, and decided the man who maintained it deserved a bit of dignity in death.

The funeral was a quiet affair, held around the corner from the bakery, at St. Mark's in-the-Bowery. A few dozen people showed up. Mostly employees, though some loyal customers, too. In the back of the church was a frail black woman, a shroud around her face, weeping softly into a yellow handkerchief, and many assumed she was family, though she left before anyone could ask.

When it came time for the eulogy, the owner of Patiserie, a slight old man, was helped to the dais. He stood there for a long time, looking down at his hands resting on the podium. Then he looked up and told a story.

One day, Creampuff had finished his shift and was getting ready to leave, when he saw a woman across the street, struggling to carry groceries into her apartment building. He didn't know her. But he walked across the street and said something to her and then took the bags from her hands and disappeared inside. He came back out and walked away and went home.

It was a small moment in the immensity of this man's life, but it was a measure of the kind of person Creampuff was. Someone who did the right thing when the right thing was required. He didn't seek thanks or reward. He did it and he moved on.

After the funeral, things slowly returned to normal.

The owners of Patiserie hired a new bouncer. This one not as reliable, not as steadfast. If someone handed him a hundred, he would allow that person to cut the line. He was prone to anger and berated people for not walking inside fast enough. He was high on the allowances of his power.

He was no Creampuff.

Occasionally, someone would ask about Creampuff, not having heard the news, and would be disappointed for a moment, before returning to their quest for a creamelé.

Something no one was able to prove was that after he was gone, the line got a little shorter. Patiserie always sold out of the day's allotment of creamelés, and the offers to buy the recipe never stopped, but it seemed like there were less people waiting.

And, eventually, people forgot.

In New York City, the space left by a memory is a vacuum. It won't be long before something fills that space.

But even then, there are people who fight against the vacuum.

On the one-year anniversary of Creampuff's body being found, early in the morning, the employees opening the store found a gift-wrapped package leaning against the closed door of the bakery. Inside was a framed photo of Creampuff. It was a candid shot, taken with a cell phone camera in the early morning hours, when the sun wasn't yet strong enough to push away the shadows.

Creampuff, staring off toward the end of the line, his arms crossed, like they were always crossed. A statue, solemn and unmoving, with the hint of a smile spreading across the boundary of his lips. His face a portrait of contentment.

That's the story of the photo hanging behind the register at Patiserie. The owner thought it important that the photo hang there. It means you can't buy a creamelé without seeing it.

You might not know the significance, but at least you will see it.

BHUT JOLOKIA

WHEN YOU VISIT Google and type in "world's hottest pepper," you find there are a lot of contenders vying for the crown.

There's the Bhut Jolokia, cultivated in Indian states like Assam and Nagaland.

The Trinidad Moruga Scorpion from, you guessed it, Trinidad.

The Red Savina, which was engineered in California.

The important thing to look for is Scoville units. That's the measure of concentration of capsaicin, the active component in peppers that makes them spicy. According to Google, the Bhut Jolokia measures in at 1.5 million Scoville units. For the sake of comparison, a jalapeo rates about 3,500.

Bhut Jolokia it is.

You order four from a specialty food website and wait for the mailman. You purchase a pair of goggles and some heavy-duty rubber gloves from the hardware store, because you will be playing with the culinary equivalent of fire.

You imagine the look on Scott Olson's stupid fucking face when he takes a big bite of your lunch.

That heavy-breathing, flop-sweated pervert.

Scott has stolen your lunch fourteen times now. Never when it's something boring, like PB&J. Only when it's good, like leftover meatball parm from the place down the block, or when you summon the commitment to make a big batch of short rib stew.

Every day around 11:30—just before the lunch rush—Scott cruises the refrigerator and makes his selection. If it's not you, it's someone else who goes hungry. You can't complain. No one can. The last person who did got canned. That's what happens when your daddy owns the company, and is also a prick.

Then there are all those times he's openly stared at your tits while discussing shipping quotas or delivery reports. You stopped counting how many times he's done that.

When the box arrives, you cut it open and upend it onto the counter. Four shriveled peppers fall out, dark red like bruised lips, wrapped in crinkly cellophane. After slicing them lengthwise, you dispose of the seeds, because it's a myth that the seeds store capsaicin. All the heat is in the flesh.

Thank you, Google.

You turn the Julienned strips sideways and do a brunoise cut, dicing them into tiny cubes. The gloves make it a little tough to maneuver the knife. You wish you had a mask, because you feel a sharp tickle in your sinus cavity, like inhaling dry air on a cold day.

The diced peppers go into the cauldron of tomato sauce and cheap ground meat and spices bubbling on the stove. When the chili is done it's deep brown and thick. You forget to put the goggles on, so when you take the lid off, steam billows out and your eyes instantly burn and fill with tears. You wash your face with a gallon of milk over the sink. Milk contains casein, a compound that binds with and washes away capsaicin.

Again, thank you, Google.

Your eyes sting a little for the rest of the night, but the pain is worth it, because when you arrive at work the next day, you are dizzy with excitement. You know Scott likes chili. You know he won't be able to resist. You used a clear plastic storage container and even wrote 'Chili' on top in black felt marker, just to be sure.

This will be a win for every office worker who has ever been treated like a gear in a machine or a stat on a spreadsheet. You wonder how long you'll have to wait before you can admit to your co-workers that, yes, you are the one.

The new office hero.

You fantasize about them carrying you aloft on your desk chair, marching among the cubicles as interns throw shredded ribbons of expense reports into the air.

This makes you smile.

You don't stay in the kitchen because you don't want to be present at the scene of the crime, so you tuck into your office with your PB&J and you wait.

And wait.

Come noontime, you walk down the hall and find nearly the entire office crowded around the door leading into the kitchen. Laughing at that asshole's misfortune, no doubt.

Except, no one's laughing.

No one is moving, either.

Hands are held at mouths, eyes stretched wide in horror. Dread so palpable your stomach twists into a knot, putting undue pressure on both ends of your digestive tract.

The crowd parts. A stretcher rolls out, guided by two paramedics. Scott is lying on top with his shirt ripped open, an oxygen mask clamped on his face, his skin shiny and slick with sweat.

He's not moving either.

You hear someone in the crowd say the words "heart condition."

You are dizzy, again, but not with excitement.

To your right is the sound of shoes scraping against carpet. You turn and find a handsome police officer. Strong jaw and white teeth and blue, blue eyes.

He is not smiling.

"Ma'am, if you could just come to the conference room in a little bit. We have to speak to everyone who was here today."

KNOCK-OFF

MONEY IS MONEY. It doesn't matter where it comes from. It only matters that you have it, and you can pay the rent, or the electric, or the grocery bill.

This is my mantra. It's what I repeat as the temperature inside the Almo costume reaches somewhere around two hundred degrees Fahrenheit, and some prepubescent goblin is driving his tiny fist into my balls.

Before you ask, yes, Almo, with an A. It's a knock-off, supposedly Mexican. Ultimately, who cares? The kids see what they want to see—an anthropomorphic red monster they know from television. I would never refer to myself as anything but Almo, lest I find a lawyer attached to my neck.

Back to my balls. You would think the fuzzy padding of the suit would offer a little protection. And maybe a decade ago, when it was new, it would have. But after a dozen owners and a hundred appearances and every bodily fluid imaginable, it's not up to the task.

Last week, I had to throw some red felt pens into the wash, just to re-dye the parts of the fur that were fading. Related to that, I am no longer welcome at my local laundromat.

The tourist couple—the ones responsible for the goblin trying to bludgeon me into castration—they're smiling and laughing. They must assume the padding is intact. Or at least I hope they do, because if not, that would make them really terrible people.

The kid finally gives it a rest when the father produces a black behemoth of a camera that costs more than probably everything I own. The kid grips his arms around my waist and smiles, like the threat of violence doesn't hang between us. I'm wondering where they're from when the father counts down in Czech—*"jeden, dva, tři"*—so that answers that.

I don't actually speak Czech, but you work in Times Square for a few weeks, dressed as a knock-off cartoon character, accepting tips for photos, you pick up some things by osmosis. Hell, you live in New York City your whole life, you're doing something wrong if you can't say "cheers" in at least six languages.

After the father is done taking his photos and has returned the camera to his side, like a gun back in the holster, there's a brief moment of awkwardness, where he assumes our transaction has ended but he's not sure what to do next. I tap the red pouch hanging from my waist that has "TIPS" embroidered in white stitching.

There's a brief flash of recognition, and his hand twitches toward the bulge of his wallet. Then he shrugs, says, *"Nemluvím anglicky."*

"I do not speak English."

Another term you get used to in this gig.

There's a giant neon clock blinking over his shoulder. I've been at this three hours, and have less than fifty dollars to show for it. Friday nights, when the square is so packed with tourists the air is thick with the humidity of perspiration, I usually pull double that.

I'm about to take a step forward—one step forward being sufficient to scare most tourists into acquiescence—when I see a cop eyeing me like we broke up on bad terms. So I bow and nod my head, although the father probably can't see me nod inside the costume, and he grabs his kid and his wife and disappears into the teeming mass.

We have a détente with the cops. We can accept tips but we can't charge for photos. Charge a tourist, then you're a business, then you get cited, and if you mouth off, they take you to booking and your costume "disappears" sometime before you work your way through the system.

It happened to a guy who dressed as Superman. He didn't call himself that, he called himself Superguy. He also called the cops Nazi Death Pigs, which highlights the importance of diplomacy when dealing with the police.

I toe the line. This is not the job I dreamed about as a kid—I wanted to own a restaurant—but you do what you have to. America is the land of opportunity until you make a mistake. Then you can get fucked. I've leveled a forest with all the resumes I've sent out. The problem is I like to be honest, so I put down that I served time on a drug charge.

It's not even like it was real drugs. Pot isn't dangerous unless you're a bag of chips. But the cops treated me like they busted Pablo Escobar, and it seems there's not an employer in this town that'll look past my status as an ex-con.

The costume thing was supposed to be temporary. But the more I do it, the more it feels like this is my only option.

Exhale. No need getting worked up inside this thing. It'll just raise the temperature and make it more uncomfortable. I could use a smoke though, so I leave my spot outside the M&M store and head for a vacant side street. It ruins the illusion if the kids see you with your mask off, sucking down unfiltered cigarettes.

Anyway, it's not like the square is promising tonight.

Christ, this place. It used to be great if you wanted a handy, or some blow, or a sucking chest wound. Now there's an M&M store. Back in the days of David Dinkins and *Death Wish*, it was like there was no way this place could get any worse. And in a way, that was true. The pendulum swung as far as it could, and it hit the end of its arc when Giuliani showed up with his militarized police force.

Now look where we are. Seizure-inducing lights and chain restaurants and Broadway shows based on Disney movies. Tourists staring into the sky, eyes glazed over and faces slack, like they've got heroin needles jammed in their arms.

I say these things like complaining is going to fix it.

I hit the corner, head toward the dark. Drunken couples stumble out of the way, point and laugh, yell things at me, but I tune them out, intent on getting to a quiet alcove where I can take off the damned head of this costume.

And when I do, it is sweet bliss. My skin is so wet it's shiny and the cool night air caresses me like I haven't been touched in a long time.

I'm halfway through my cigarette when the shadow in the doorway grows deeper. I look up and find two silhouettes outlined in the street lamps. One of the silhouettes says hello, like he knows me.

The two of them step in the light. Billy and Richie. Two market-price thugs, and the last two people I want to see right now. Richie smiles, his hair slicked back, his eyes twinkling like he's trying to sell me something that's broken. Billy lingers behind him, just like he always does.

Richie says, "We've been looking for you. Heard about the new gig." He taps the Almo head with the tip of his boot.

I shake my head, wave him away. "I'm on parole. Absolutely not. Under no circumstances."

Richie puts his hands up in a 'calm down' gesture. Says, "It's just an idea. Hear me out?"

I tell him, "Dude, no. Please, kindly piss off."

He exhales. "Look, nobody hanging out in Times Square dressed like a muppet is doing it because they've made good decisions. I've got a proposition that'll make you an extra couple of bucks. Low impact, low risk."

I'm about to tell him to piss off again, when I remember the rent is due in two days and I'm still three hundred short. I do not expect to make that much between now and then. I know I'm making a mistake but I ask for the details.

He says, "You sling a little while you're doing the muppet thing. And it's perfect…"

I cut him off. "Have you ever been to Times Square?"

He inclines his head, looking at me like I'm a sphinx.

I tell him, "Let me rephrase. Have you ever gone to Times Square and seen the army of cops? Half the police force is there. You know why that is? Because all this city cares about is protecting the tourists so they come here and spend their money. You want me to sell drugs in the place where the majority of this city's cops hang out. Seems pretty dumb."

Richie puts his hand on my shoulder, bunches up a wad of red felt in his fist. "You make it sound like you're going to be doling shit out in the wide open. I thought this through. Well, Billy thought it through. Billy, tell him the idea."

Billy clears his throat. "Well, think about it. We tell someone they buy from Elmo…"

I interrupt. "Almo."

He pauses. "Almo, whatever. We have them look for the… Almo. They come, take a photo with you, right? When their arm is wrapped around you for the picture, you've got like a sleeve or something with the coke. You hand it to them inside the costume, and then they slip the payment in your tip bag. At the end of each shift we split the pot, thirty percent to you, the rest to us."

"Bullshit thirty. I'm taking all the risk."

Richie says, "You're not getting the product. You're not transporting it. You're not getting the customers. You're not doing anything but standing there. So it's twenty, or we go talk to the asshole dressed like SpongeBob."

"He calls himself SpongeTodd."

"Whatever. Fuck that guy. We're being nice, trying to give you first shot at this. You don't want it, it goes to someone else."

I take a deep breath. "Where would I get it?"

"You know the ice cream truck on 43rd, a little off Seventh?"

"I don't know, yeah? I don't really notice the ice cream trucks. They're everywhere."

"That's the point," Richie says with a smile. "You go up and ask for a vanilla sundae with extra marshmallow and two scoops of peanuts. You get what you need."

"Wait, wait…an ice cream truck? Really?"

"Most ice cream trucks are drug fronts," Billy says.

"The things you learn…" I flick my now-dead cigarette to the curb. Reflect on what my life has become. Finally, I tell them, "Let me sleep on it."

Richie puts up his hands up in a 'sure thing' gesture. Says,

"That all I ask. Call me. Number's the same."

I watch them disappear around the corner, then put the Almo head back on, trudge to my spot, their offer trailing behind me like a desperate stripper.

Money is good. I like money. Coke is not so good. Nor is getting caught with it. When I turn the corner, back into the searing light of the square, there's a bunch of cartoon characters standing around in a circle, while a cop wrestles with a pile of black and red felt. I jog over and find Mickey Mouse's crack-addicted brother lying on the ground in a fetal position. One cop is holding what looks like a gun in his hand, but then I see the wires and realize it's a Taser. Another cop is trying to take the mouse's head off but it's stuck.

Next to me is giant, bulbous Hello Kitty. It leans toward me and a male voice with a Mexican accent spills out of the mouthpiece. "Some family wouldn't tip so he pushed the kid. Kid hit the ground. Everyone lost their shit."

The cop gives up trying to get the head off, and they pull him to his feet, drag him off. I push through the crowd of people taking video on their phones, head back to my position. Within minutes the cops box me in against a light pole, wanting to know the guy's name, where he lives.

I tell them, "It's not like we're in a union or something."

One of the cops, the same one who was eyeing me earlier, he presses his baton into my side. "Got ourselves a comedian here, Officer Ruiz."

The other cop, presumably Officer Ruiz, says, "I bet you're all a bunch of sickos. Get your jollies feeling up kids or something, right? You keep it straight, sicko, or we'll bust you down."

I nod, resist the temptation to do anything else but that. And I have a lot of temptations.

After an hour, and four dollars in tips, and the tourists avoiding me like I have hepatitis—which, with this costume, maybe?—I pack it in and head home.

And when I get there, I find the icing on tonight's cake: a note attached to my door, saying my rent is going up fifty bucks a month.

ALL TOLD, IT'S not a bad system. I go to the ice cream truck. Between the bald tires and the menu pictures mostly scraped off, there's rarely a line. I order the sundae, as described by Richie, from a man whose heavy brow and bushy beard make him look like he moonlights as something that hides under beds to terrorize children. With an uncomfortable wink he serves me a big sloppy sundae in a plastic clamshell with marshmallow and crushed peanuts, and I find a quiet alcove to eat it, and at the bottom find a plastic bag, which is stuffed with even smaller bags, which are stuffed with coke.

At least I get some ice cream out of this, along with the thrill of wondering whether the bag is intact, or if my ice cream is now loaded up with cocaine.

Then I make my way to my post, where I am now one of the most popular characters on the block. Mostly it's drunken kids stumbling up to me, their friends holding up iPhones, looking around nervously for cops, ready to take pictures.

Tonight is no different. The kid who has his arm around me looks like he wants to grow up to be a professional college student. He grips my shoulder and leans in close and says into my mouth, "I'll take one, please." I can smell the beer through the mesh.

He's using his right hand, not his left like he's supposed to. I poke at him until he realizes his mistake. Then he finds the hole I made in the costume. His hand reaches in—there is something so disturbingly sexual about this—and I slip a baggie of coke into his hand, leaving the empty arm of the Almo costume to hang in the air like a noose. It actually probably looks nothing like a noose, but that's just what it feels like.

We pose for the photos, his friend snapping away, sweating, looking around for the cops. The guy posing for the photo turns his body toward me to shield himself from view, shows me three twenty dollar bills, and shoves them in my tip bag. And then they're gone.

Things have been tense with the cops—between Mickey Mouse last week, and then last night, Roger Rabbit went haywire. He was running in circles, screaming anti-Semitic comments, before charging at random people. Three cops to bring him down. I'm thinking PCP, but the guy who dresses as Spider-Man thinks it was meth. We have a pool going.

So, anyway, the cops are on edge but they think we've all got mental problems, and don't like coming near us. As long as I don't punch any kids—not always the easiest impulse to ignore but I do my best—it means they give us a wide berth. And I get to hide in plain sight.

There's a tap on my shoulder and my heart skips. I turn and find Marvin the Martian. Except his costume is such a bad knock-off, the colors wrong and the head too small, so he looks like Marvin the Martian's older, socially-inept bother. Flanking him is a Disney princess. I don't know which one exactly, but given the sunken eyes and stringy blonde hair, I'd say it's whichever Disney princess made the most mistakes in life.

Marvin leans toward me and mumbles something I can't make out.

I put my hand up to my ear—or to Almo's ear—to indicate I can't hear him. He adjusts his headpiece, says, "You have to stop."

"What are you talking about?"

He says, "We control the coke game here."

"Dude, I'm just taking photos with people."

The princess says, "You must think we're kidding."

She holds up her sequined clutch, looks around to make sure there's no one watching us, and pulls out something black and plastic that looks like a comb. She presses a gloved finger to the side and a blade flicks out.

Purely on instinct I throw my arm out to block it, and for once the padding comes through—the knife barely grazes me, instead flies from her hand and skids across the ground.

She looks at it, looks at me, shrugs, and plants her foot in the back of my knee.

It hurts. I go down, the suit not doing a great job of cushioning the fall. Nor does it help when they start kicking me. The princess, driving the sharp tip of a ruby red slipper into my stomach, is yelling, "You can't fucking sling here, motherfucker."

When there's a lull in the kicking, I look up and see that there's a kid watching us, his face flushed red. In one hand is an ice cream cone, in the other is the princess' switchblade. Through a veil of tears he asks, "Why are they hurting Elmo, Mommy?"

The mother plucks the blade from the kid's hand, her mouth opening and closing like she wants to speak, or puke, but can't figure out which. She drops the blade to the ground and runs away so fast she leaves a sandal behind.

A cavalcade of cops is headed in our direction from across the square. And I've still got eight bags of coke on me. I consider swallowing them but I'm not sure if it's enough to kill me, and anyway, I don't even know if I can reach them, because Marvin and the princess are back to kicking me into submission.

The pain builds to crescendo. The cops crash into us like a wave, and as I'm rolled across the sidewalk, I see glimpses of the tourists huddled around us, taking videos, snapping pictures, pointing, documenting the story they'll carry with them for the rest of their lives, or at least for one good status update on Facebook.

And I can't help but laugh, even though it makes my ribs hurt.

The thing about pendulums is, eventually they swing back the other way. It doesn't matter how many lights you add, how many cops you enroll, how hard you scrape at the scum—this is and always will be Times Square.

LAKE PARADOX

ESTEBAN'S STOMACH TWISTS like he's going over that first dip on the Cyclone. Everything floating in the moment before gravity takes over. Except they're not floating. Gravity pushes him into the seat as they fall forward into the dark, barreling across I-87, the gray asphalt black and the lush green treeline black. Even the inside of the car black, save the edges highlighted neon blue by the glow of the dash displays.

3:07 a.m. 55 mph. Gas almost halfway between F and E.

Esteban grips the wheel so hard the joints in his hands ache.

"How much longer?" he asks.

Brad mumbles, whirring like an old computer. After a few seconds he says, "Given the speed and time elapsed, the next exit should be in two miles. Prepare to move left. Carefully."

"Yeah. Carefully. Thanks."

"It's just that it's very dark."

"I didn't notice."

"How could you not notice?"

Esteban shakes his head, reaches for the turn signal. He pulls his hand back without flipping the lever, and reminds himself: no lights. He drifts, squinting at the dark, finds a green exit sign and a branch off their current path. He wishes he could risk the headlights, get his bearings, but Brad will have a fit, so he eases off the gas and coasts to the end of the exit, arriving at a T-junction.

"Right," Brad says. "Keep going until I say."

Esteban turns down the road. It looks like he's driving into the mouth of a cave. He takes it slow enough to be safe but fast enough to outrace the apprehension. The silence in the car is like an echo, constantly reminding him it's there.

He runs through topics of conversation in his head. Something to fill that silence. Most guys can kill an afternoon talking about shitty cafeteria food or shittier hacks. Six months together in a cell, three months of planning and prep, two hours of crawling through the guts of the Dannemora, and they'd never talked about anything but the gig. It didn't feel so odd until now.

Brad, the guy who sat in the corner, plain as an unpainted wall. Tiny bird body swimming in his dark green prison issues, big wet eyes staring off like he was watching a movie no one else could see. Everyone wondering how he ended up there, because no one knew. Not even the hacks.

That's it.

"So tell me, *hermano*," Esteban says. "How'd you end up in Danny?"

Brad doesn't move. He keeps on not moving. Esteban wonders if he heard the question. He's about to repeat it when Brad says, "Slow, slow. Coming up on a left."

"That's it, then?"

"Don't miss the turn."

Esteban rolls to a stop. Brad says, "Pull the car up into the brush. Careful, careful. We're a few feet from the ravine." Esteban presses the brake, jerks the car into park. Wonders how the hell Brad is able to calculate such precise distance in the pitch black like this.

"Let's see if your friend Gordo came through," Brad says.

"He came through. The car was right where he said it would be."

Esteban climbs into the humid-thick night. It smells like green. Insects make insect noises in the bushes. He moves around to the trunk and pops it. A small yellow light illuminates four plastic jugs of cheap vodka, three sixteen-ounce bags of black pepper, and a maroon athletic bag.

"No light," Brad says.

"Just a second."

Esteban pulls the pepper, vodka, and bag out of the car, placing them on the ground, and slams the trunk closed. Brad is doing something at the front of the car. There's a click and he says, "Now push."

It doesn't take much. A few feet and the car falls away from Esteban's outstretched hands, pitching forward, crashing into the darkness. A few seconds later and it's like there wasn't even a car. He turns, and Brad is holding a bottle of vodka, standing under a small sign. Yellow print on French blue.

WELCOME TO LAKE PARADOX.

"So I guess there's not really a lake," Brad says.

"What?" Esteban asks.

Brad looks back and forth, between the sign and the items on the ground. Esteban picks up a bottle of vodka, unscrews the top, and tilts it over his head. The cool liquid stings where it hits his mouth and eyes, the burn forcing up into his sinus cavity.

"Do you know the Ship of Theseus?" Brad asks, still holding a bottle.

"Ship of what now?"

"It's a thought experiment. A paradox. You have a ship. You replace all the parts of the ship. Is it still the same ship?"

Esteban tosses the empty jug into the ravine after the car and picks up another. "What's the point?"

"Our cells constantly die off, and they're replaced by new cells." Brad unscrews the top of the vodka, sniffs, and recoils. "When all your cells are gone and replaced, how can you be the same person? Will the dogs still be able to find us then?"

"Hey, we have a plan," Esteban says, dousing himself, then emptying the last of the bottle down his throat. The alcohol kicks a path to a soft spot in his brain. Ten years since he's had a drink that wasn't prison wine. It's like a warm hug. "We wait for Gordo. Now, wash yourself down, *hermano*. We've got some walking to do."

"I'm not your brother."

"It's a term of endearment. We're going to be stuck together for a little while. Let's at least pretend to be friends. For example, you can answer my question from earlier. How did you end up in Danny?"

Brad shrugs. "Mistakes were made." He pours the bottle over his head.

Esteban gives up, tears open the first bag of pepper and dumps it into a pile on the ground, kicking at it so it mixes with the dust.

"The vodka, I understand," Brad says. "Why the pepper?"

"Never seen *Cool Hand Luke*?"

"Never."

Esteban sighs, wondering how long it will take Gordo to show up. Worried that this might be his punishment. Eternity in the woods with this weirdo.

DAYLIGHT LIFTS A tentative eyebrow over the horizon as they reach the cabin. It's small, built in a rush from mismatched wood. Nothing covering the door or the windows. There's a spigot out front. Esteban gives it a pump. A weak but steady stream of water spills out.

Inside there are two cots and a table and a stack of books and some debris from previous occupants. Their footsteps echo on the floorboards. Esteban drops the maroon bag on the closest cot and unzips it, finds a stash of granola bars and protein bars and some bottles of water. Underneath that, a plain white envelope, folded in thirds.

Brad sits on the other cot and folds his hands. "So how long until Gordo gets here?"

"When it's safe, *hermano*," Esteban says.

"How long until it's safe?"

"No idea."

Brad nods. "Still no lake."

"What are you talking about?"

"I need to sleep."

Brad swings his legs onto the cot, facing away from Esteban, circling his body inward like he's trying to close up around something.

Esteban steps outside, pulls off his top, bare-chested in the dewy morning air. He sits on the single step leading to the doorway and undoes his tan work boots, tossing them aside, his feet aching from the long trek through the woods.

He wishes he had a cigarette. More vodka. Something to eat that wasn't in bar form.

A normal bunkmate.

Esteban opens the envelope. Gordo came through. He removes the small silver crucifix and hangs it around his neck. He closes his eyes, rests his hand on it, and pictures the face of the man he killed. He says a quick prayer.

If prison was hell, then this is purgatory. The in-between place where he'll be purified of his sin before reaching heaven: his ex-wife's bed and a torta from the corner deli. If the corner deli is still there.

Something cracks to his left. A black cat with deep yellow eyes passes in front of him, regarding him like he might be a threat. Esteban reaches out his hand but the cat doesn't come any closer.

"Don't worry," he says to the cat. "We won't be here long."

THE SILENCE IS the worst part. In prison, there's always noise. Fights during the day. Someone weeping during the night. Footsteps echoing from deep within the building, bouncing off hard surfaces.

Here, the woods are quiet. In the first few days there were insect noises, things cracking leaves and twigs in the distance, things scurrying through the brush. That seemed to fade, like the land has fallen ill, the forest clatter replaced by a faint sucking sound.

Some days, Esteban tries to engage Brad. Ask him questions about his life before prison. Brad keeps asking about the ship. If when you replace all the parts it's still the same ship. Some days they orbit like planets suspended in the darkness on paths that can't cross each other.

At least there's the cat.

After a week, it lets Esteban pet its matted fur.

ESTEBAN WAKES FROM an uncomfortable sleep. In his dreams, the man he killed is smiling, even though he wasn't smiling when Esteban killed him.

He rolls onto his side, the heat making his skin stick to the flimsy material of the cot. A toothbrush would be nice. His mouth tastes like he's been sucking on a dead thing.

Something feels missing. He pats himself, chest and stomach, before reaching his hand up to the empty space on his neck. The crucifix is gone.

He sits up and Brad is perched on the edge of his own cot, in his yellowed tank top and flimsy boxers. He's cramming a protein bar into his face and staring at Esteban with those big wet eyes.

There are two ways to kill time in prison. Lift weights and read books. Esteban lifted. Brad read. Their skills complement each other. It also means Esteban outweighs Brad by a hundred pounds of bulk. Maybe more than that.

And still, the way the smaller man stares unsettles Esteban's core.

"Last one," Brad says, folding up the cellophane wrapper.

Esteban checks the floor, then gets up and inspects the cot. "Have you seen my cross?"

"Gordo better be on his way," Brad says. "We're covered on water but I haven't seen any animals around here except the stray squirrel. I would say we could eat the cat but I suspect the cat is dead."

Esteban's head swims. "Okay, wait. No, we're not eating the cat. Second, have you seen my cross?"

"The crucifix?" Brad places the folded-up piece of cellophane on his cot. "I borrowed it."

Heat rises to Esteban's face. He stands, casting Brad in shadow. The small man regards him like a vaguely interesting sculpture.

"What the fuck do you mean?" Esteban asks.

Brad stands and pushes past Esteban, like the bigger man might not snap his neck in this very moment. He walks to the table in the corner, to a pile of electronics that looks like something smashed with a hammer. "I found this. It's a radio. If I can get it to work, we can listen to news reports. Some of the metal pieces are missing. I needed the silver."

"Give it back."

"You understand it's a meaningless symbol, correct? Jesus of Nazareth was no more the son of God than..."

Esteban pounds his fist onto the table so hard that the corner of it cracks and splinters off. "Now!"

Brad reaches into the clutter and comes out with the crucifix.

Esteban snatches it away and places it around his neck. "Take this again and Gordo will be picking me up alone, okay, *hermano*? And now what the fuck do you mean the cat is dead?"

Brad nods his head toward a box in the corner. "It climbed in there."

Esteban crosses the room and looks down into the cardboard box. The cat, curled up on itself, looks up at him and purrs.

"The cat is fine."

"I guess it just depends on your perspective, then," Brad says.

ESTEBAN STANDS AT, far wall of the cabin. He counts the marks he scratched into the wall with the rusty nail he found half buried in the dirt outside. One mark for every sunrise, twenty-two marks in total.

Hunger has become a third person in the cabin. It looms over Esteban as he tries to sleep. Whispers in his ear as he crunches through the leaves outside the cabin.

Sometimes it roars.

There is plenty of water from the spigot out front. It tastes funny, like old loose change, but it's water. The forest refuses to provide much else. Esteban has been able to catch the occasional bird or squirrel by throwing rocks. Cooked over small, brief fires, they only ever yield enough meat to make him feel hungrier.

One day, Esteban saw a deer. He was sitting on the steps and he heard it before he saw it. The sharp crack of a stick in the distance, and he expected to look up and see a wave of police officers coming through the trees. He was almost disappointed when that's not what he saw.

The deer was there and then it was gone. He considered chasing it, but was afraid to stray too far from the cabin. He sharpened the end of a long branch in case the deer came back.

Brad hasn't been concerned about the lack of food. He's never complained or asked for a share of Esteban's primitive hunts. He just sits at the table, fiddling with scraps he found in the cabin and things he scavenged from the woods. Making like he's building something, but whole days pass and nothing ends up built.

As Esteban makes the twenty-third mark on the wall, he realizes his pants are loose, and wonders if he can find some rope to fashion into a belt.

ESTEBAN'S STOMACH TWISTS like it's trying to devour itself. Nerves misfire as time unravels like a ball of twine, spilling into a jumble on the floor. No longer linear, crossing over on itself.

He wakes at the slightest noise.

Sometimes Brad is on his cot. Sometimes he's not.

Sometimes they argue about Gordo.

Sometimes he hears sirens in the distance and they turn out

to be nothing.

Sometimes he thinks of his father, sitting on the other side of the glass partition, his face collapsed like a bridge, telling him, "I did this to you."

Sometimes he finds Brad standing in the woods, staring into the distance, at where the world disappears beyond the trees, and he asks, "Don't you think there should be a lake?"

Sometimes Esteban thinks about ships. Which makes him think of himself as a ship. If all his parts are new, cells and hair and skin replaced in the years since, is he still the same man who pulled that trigger?

Mostly, Esteban sits on the step of the cabin and looks out on the forest and waits for Gordo and wishes he had something to eat.

ESTEBAN COLLAPSES TO the floor, pain gushing through him like water. He rolls onto his side. Exhausted, starving, he surrenders to the pain.

When he's able to pull his brain out of the mud, he works himself into a sitting position, his hands tied behind his back. He flexes his arms but the bindings don't budge. A bloodied stick as thick as his forearm rests on the floor next to him.

Brad is sitting at the table, in only his boxers, even though the air has turned to chill at night, poking at the innards of the gutted radio with a stick. The room smells of metal and feces.

Esteban looks the wall and sees the cat nailed into place, limbs pointed in odd directions, gutted from chin to groin. Dark brown blood caked and smeared on the wall, like a child gone crazy with finger-paint.

His first thought is: now he is alone.

His second: where the hell did Brad get the other nails?

"I told you the cat was dead," Brad said. "You shouldn't have looked in the box."

Esteban struggles to form words. They're like raw dough in his mouth. "What...why..."

"The radio," Brad says, not looking up from his project. "I thought I would be able to communicate with Gordo. Find out where he is. Or maybe find out where the police are focusing their search. And then this happened."

He turns a dial on the broken face of the radio and cocks an ear to it. His wet eyes so wide they look ready to fall out of his head. There's nothing but silence.

"Don't you hear that?" Brad asks.

"Hear...what?"

"They've already caught us! At first I thought it was a ploy to make us feel safe. And then I heard you, your voice." He jabs the stick at Esteban. "You ran, and you lead them right to us. Gordo never showed. Do you need me to turn it up?"

Esteban looks around the room for some sort of weapon.

"That's why you're tied up," Brad says. "Don't you understand?" He leaps to his feet. His slight body towering over Esteban. Clutched in his hand, so tight the skin is taught and white, is a rusty hunting knife. An antique with a wooden handle given way to rot, the blade blunted nearly flat on the edge.

That poor cat.

"Look. I know Gordo will be here. Just untie me..."

"Do you know what prison is?"

Esteban shakes his head.

"It's a box," Brad says, pacing toward the cat, then away. "You go into it and you're both alive and dead. Alive inside but dead to the world outside. We left and we were alive and we came here and we died. I can't figure out if this is our fate or if there's a way to change it."

"Listen…"

Brad spins, holds the knife toward Esteban. "Do not speak. You couldn't possibly hope to understand this."

Esteban nods again. Realizes there's only one way out. Going back to prison has to be better than dying. Maybe going back is the thing he deserves.

Brad paces the room, between the cat and the radio, examining the innards of both. Occasionally, he pauses, listens to the silence, and says, "I love this song."

Esteban realizes his mistake: the pills. Brad used to take pills. Every day, delivered in a small paper cup by the hacks. Weeks out here and the medication cleared through his system. The broken part of his brain is back in control.

Esteban curses himself. He should have seen it. Should have asked Gordo for meds.

Brad sighs. "I think I need to sleep. You need to stay there. If you leave, if someone sees you, then you may very well kill us both. Do you understand?"

"Can I have some water?" Esteban asks.

"In the morning."

"Please. Just a sip. Something to hold me over."

Brad stares at the knife, considering the request or something else, Esteban isn't sure. Finally, he nods, picks an empty bottle off the table, and steps outside to the spigot. Esteban braces himself, and when Brad reappears, throws his foot out.

It catches Brad in the knee. There's a crunching sound, like a handful of dry spaghetti cracked in half, and the small man tumbles to the ground. Esteban lifts his right foot up as high as he can and brings it down onto Brad's forehead. Another crunch. This one deeper.

He climbs to his feet, reaches back, and slams his bound wrists against his ass.

Once, twice, three times. On the fourth blow, the ropes binding him snap.

Esteban picks up the knife and drops to a knee, turns Brad over.

Brad looks up at him with sad, pleading eyes, blood spilling from a gash on his forehead. Esteban holds up the knife. Not wanting to be that man, but also not wanting this man to kill him.

Maybe with his parts replaced he's no longer a killer?

Brad pushes, trying to get up, and he's strong. So much stronger than Esteban would have expected. It scares him, so Esteban pushes the knife in under Brad's chin, pressing his weight into it until it catches on the hard wood floor. Blood erupts from Brad's throat and forms bubbles on the corners of his mouth.

Esteban climbs to his feet and runs out the door, crashing through the woods, falling forward through the darkness.

HOURS LATER, OR maybe just minutes later, he's not even sure anymore, Esteban sees something ahead. A thing somewhere between light and movement, off beyond the trees. He walks toward it. Slow enough to be safe but fast enough to outrace the apprehension.

He thinks of the man he killed. The first one. He was sitting on a park bench. He was a man who did something another man didn't like, and Esteban was tasked to kill him. He can remember the dead man's face, but not the transgression that put them on a collision course.

When Esteban held up the gun, the man's face twisted in anger. Not fear or regret. Anger.

Esteban looks at his blood-soaked hands. His head spinning from hunger. Even with his parts replaced he is not any different. The ship is still the same ship.

He reaches the clearing and before him sits the cabin.

He stares at it, his hands cold where they're wet. It has to be a different cabin.

But it's not.

Weeks now he's been looking at it, he knows every shade of wood, the shape of the spigot and its distance from the front door.

He knows he stuck to a straight line as best he could. And yet there it is.

From the inside he hears an electric hum.

He touches his hand to the cross and steps forward, plants his boot on the first step as daylight lifts a tentative eyebrow over the horizon. His body screaming at him to run in the other direction, even though he knows it won't change anything.

Brad is sitting at the table in his dark green shirt and pants. No blood. Just those big wet eyes staring at him, petting the cat, curled up and purring under his hand.

A smooth-stern voice buzzes from the radio. "*... the men were found in a cabin, apparently starved to death...*"

"There is no lake," Brad says. "*Now* do you understand?"

LEARNING EXPERIENCE

GINNY TONIC HOLDS out her left hand and finds a splotch of blood on the green gemstone of her peridot ring. She pulls it off her finger, intent on buffing it clean on the hem of her dress, but instead discovers a jagged edge on the tip of her crimson fingernail.

She shakes her head. "More's the pity."

Then she turns to the man bound in duct tape, a black bandana crammed halfway down his throat. She holds up the broken nail into the harsh light of the bare bulb buzzing in the ceiling. "You are going to pay dearly for that."

The man fights against the tape, the muscles in his neck taught and bulging. He squints away the blood trickling from his hairline. The creaking wood of the chair bounces off the basement's stone walls. The room reeks of sweat and stale water.

Ginny turns to Jacqueline Coke. The glitter in Jacqueline's blonde wig scatters the light. The young queen's contact-lens green eyes look at the floor, the wall, the light. At everything but Ginny, who's shaking her head.

"This is getting out of hand. Now I'm breaking nails." Ginny pauses, rubs two fingers on the bridge of her nose. "Tell me again what happened."

Jacqueline lingers in the shadows, speaking so soft Ginny can't hear over the scraping and struggling of their captive.

Ginny shakes her head. "Darling, please. Chin out, adult voice. Speak like you have something to say."

Jacqueline clears her throat and starts again. "I was making the buy like you told me to, Ginny. Johnny only had half because he said there was a new guy in town."

"Spreading the wealth," Ginny says. "So generous. Do continue."

Jacqueline's words stumble out in stops and starts. She fights to maintain the feminine lilt of her voice, but bass-driven syllables slip out. "I was walking to the car and Samson saw this guy following me. He works for the guy who took our half. So we— I— thought it was best to bring him to you."

Ginny nods, walks over to the man in the chair. She puts her hand on his shoulder and squeezes. "And you brought him straight to me, correct?"

"Of course, Ginny. I thought that's what you would want."

"It's what I would have wanted."

Jacqueline cringes. "Ginny."

"Straight to me." Ginny flips open her cell phone. "And here, I have a text from Samson saying you got here four hours ago. Which means this man has been sitting here for four hours." She snaps the phone closed. "What kind of host makes a guest wait four hours?"

"When we came back, you were busy. I thought you don't like

to be disturbed when you're busy."

"Except for something like this. You should have told me right away."

"Please don't be mad, Ginny. I just...you were in a meeting with the district leader from Harlem and I thought you didn't want to be disturbed during your meetings and I just...I'm sorry."

Ginny places a hand on Jacqueline's elbow and smiles. "You're still learning, darling. In the future, you need to tell me about these things much sooner. But you did the right thing."

Jacqueline brings her hand to her mouth. "Oh, Ginny, you scared me. I was so scared just now that you were unhappy."

"Don't misunderstand me. I am unhappy. But you're still learning." She moves up Jacqueline's arm, pressing a nail into the exposed flesh of her shoulder. "Don't let it happen again."

Then Ginny leans down to the man bound to the chair. He's handsome in a Wall Street way, his Brooks Brothers suit cut clean to his stocky frame. Ginny runs her hand along the wet lapel. "Pity the blood."

She turns her attention back to Jacqueline, who's shaking so hard she's vibrating. The new queens take so long to break in, but this one had seemed so much more promising. Still, no reason to give up on her yet.

Ginny says, "Darling, this gentleman and I need to have a talk. I think you should stay, so you can learn." Ginny smiles for effect, pats the shoulder of the bound man. He moves away like her hand burns. "Jacqui dear, would you like to stay?"

Jacqueline freezes. Not the response Ginny was looking for. Hesitation won't do, not for this job. Ginny is drafting the want-ad in her head when Jacqueline nods.

"Good girl," Ginny says. Then she turns to the man in the chair. "I'm going to take this gag out of your mouth. You are going to play nice."

The man shakes his head in what looks like a nod, then juts his chin forward. Ginny pulls out the cloth and the man coughs like he's trying to clear a milkshake from his lungs.

Ginny snaps her fingers. "Water."

Jacqueline appears with a half-empty bottle and tips it to the man's mouth. He drinks the little bit that doesn't splash down his face, takes three deep breaths.

Then he hits Ginny on the cheek with a wad of spit.

The guy takes a few more wheezing breaths and says, "Fucking faggot."

Ginny can feel the blood rushing to her face but she ignores it. She pulls a handkerchief from her sequined evening bag and delicately places it against her face, blotting away as much spit as she can without smearing her foundation.

Jacqueline's voice is barely above a whisper. "I'm so sorry, Ginny. He shouldn't have. I should have stopped him."

Ginny shakes her head and drops the handkerchief to the floor. She places a thin cigarette between her ruby lips. Jacqueline's hand appears under the flame of a chrome Zippo.

The man and Jacqueline hold their breath.

Finally, Ginny says, "I did not appreciate that."

The man says, "I don't give a fuck. If someone didn't already take your balls, I'd slice them off myself."

Ginny rubs the bridge of her nose. "Christfuckingdammit. I will never, ever understand why I need to explain this as often as I do." She grabs a folding chair from the corner and drags it, screeching, across the floor. She sits on the edge and stretches the hem of her cream-colored Zac Posen dress over her knees. "Honey, I am not a transsexual. I am a drag queen. There is a difference."

"Still a fag."

"You are not the brightest pole in the marble bush, are you?"

"What the fuck does that mean?"

"Nothing. I'm testing your comprehension level. I want to make sure you understand what I'm about to say." Ginny drops her cigarette on the floor and grinds it out under the point of a strapped Kelsi Dagger heel.

"I have a bona fide, fully-functioning penis," she says. "Lucky for you I don't feel inclined to prove it. But despite my penis, I like to look pretty. That doesn't make me any less dangerous. And in fact, you should concern yourself with what a lifetime of abuse and ridicule has turned me in to. Do you understand?"

The man shakes his head. "Whatever. You're fucking dead when I get out of here."

"I'm terrified, completely." Ginny leans forward and drops her voice. "Now, I need the name of your employer."

"Who the fuck do you think you are?"

"I am Ginny Mother Fucking Tonic, and everything in this town between the Bowery Ballroom and Union Square belongs to me. If your boss is going to work this neighborhood then he needs to make me an offer."

"Fuck you."

Ginny leans back in her chair and smiles. She changes her tone, bringing the tension down a few clicks. "I know this guy you work for is new in town. No one who does business here would cross me. And your accent tells me you're a native. Queens, I think. Logic dictates you're a recent hire. The question you should ask right now is, have you known your boss long enough that he cares what happens to you?"

The man's lips part, then he purses them together until they go white. He sniffs. "Don't try to fuck with my head, faggot."

Ginny nods, puts another cigarette in her mouth. Jacqueline

lights it. Ginny takes a deep drag. "I hate that word. Not for the history or the intent. Because it lacks creativity. I'm going to get you a thesaurus for Christmas. As for right now, all I can give you is this."

She lunges forward and places the glowing tip of her cigarette underneath the man's left eye.

The crackle of singing flesh is quickly overtaken by a white hot scream. The man jerks back and twists his arms against the tape, trying to reach the mottled skin flecked with black ash under his eye.

Ginny puts the cigarette back in her mouth and lets it hang. "How did that feel?"

"Fuck. You."

"You must be a wonderful conversationalist. Now, you've got two options before you."

Ginny unfurls her right hand, palm up. "You can choose to play ball and I'll let you leave here with all your parts intact." Ginny holds up her other hand. "Or you can pursue this tough-guy routine and end up on the bottom of the East River. To be perfectly honest it makes no difference to me."

The man opens his mouth to say something but Ginny puts up her index finger. "I want you to think very carefully about the next thing you say. You did break one of my nails with your skull. I'm not feeling especially merciful."

The man's eyes dart hard to the left, at an empty space on the other side of the room. "You don't scare me."

"Yes, I do. Now, decide. What's it going to be?"

The man doesn't even think about it. He smiles like he's proud. "I ain't no rat."

"More's the pity." Ginny turns to Jacqueline. "Darling, go upstairs. Next to my makeup kit is a toolbox. It's blue. Inside, there's a rotary tool. You know what that is, don't you?"

"Yes, Ginny."

"There's also a little case of attachments." She sneaks a quick smile at the man in the chair. "You know what? Just bring down the whole damn box. I'm not actually sure what I'm in the mood for."

Jacqueline nods and bounds up the metal stairs. Ginny yells after her. "And grab a bottle of red. Cab sav, if we have any left."

Ginny gets up, smooths the wrinkles in her dress, and walks to the stereo in the corner. She pulls the iPod from the top and runs her finger around the scroll wheel. "What are you in the mood for? I'm feeling a little jazzy, but the next hour or so is going to be very unpleasant for you, so I guess it's only fair to let you pick the music."

The man says nothing, just stares at the water stains on the stone wall across from him.

"Fine," Ginny says. "I hope you like Thelonius Monk."

The music fills the small room. Ginny snaps her fingers in time with the high notes of *Bemsha Swing*.

Jacqueline comes down the stairs balancing the items she was sent to fetch. As she sets the rotary tool and its attachments on the workbench, Ginny puts her mouth next to her captive's ear. "You can consider this a valuable learning experience. For you and for my friend."

The facade cracks. The man looks past Ginny, at Jacquelyn, with pleading eyes.

Ginny purrs in his ear. "She can't help you."

She sways to the workbench in time with the music, regards the attachments as though they're a display case of diamond rings, hovering over them, afraid to commit to just one.

Then her hand darts out. She picks it up and holds it to the light.

"This one is my favorite," she says. "The pumpkin carving attachment."

ANOTHER DRESS, RUINED. Ginny never had the good sense to wear black for these things. Instead, she went in wearing a light-colored cap-sleeve mermaid gown, now completely awash in splotches of brown.

"Occupational hazard," she says to her empty bedroom as she strips off the dress and tosses it in the corner. She shuffles to the corner and plugs her iPod into the stereo. Thelonius Monk starts back up, but it sparks sour memories. She changes it to Nina Simone and lets out a long, exaggerated breath.

That could have gone better. An hour in, it became fairly evident this guy was, indeed not a rat. Or maybe he didn't actually know his boss' name. Either way, he endured a hell of a lot before that conclusion was reached.

Ginny pulls off her auburn wig and places it on a disembodied mannequin head next to the vanity mirror. She leans in close into her reflection and finds a dried splash of blood across her chin.

Her body sags as she reaches for the container of baby wipes to take off her makeup. It's been a long day and she has little interest in doing anything else tonight. As she wipes away her midnight eyeshadow, she considers Jacqueline, who did a decent job tonight, but requires further molding.

Ginny would have given up on her already if it hadn't been for occasional bouts of severe cleverness, and the glint in her eye as they started in on their captive. At least the girl wasn't squeamish.

Just a few months ago she was some skinny kid named Mark, fresh off the bus from Alabama. Now, Jacqueline Coke was on her way to becoming a lieutenant in Ginny's army of queens. She just needed a bit more nerve.

After removing her makeup and stockings, Ginny stumbles to the bathroom and swallows the white OxyContin pill waiting on a silver tray by the sink. It gets caught in her throat and the water she drinks from her cupped hands strips away the outside coating. It takes a moment to get it down, not before leaving a bitter taste of aspirin in her mouth.

She spits a few times, then pulls out her straight razor and shaving cream. She looks in the mirror and frowns, pulls her cheek taught, and brushes her finger across the stubble. Long ago, she had accepted the fact that her five o'clock shadow was an around-the-clock fixture, peeking through even the thickest foundation, but that was no reason to give in.

She sits on the toilet with a hot towel draped over her face, and just as her head is bobbing back from the Oxy, there's a knock at the door.

Ginny considers ignoring it, then tosses the towel in the sink and trudges through the living room, kicking aside mismatched heels. Before she reaches the door, she dashes back to the bedroom to yank her wig back into place.

She puts her face against the inside of the door. The wood is cool on her cheek. The drugs are whisking her away and she's not interested in company. "Darling, if we are not in the midst of the apocalypse, I hope you have a good reason for disturbing me."

"It's Ash."

Ginny rolls her eyes so far back it hurts. If Ash is here, it's for good reason.

She opens the door and he towers over her like a slab of granite. Most people would be nervous around him, and they would be wise to do so. He's grown a beard, and it looks pretty good, not that Ginny would admit that. She steps aside from the door and stretches her hand toward the Victorian walnut easy chairs in the corner. "Sit. Can I offer you a drink?"

"I'll take a glass of Jay if you've got it."

"I only have vodka."

"That'll work." Ash strides to the far chair, sits, and stretches his legs out, his heavy boots *thudding* on the floor. Ginny offers him the half-empty bottle. He takes a long swig and holds it out to her. She shakes her head and sits, adjusting her nightgown and robe.

"So, Ash. The beard is an interesting addition. Very Joycian."

"I *am* Irish."

"Still, I admire your bravery." Ginny fights through the drugs that are clawing her eyes closed, and reaches for the pack of cigarettes on the edge of her vanity. "Darling, I am not long for this evening. Is this a social call? Because if it is, I'm afraid I'm not going to be good company."

Ash takes another gulp of vodka, puts the bottle on the floor next to him. "Not tonight. I come on business. I have something you may want."

With an air of exhausted exasperation, Ginny asks, "Rob Lowe in a leotard?"

"Nope. The name of the guy Johnny is fucking you over for."

Ginny cocks her head, suddenly awake, and claps her hands together. "Ash, my love, you don't understand how badly I wanted to know that." Then she narrows her eyes. "How did you know I was looking for that?"

"I ran into Samson at the bar downstairs. And before you say it, no, he wasn't just offering up intel. He said something about Johnny and I said something about Johnny and it just went from there. He suggested I come talk to you."

"Well, gold star to him, then. What do you have for me?"

"Two names. One is the name of the guy. The other is the name of the bar he's at tonight."

"How did you learn this?"

"Doesn't matter, does it? Important thing is I'm giving it to you."

Ginny opens her mouth to say something. Ash shakes his head. "Christ, Ginny, I've known you since your name was Paul. Do you really think I'm going to fuck you on this?"

Ginny exhales. She slides down in the chair and looks past Ash. "I'm sorry. Please don't think me insensitive. You are one of very few people I'd actually allow in here." She waves her hand across her face. "To see me like this."

"Fine. Just, you know, don't forget who your friends are."

"You give me these names, and what do you want in return?"

"I hadn't thought of that."

"You're lying."

"Am not."

"Everyone wants something."

"The things I want I can get on my own. I came here because you're my friend and someone is cutting into your business. Can't that be enough?"

"I don't believe in freebies, Ash."

"Fine, then owe me one. A favor. And you know that just means I'm going to stumble into your bar one night and demand free drinks. Can you live with that?"

"That works."

"The man you're looking for is Daley. First or last name, I don't know. The bar is called The Soviet. Do you know it?"

"Well enough."

Ash slaps his hands onto his knees and gets up. Then he reaches down for the bottle of vodka. "Taking this with me. Doesn't count toward your debt because I still want my whiskey."

"Understood." Ginny rises and takes Ash's hand. They shake and he turns to leave.

As he twists the knob to the door, Ginny says, "Ash."

He doesn't turn around. "Yeah."

"Thank you."

"That's what friends are here for."

GINNY LAYS TWO lines of coke on the pearl-handled hand mirror on her vanity, then coats the inside of each nostril. Just enough to balance out the Oxy.

When the blow kicks in and her head stops swimming, she goes about applying her makeup. Using a paintbrush, she dabs foundation around her face and rubs it in with her fingertips until it disappears.

She applies a pale silver highlight to her eyelids, blending it with a pinky until it just barely disappears into the skin of her face. Then she attacks her lips, first with a pencil, to lay down the thick brown outline that will stand out in the red lighting of The Soviet.

She leans into the mirror to inspect her face. She looks like a cheap hooker at the end of a bad shift, but the thought of more makeup is exhausting.

Then there's the closet. She flips through her clothes, sliding hangers across the chrome bar, passing over dresses that are too short or too tight or too elegant. She settles on a matte Jersey infinity dress with a flare skirt by Donna Karen. Something simple, a little fancy, but more importantly, she can move around in it.

She drapes a beige pashmina over her shoulders and tugs her wig in place. As she inspects herself in the mirror, she frowns;

something is missing. Then she remembers the obnoxiously huge Russian fur hat she got as a gift and subsequently buried in the back of the closet. It doesn't take long to locate. An ushanka, she thinks it's called.

The hat works with the outfit. Certainly appropriate for the destination, and anyway, it's a little chilly. She inspects herself in the mirror one more time, and confident that her armor is intact, she heads for the door.

Then she stops. It would be silly to go into this naked, so she goes back to the vanity, hikes up her dress, and straps on her garter holster. From the right drawer she pulls out a Kel-Tec P-32, so small it nearly disappears in her hand.

She checks the clip, finds it full, and slides it into its strap.

As she exits her apartment, she clicks at the face of her phone, sending a text to Samson: *Car.* By the time she exits the building, Samson is leaning against the black Lincoln Town Car, smoking a cigarette and staring through reflective sunglasses at the drunken women littering the sidewalk outside Chanticleer.

Ginny snaps her fingers at him. "Find something to play with later."

Samson flicks his half-done cigarette onto the pavement and moves to open the door of the car, moving quicker than his size would indicate he could. Then he climbs in the front and pulls away from the curb.

Ginny takes a glass vial of white powder out of a pouch in her purse and leans forward to blow another line.

That one sets her just about right.

GINNY WRAPS THE pashmina tighter around her shoulders and curses herself for not wearing a warmer jacket. The hat helps, but it's also a little too big, and she has to concentrate to keep it straight.

She sucks down the last drag of a skinny cigarette and lets it drop to the asphalt. This is stupid. She should send in Samson. He doesn't say much, because as a bald black man with shoulders as wide as he is tall, he doesn't need to. It helps that he doesn't smile, either.

But still, Ginny feels compelled to handle this. Part of her success in this neighborhood has come from her hands-on approach. She doesn't ask anyone to do anything she wouldn't do herself. People see that and they respect it.

This guy, Daley, whoever he is, he's trying to move in on her land, and if she sends someone else, it'll convey a message that maybe she's not too concerned with the value of said land.

So Ginny draws up from her slouch to a razor-sharp pose. She sets her lips into a sneer and arches her back. Over her shoulder to Samson, she says, "Keep it running, darling. I don't know how long we're staying."

She pulls out her cell again and hits a few numbers. Then she holds her arm up like she's lofting a martini, clicks the phone off, and sashays into The Soviet.

IT'S A WEEKDAY so the bar is crowded but not packed. When Ginny walks in, every conversation stops.

From the first time Ginny smeared her mother's lipstick across her mouth as she stood on the bathroom counter, she knew what she was doing wasn't a mere indulgence. She also knew, even from that young age, she would never make a convincing woman. Her Adam's apple was too pronounced. Her slight body too straight and bony. That became part of the game.

But regardless of why the people in the bar had stopped to stare—aghast, disgusted, intrigued—they were still looking, and that's all that ever mattered to Ginny.

She slides up the bar and puts a long hand on the wooden top. The bartender looks up from the glass he's polishing, and without saying anything, points to the back, toward a bank of three doors. One of them isn't a bathroom, so that's the one Ginny picks to walk through.

It's a small room with plain walls. More like a large storage closet with room enough for six people to stand in and have an intimate conversation. Pushed up against the back wall is a poker table with a man sitting behind it.

The man is in his thirties, with hair bordering on gray and an easy look about him, like a movie star who's growing old and isn't too concerned about it. There's an ashtray on the table in front of him and half a cigarette sending tufts of smoke into the air.

The door closes and the sound of the bar is cut off. Soundproofed.

The man doesn't say anything. Ginny doesn't want to be the first one to talk, but she has no choice when it becomes clear that the man isn't budging. In fact, he hasn't budged at all, to the point where she wants to check for a pulse.

"So," Ginny says. "What does it take for a lady to get offered a seat in a joint like this?"

The man smiles. "Forgive me. I've been rude."

He gets up and pulls out the chair across from him and helps Ginny into it, like a gentleman on a first date. He returns to his seat and picks up his cigarette, which has gone out. He relights it with a wooden match and takes a deep drag before setting it back down again.

Ginny says, "Daley. I wish I could say it was a pleasure, darling."

Daley smiles again. It's such a warm smile. He speaks with a slight Russian accent. He says, "But I find this very pleasurable."

"Not for long, maybe."

"We'll see. Would you like a drink? Dare I say, a gin and tonic?"

"I'll take a seltzer with lime."

Daley leans over and presses a button on a small box next to the ashtray. He says, "Seltzer with lime."

He leans back and smiles, waiting. A few moments later, two men come in the room. Big guys. Ginny doesn't turn to look; that'll make her look afraid. She can tell from their footsteps, and how they block the light.

One of the men puts the drink down in front of her, and the other places a rocks glass of amber liquid, straight, in front of Daley. The two men take guard at Ginny's shoulders. Just close enough that she can't forget they're there.

Daley takes a sip of his drink and glances down at Ginny's untouched glass. "Please."

Ginny laughs. "How do I know you didn't spike it?"

"Because if I wanted you dead, I would have shot you as soon as you walked in and that door closed."

Ginny draws in her breath, involuntary, vulnerable. She leans forward to hide it, then picks up the drink and sips to show she's not afraid. She sets the glass down. "Wonderful. I was parched."

"That is a very interesting name," he says. "Ginny Tonic. What made you choose that?"

"Why so interested?"

He waves the glass. "Because I'm curious to know more about you."

Ginny takes another sip of the seltzer, her brain crackling from the coke. "Gin tastes like Christmas."

"It does taste like Christmas, doesn't it?" He takes another sip of his drink, leans forward. "I'm a scotch man myself. I like the smoke. I like a drink that tastes like fire. I guess that's the difference between us." He raises his fist, pumps it, scrunches his face. "I like my drinks a little more...masculine."

"Scotch all tastes the same to me," Ginny says. "And it gives me a headache. So, apparently, do scotch-drinkers. Darling, how about we get down to it?"

Daley sits back, curling his lip. "You mean my position as your new partner."

"I don't even get dinner first?"

"I'm not one to drag things out."

Ginny can't tell if it's a pun. Her cell phone buzzes in her purse. She reaches for it and he puts one hand up, the other close to the inside of his jacket. He says, "It's rude to reach for something like that."

"Just my phone."

"Would you mind putting it on the table? I'm sorry to ask, but I think it's only fair that we can see each other's hands."

Ginny doesn't nod, doesn't acknowledge him, just places her cell phone on the table and hits the button on the side to make it stop vibrating. She pulls out her own cigarettes and puts them next to the phone, then places one between her lips. Daley leans over and lights it for her.

"You're quite the gentleman for someone who's trying to fuck me. And not in the nice way."

"I'm not fucking you. It's a mutually beneficial relationship."

Ginny almost chokes on her cigarette. "Honey, I've been running this show for three years now by myself. Why would I need to go into business with someone?"

"Because I can bring a lot to the table."

"What do you have that I could possibly need?"

"Manpower. Knowledge. I have hooks into the district leaders in the northern territories, and I have knowledge of how business works in other parts of the city."

"So do I."

"I also have extensive connections in the police department."

"And I blow the detective inspector from the precinct down the block from my bar. So what?"

The smile fades from Daley's lips. He picks up his cigarette, lights it, takes another drag, places it back down. "Together, I believe we could be very powerful."

"Then why did you move into my territory without asking me first? Was I supposed to be impressed that you were encroaching on my businesses?"

"No, the reason for that was that I plan on moving into this neighborhood regardless of how you answer. I'm offering you the opportunity to maintain a foothold. I, of course, will be running things. But you will answer to me."

"That doesn't sound like a partnership."

"To you and your people it will be."

"So, you're trying to overthrow me."

Daley shrugs.

Ginny's cell buzzes again. Her finger lingers on the side. She never takes her eyes off Daley. Then she shrugs back and hits the button. Then she says, "I refuse."

"That's not an option."

"Of course it is. I've never heard of you. I've never seen you. I have broken so many nails to get where I am. You're not welcome, you're not my partner, and I will give you one chance to pack up and leave, or else you will be dead by the end of the night."

Daley nods. He looks sad, like a friend died. Then he says, "Well, then you leave me no choice."

He snaps his fingers again. Before she can turn, something heavy snaps across her skull and the lights dim.

STONE STEPS. THE smell of hard water and stale beer. Darkness and a harsh light. Ginny fades in and out until finally she's doused with a bucket of water and manages to shake off the buzzing in her skull.

She looks up at Daley, holding an empty bucket. He's smiling, except now it's a lot less warm. He leans down in front of her and places a hand on her cheek. Ginny tries to say something but she's still a little loopy from the blow to the head and the cocktail of drugs in her blood. The pain rolls around her brain, making it hard to think.

"So, this is where you find yourself," Daley says. "You could have accepted my offer. I wouldn't have hurt you. You must understand, you made me do this."

With great effort, Ginny manages to string words together. "You know, funny, this is how I started my day. I guess I'm paying some sort of karmic debt."

"Yes, my messenger. He was collateral damage. I wasn't expecting to get him back."

"Then I can't disappoint you."

Daley drags a chair across the floor and places it in front of Ginny. Her vision is steadying and she takes in her surroundings. It's a basement. Another basement under a bar. They're boxed in by kegs. Her hands are tied down with thick pieces of rope. Her legs, too.

Daley places a cigarette between Ginny's lips and lights it for her. She takes a few drags as Daley leans back and crosses his legs.

Ginny says, "Why not just kill me?"

"Because there are things I need to know, about how things operate around here. You're going to tell them to me. If you tell me enough, maybe I'll let you live."

"Somehow I doubt that," Ginny says, trying to not drop the cigarette.

"How would you feel if I told you that your driver has been detained, and I can make the next few hours of his life exceedingly uncomfortable?"

"Samson is a loyal soldier. He knows the risks."

"I'll just have to make life exceedingly uncomfortable for you."

"Then just keep talking, darling."

Daley nods and produces something from his pocket. He brings up his hand into the light. A shiny straight razor with a pearl handle. He pulls up the hem of Ginny's dress, revealing her bare knees.

He shakes his head. "I don't understand why men want to dress like women."

"The day men's clothing is as fabulous as women's, then I'll come back."

Daley presses the razor to the exposed flesh above the knob of Ginny's knee. He presses down, enough to indent the skin but not enough to break it. "But how can anyone take you seriously? To dress like that, like a woman, how is that a sign of strength? How do you expect people to respect you?"

"They don't need to respect me. They just need to be afraid."

He presses down on the razor. The skin separates and a small trickle of blood rolls down the outside of Ginny's leg. She doesn't move, doesn't change the tone of her voice. She just looks straight at Daley. "You may believe the way I look to be a sign of weakness, but the first time you get your ass kicked by a man dressed like a woman, that changes your perspective."

"But you aren't kicking my ass."

"Give it a few minutes."

Daley drags the razor toward Ginny's crotch, cleaving the skin. She breathes in sharp and tenses her shoulders. It hurts and she wants to cry out but she bites the tip of her tongue and asks, "Before I answer any questions, I need to know something."

"Hmm?"

"Ash is loyal as a clock. How did you get him to flip?"

There are footsteps in the corner, outside the range of light. Ginny didn't realize they weren't alone. A manicured hand appears on Daley's shoulder. "No, dear, Ash didn't do this. At least, not directly."

That voice. The figure steps into the light, the glitter in her blonde wig scattering the light.

Jacqueline Coke says, "Ash wasn't your problem."

"Well, Jacqui, I guess I made a mistake by putting my trust in you."

"You did."

"What are you getting out of this?"

"I'll be king of the queens when you're gone. Daley's liaison into the community."

"That's lovely for you, dear. But indulge me, please. How did you get Ash in on this?"

"He likes to drink and he likes to please. Wasn't hard."

"Well, good to know, for future reference."

Jacqueline leans down to Ginny, her voice guttural and mean. "You think you're so clever. Sitting up on high, giving orders. Making people dance for you. You never realized that I was a plant. I didn't even think I was that good an actress. And yet, somehow, I managed to take everything away from you."

Ginny laughs, then spits in Jacqueline's face.

Jacqueline draws the back of her hand across her cheek, then balls up her fist and smashes it across Ginny's face. Ginny's head snaps back and she feels something in her jaw go loose. She drops her head and blood leaks from her mouth onto the floor.

Jacqueline takes the straight razor from Daley and presses it to Ginny's face. "I'm going to take something from you. Something you value. And then we'll see if you're interested in talking."

Instead of moving, instead of flinching, Ginny laughs. Long and hard, her voice echoing off the stone walls. So loud and so hard that Daley and Jacqueline are visibly upset by it.

When Ginny has finally calmed down, Daley asks, "Did I miss a joke?"

"Not really, but where my phone?"

"I left it upstairs."

"Did you break it? Do anything to it?"

"No."

"Good. Then this will all be over soon."

Daley leans forward. "How so?"

"I have this fun little program built into my phone. When I activate that program, it buzzes every ten minutes, and unless I turn it off, it broadcasts an emergency text and my current location."

Daley smiles. "I remember you reaching for your phone. I should have put that together. But I think it's been twenty minutes or so. So where are the reinforcements?" He looks up at the stairs and hears nothing but silence beyond them. "I think you are bluffing."

"Honey, I don't bluff."

Daley looks at Jacqueline. "Did you know about this?"

She's breathing hard. "No, I didn't."

Daley looks less sure but then shakes his head. "You are bluffing."

"I'll tell you what." Ginny smiles. "You untie me, no one dies. That is the most mercy I've shown anyone in a very long time. I'll give you until the count of five to start."

Jacqueline and Daley stay frozen. Ginny shakes her head.

Daley says, "You are lying to us."

Ginny says, "Maybe I am. Five."

"What?"

"Four."

"What are you doing?"

"Counting. Three."

"You are lying."

"Two."

"Stop it."

"One."

Everyone freezes. They look up toward the stairs. And nothing, not a sound. Daley laughs. "You really thought you would scare me into untying you. You are ballsy for a man without balls, I will give you that."

Ginny presses her lips together. "Christfuckingdammit."

From upstairs there's the sound of a wooden ruler smacking against a desk. It happens three more times in rapid succession. Something topples to the floor and there's a scream.

Jacqueline looks at Ginny, her eyes rippling with fear. "How did you know they were here?"

"I didn't. It was a guess. But how amazing would that countdown have been if my timing was better?"

Daley reaches inside his jacket. "A shame they weren't faster to respond."

Ginny looks up at Jacqueline. "Restrain him and you won't die down here."

Jacqueline doesn't hesitate. She tackles Daley into pile of kegs

96

and they crash to the floor, outside of Ginny's field of vision.

Ginny listens to them struggle and smiles, waiting for someone to untie her.

JACQUELINE WAKES TO find herself in the same chair in which she and Ginny tortured a man earlier than night. Bound with the same roll of duct tape. Something thick and wet soaks the bottom of her dress.

Ginny leans against the wall, just outside the circle of light. A thin cigarette dangles from her lips, smoke billowing from her lungs.

Jacqueline says, "You said you wouldn't kill me."

"I said I wouldn't kill you down there. Did you really think I'd give you a pass on this? It was a fairly large transgression."

"Please, Ginny."

"Don't beg. It's not becoming of a lady. Now, we have some things to discuss. I need to know everything you told Daley, and if there's anything else I need to be concerned about."

"Fuck you."

"Ah, this old dance. Don't worry. You will talk. And in case you're not feeling inclined…"

Ginny plugs in her iPod, setting it to *Bemsha Swing*. Then she turns, the rotary tool in her hand.

"I believe you remember the pumpkin carving attachment, darling."

CONFESSIONS OF A TACO TRUCK OWNER

MONDAY

WHEN I WENT to close up today, the back tire closest to the sidewalk looked like it had melted. Upon closer inspection, I found the handle of a paring knife sticking out of the side.

Assuming a forward thrust, the angle of the knife indicates the assailant was walking east to west. That narrows down the list of suspects considerably.

It couldn't be those whale-hugging hippies from the vegan cupcake truck. They don't eat enough protein. No way they've got the upper body strength to get a knife through the thick wall of a tire.

It couldn't be the soft-serve ice cream guy. If he was intent on sending me a message, that knife would be sticking out of my chest.

A week in the world of New York City's food trucks, and this is what I've learned: you do not fuck with the soft-serve guys. I've heard they drain the blood of their enemies to artificially color the strawberry ice cream. Which I'm sure is hyperbole. What's not hyperbole is the fact that the vast majority of ice cream trucks are actually drug fronts.

So, who does that leave?

The hot dog vendor around the corner isn't a fan of mine. You'd think tacos and hot dogs would not be adversaries, but both can be served up quickly, and my carnitas tastes way better than his ground-up circus animals.

The kids in the Korean barbecue truck, maybe. They certainly seem like the type.

That's not racist. I'm not saying Koreans are knife-wielding tire slashers. It's just that one kid, the one in charge, is always wearing a *Scarface* t-shirt. And anyone wearing a *Scarface* t-shirt is probably an asshole.

The only other food truck in that direction within a few blocks is the waffle truck. But the guy on the waffle truck has been nice to me so far. He came over on my first day, gave me a free waffle, I gave him a free taco, I figured we were best friends now.

Unless it was a ruse.

A keep-your-enemies-closer kind of thing.

TUESDAY

SOMEONE MIGHT BE trying to kill me.

The thing I didn't write about yesterday, because I was real angry about the knife in the tire, is that I had a good run of business. I was working so hard and so fast that I ended the day with a sprig of cilantro in my sock. And I was wearing long pants. How does that even happen?

There was a conference at the college across the street. That's why it was so busy. I don't know what the conference was for. But the line was full of pasty introverts with crippling egos and no fashion sense. I'm guessing they were writers.

So for once, it seemed like I'd be in the black for the day. And then I got to the storage yard in Queens this morning, ready to spend a little extra time on cleaning and prep. The guy who gives my truck the once-over in the mornings says there's a problem with the brake line.

Says it looked like someone tried to cut it.

Not all the way, but enough that it would snap if I stopped short.

The guy allows it could be the chewed-up roads shot something up into the chassis. I don't know. After the tire, I'm a little antsy.

So the money I made yesterday is going to fix this. Which means it's not going into my rent. Handing that wad of cash over was like a fillet knife twisting around my guts. Wear and tear is one thing. Attempted murder is another.

Makes me miss Portland. Everyone there is either too polite or too high to pull shit like this.

WEDNESDAY

THE HEALTH INSPECTOR came by today.

He comes up to my truck wearing khakis and a white button-down shirt and a bad attitude. Like I kicked his dog into a coma and then forced him to do a surprise inspection.

I don't fuck around. My Mobile Food Vending Permit is in order. Since I handle raw meat on the truck, I have a sink for hand washing. And soap dispensers. And paper towel dispensers. The hot food is held at 140 degrees, and the cold food at 40. My prep surfaces are sterile as an operating room.

This guy, though, he was looking around like it was a fresh crime scene.

Like everything was something I should be guilty about.

He stuck the needle of his thermometer through the plastic wrap covering the guacamole, and told me I had a problem. He said: hot food needs to be held at 140 degrees.

Very politely, and without using words like "fuck-brain" and "douche-rocket," I explained to him that it's guacamole, which is served cold, and therefore needs to be held at 40 degrees.

He shook his head. Said: hot food needs to be held at 140 degrees. Like he was reciting it directly from a rulebook.

This is the point in our conversation where I did use the words "fuck-brain" and "douche-rocket."

You might be surprised to hear this, but I failed the inspection.

THURSDAY

NOW I SEE how business is done in this town.

I was up until four in the morning going over paperwork, trying to figure out how to appeal. Then I spent another hour going over my truck, just to make sure it wasn't booby-trapped.

So I drove into Manhattan and found a spot in Gramercy, set up the generator, tweeted my location, and finished the last of the prep. I was so tired I nearly took the tip of my finger off dicing jalapeos.

Just before I was ready to open, there was a knock at the back of the truck, and standing there is this young guy wearing a suit. A bad suit, like it belonged to his taller, skinnier brother.

Without me inviting him in, he just climbed up to join me. Without offering me his hand or his name, he told me he could help me with the inspection problem.

I hadn't told anyone I failed, and I asked him how he knew.

He said he works for a company that helps food vendors sort through inspection issues. When I asked him the name of the company, he didn't answer. I asked him how much his help would cost. The number he quoted me was about what I was hoping to make in the next three months.

That asshole may look at me and see a country mouse, but I know a shakedown when I see it. So I told him to get the fuck off my truck.

He said the permitting process is convoluted. Said that without friends—he pressed a finger into his chest when he said the word "friends"—that new food vendors can have an exceedingly hard time.

The way he said it made it sound like a threat.

FRIDAY

THREE HOURS AND not one damn customer. People looked at the truck and then they walked faster. I figured, it's New York City. Everyone's always in a rush.

I should have been smart enough to get out and look around. But it was three hours before I left the truck to go over to Starbucks for a piss break, and that's when I found the fliers.

There were five of them, applied with clear packing tape. Must have gone up after I parked, while I was prepping to open. At the top they said, in big, bold letters you couldn't possibly miss: REGISTERED SEX OFFENDER.

To be clear, I am not a registered sex offender.

I tore them down, and spent the next two hours fuming, and it made me careless, snapping at customers and fucking up orders. Which made me even angrier.

I know this is a tough town. I know we're all fighting to make it. But is this really the standard of New York City's business community? I just want to sell some tacos.

It's bad enough that the brick-and-mortar restaurants are lobbying the City Council to restrict our permits, and it's worse that the City Council is listening. You'd think the food truck guys would band together and go at this like a team.

Just as I was about give up for the day and head home, the waffle guy stopped over. Said I looked stressed out and asked how I was holding up. I told him about the past few days. He assured me the fixer probably wouldn't be necessary, and that his waffle batter had more reasoning ability than most of this city's health inspectors.

He told me we could grab a beer if I ever needed to vent, which I might take him up on. I don't have any friends in this town yet.

It calmed me down, him stopping by, so I got through the day. As I was gearing up to close, I noticed the bodega across the street had a camera. I went in and told the kid working the counter what happened with the fliers, and asked if I could see the tape from that morning.

I did not expect what happened next: he nodded, went in the back, returned with a DVD, said I could have it. Wished me luck, too.

I guess not everyone in this town is an asshole.

SATURDAY

THERE'S SOMETHING I think needs to be clear right now.

I drove across the country with a wad of cash and three changes of clothes and my favorite chef's knife. I'm living in a closet in Bushwick, which I'm renting from some asshole who glues pieces of wood together and calls it art.

I had a plan. Bust some ass, make enough money to hire some people, maybe graduate to a storefront. I'm not going to pretend like I wasn't afraid. Those late nights, driving across the northern tier of the country, nothing but darkness beyond the yellow arc of my headlights, there were times I almost turned back.

But I didn't. Because this is it. This is my one true love.

I watched the tape. And who was it that put up the sex offender fliers?

Waffle truck guy.

Soon as I saw it, I thought, I need to strike back. Let this motherfucker know I'm not weak. Problem was, I wasn't sure what to do. I could glue his tires to the roadway using two-ton epoxy—which is a thing a friend of mine did to someone in college—and the tires will shred before the truck moves.

But that would take time, and planning, and effort, so instead, this morning, I parked my truck in Gramercy, didn't bother tweeting my location. But I did take that paring knife I found sticking out of my tire, and slid it into the pocket on the front of my apron. Figured I would stab the shit out of his tires.

It wasn't creative, but it would make me feel better.

So I went looking for him, and as I turned the corner of the street where he's usually parked, I saw him talking to the guy in the bad suit. They shook hands like they were buddies. Another layer of subterfuge. It made me wonder if he sicced the health inspector on me, too.

And as soon as he saw me, he knew I knew he did what he did.

But he didn't see the knife. It was still in the pocket on the front of my apron.

He came at me with a big smile on his face, like it was a joke, or no big deal that he lost me thousands of dollars over the course of a week. I snapped. Called him a coward. Called him a dumb fuck. Said I was going to kick his ass.

He got close to me and his right shoulder dropped, broadcasting the punch he was about to throw.

And here's where things get hazy. How the fight-or-flight response can smear time like grease on a countertop. Because I can't, for the life of me, tell you how the paring knife that started in my tire and then I put in the pocket on the front of my apron ended up in his chest.

It just did.

When the world came back into focus, his eyes were frosted over, blood blooming on his white t-shirt, growing wet and thick and tugging on the fabric.

He began to fall backward.

Someone screamed.

I ran.

And here I am. Sitting in my little closet of a bedroom.

The shock of it hasn't settled into me yet. There's a hot, terrifying thing rumbling on the horizon like a thunderstorm, and I'm afraid of what'll happen when it crashes into me. Until then, I'm just numb.

At this moment, someone is banging at the door, and my artist landlord is passed out on the couch, high as fuck, and nothing's going to get him up. Of course it's the cops. Because I don't fuck around, and my Mobile Food Vending Permit is in order. Complete with my current address.

So now I just have to decide what to do with this. My journal. I could burn it or shove it in the toilet, but is it even worth the effort? There had to be a dozen witnesses. I'm fucked no matter what angle you take this from.

Since this will probably be presented as a courtroom exhibit, I would like to point out that I did not intend for any of this to happen. Even though that guy was a dick, and tried to ruin my business, I'm sorry I killed him. I shouldn't have taken the knife.

Though, I guess that's the folly of these things. Am I apologizing because I'm sorry, or because I'm about to be caught?

This is not the time to be philosophical. Because at this moment, there's a crash and a crack from the front of apartment. Cops breaking down the door, probably.

I had another plan for the future, too. After I built my taco empire, I was going to take this thing and turn it into a book. Even had a title planned out.

Confessions of a Taco Truck Owner.

I figured, in ten or twenty years, I would have mined enough material that I could have told a pretty good story. How to make it selling tacos in New York City.

Instead, it really did turn into a confession.

LAST REQUEST

CYNTHIA MARKS HAD dreamt her entire life of seeing New York City.

She wasn't worried about the sharp edges that made out-of-towners afraid to wear jewelry on the subway. The bad old days were long since gone and she knew that.

Her New York was Audrey Hepburn staring into the gem-filled window at Tiffany's, still wearing her dress from the night before. It was Ross and Rachel, playing out their will-they-or-won't-they romance around the comfortably worn couch at Central Perk. It was Billy Crystal's rambling profession of love to Meg Ryan at a New Year's Eve party, surrounded by the buzz of perfectly oblivious revelers.

It was a place where magical things happened, and there always seemed to be lights strung up somewhere in the background, twinkling like the stars you couldn't actually see in the night sky.

That's what it was supposed to be.

Instead, Cynthia found herself dodging greasy paper plates blown about by the wind, inching forward on a filthy Brooklyn sidewalk toward a pizza take-out window carved into the side of a brick building. She gazed at the red metal picnic tables, packed with people tearing into thick, square slices of pizza.

She didn't know pizza came in squares slices.

She wished she were sitting. With the way the sun was hammering down, her stiff gray uniform clung to her skin, sweat acting like glue.

Cynthia could have packed a change of clothes, a pair of shorts and a blouse to wriggle into after the plane touched down. But even if she could have gotten the clothes out of the house without Doug noticing, what would have been the point?

This entire trip, beginning to end, should last no more than nine hours.

Get off a plane, catch a cab, get the pizza, catch a cab, get on a plane.

Who was there to impress?

Not that a little part of her didn't hold onto a wistful fantasy that she'd meet a handsome man along the way.

Maybe waiting for a cab outside the airport. A man in a suit with windswept hair would make a clever comment, and she come back with a witty retort, and by some mystical turn of events they'd wind up in a place where "maybe" wasn't just a wish. But no, there was just a line of harried travelers, screaming into phones, choking on exhaust fumes that hung heavy in the humid air.

Maybe the cab driver would be a dark-haired rogue looking for someone to keep him company on the late shift, and they'd eat in a late-night diner where he'd regale her with wild tales from the job. Only in New York-type stuff. But no, her driver was a hunched

Eastern European man who reeked of sizzling meat.

The pizza line was her last hope.

But no, she found herself stuck. Between the Mexican family behind her, and in front of her, a man wearing a worn tank top, stained yellow with age. Although he didn't look capable of it, he smelled like he ran a marathon to get there.

Nothing about any of this trip was magical.

And for the hundredth time since she got to the airport this morning, she wondered what the hell she was doing this for. She settled on the same answer, even if she wasn't sure it was the right one: that everyone, no matter what sin they've committed, deserves a little dignity in death.

She looked up at the sign, stuck atop a black pole at the corner of the lot, looming over the line. Red cursive on white background.

M&C Spumoni.

What the hell is *spumoni*, she wondered.

THE JOKE WAS, Cynthia was chosen for her strawberry-blonde hair.

"He only kills brunettes," Cap had said.

Like it was supposed to be encouraging.

The truth was, budget cuts and staff reductions meant the administration had to think creatively. They realized they could move Cynthia's desk from her office in the main wing over to death row, and they wouldn't have to pay someone else to sit there all day.

"If anything happens," Cap said, "just call a real guard."

The day she arrived, she put down a small potted cactus, and her little faux-crystal Statue of Liberty—a souvenir from a friend who had spent a week in New York and needed someone to feed her cat. Sometimes Cynthia stared at it, wondering how the real thing would compare.

Her desk was at one end of a long, dreary hallway. Along the left wall, which was water-stain mint green, there were barred windows that looked out onto the activity yard. On the right was a line of five cells, and at the end was a blank wall with a small, off-center crucifix.

The day Cynthia moved in, only one of the cells was occupied.

The one holding the Southpaw Killer.

Cynthia stood at her desk for a long time, working up the courage to walk down to the end of the row and back, which she was told to do once every hour. She'd interacted with prisoners before. Never one she heard of before she laid eyes on him.

She took some time to adjust the plant and the statue so they were perfectly framing the boxy gray monitor. She logged on to her computer and checked her e-mail. She took a deep breath and got up and walked. As she got closer to the third cell, the one that was occupied, she drifted toward the wall with the windows, away from the bars.

The man was in his beige uniform pants, no shirt, his muscled torso catching the light and casting shadows that made him look like he belonged on the cover of a romance novel, a thought that immediately turned her stomach. He was sitting on the slab bolted into the wall that served as his bed, reading *Pride & Prejudice* by Jane Austen. On one side of the slab was a toilet with a sink built into the top. On the other side was a showerhead sticking out of the wall like it was an afterthought.

He wouldn't leave the cell until it was time to die. No physical activity in the yard, even. As Cap would say, dead men and nearly dead men had just about the same amount of rights.

The man looked up and put the book down. His smile was sharp, showing off his teeth like an anatomical drawing. But his eyes were soft. He had a thin beard, black and dashed with salt to match his hair. Cynthia didn't know what she was expecting, but she didn't expect him.

He nodded. "I must have finally done something good to get a guard pretty as you."

Something hot flashed in the middle of Cynthia, but she paved it over with fear and revulsion.

"I'm not here to chat," she said, continuing on her way, toward the end of the row, past the last two empty cells. She stopped at the crucifix, turned, and headed back the other way, not looking at the man as hard as she could.

"I didn't do it, you know," he said.

"They all say that," Cynthia responded.

As she neared her desk, he called, "I'm James."

She paused, wanting to say her name back, like a reflex. Instead, she sat down and gazed at the Statue of Liberty, its torch barely touching the bottom of her computer monitor.

THERE WERE TWELVE known victims, spread across three states, though authorities speculate there might have been more. All of them were college-aged, doe-eyed, brunette. When the local paper ran all their pictures together on the main page, they almost looked like sisters.

Each one was found missing her left hand.

Cynthia turned blue links purple, scrolling back and forth through Google, reading article after article as the computer choked and chugged like an old car.

James Winston was arrested on a description provided by two young boys who said they saw a man burying a body along a creek. Winston was a drifter, claimed to be passing through town. There was no evidence tying him to any of the crimes, no DNA, no proof he was actually at the place where those two kids said they saw him.

Just someone matching his description.

The jury deliberated for two days.

Cynthia wasn't an expert in anything. But looking at the scant evidence, she wondered how they could have wrapped up that quickly.

Meanwhile, the district attorney, the police chief, and a local state senator were all up for re-election. All three of them were running ads claiming they'd captured the Southpaw Killer and sentenced him to death.

The front door slammed open. Cynthia closed out all the windows on the computer, her finger slipping on the mouse, her heart racing.

Doug stomped into the kitchen, reeking of blood and raw pork. No matter how hard he scrubbed in the locker room showers, the smell of death always followed him home from the plant.

He stood in the middle of the kitchen, waiting. His brown eyes sunken, his thinning hair disheveled. Cynthia kissed him on the cheek, lips scraping against stubble, and she tried not to gag at the stink.

"Dinner?" he asked.

"We're overdrawn," she said.

"Well, what about a line of credit at the grocery store? I heard they do that sometimes. Those bastards can't just let good people starve, can they?"

Cynthia twitched a little at "good people."

"They put interest on it," she said. "We're going to wind up paying so much more. I know it's not ideal…"

"Dammit, Cyn," Doug said, smacking the flat of his fist into the fridge. An overdue bill tacked up with a magnet depicting the New York skyline came loose and drifted to the floor. "What the hell are we supposed to eat?"

"We got some pasta and I can dip into the pantry," she said. "Were you…were you able to bring home anything from work?"

Doug holds up his hands, gesturing to the empty space around him. "Do you see me carrying anything?"

"Well, no…"

"So I should bring the food home with me. Should I cook it, too? Do you want me to do everything? I work twelve-hour days just to keep the goddamn lights on. What more do you want from me?"

Cynthia nearly said it.

She nearly said that he ought to stop handing so much of their income to the bar around the corner. To the machine at the grocery store that sold lotto tickets.

Instead, she opened up the fridge, a beam of yellow light shooting between the two of them. She pulled out a can of beer and cracked it and offered it to him. "Just go on into the living room and put your feet up. I'll make something. It'll be good, promise. Tomorrow, I'll see about that line of credit."

He ripped the beer from her hand, white suds erupting from the top, splashing her arm. He stalked off but the smell of death remained.

Cynthia pressed both hands to her mouth and fought to keep from crying.

Hours later, after they had eaten pasta with jarred sauce and watched some television and Doug had passed out on his recliner, the living room scattered with beer cans like corpses, Cynthia retreated to the back porch with a glass of wine and the copy of *Pride & Prejudice* she got from the library.

"I HATE JANE AUSTEN," James said, putting aside the car magazine he'd been reading.

"Seems like an odd choice, then."

"Well, Cynthia, it's not like I have a whole lot of options."

Cynthia watched James, legs curled up onto the slab bed. A killer of women, and yet she couldn't get past those kind eyes. The sadness that permeated the space between them.

"What would you like to read?" she asked. "I can see if we have it."

James smiled and swung his legs around so he was sitting, facing her. The closest he'd gotten in all the times she'd passed by, because he always seemed to be curled up on that bed whenever she got close.

"What's your favorite book?" he asked.

"I don't have a whole lot of time for reading lately," she said.

"C'mon," he said, smiling. Showing his teeth. "Everyone has a favorite. Just name something."

"I really liked *The Stranger*," she said. "Albert Camus. I read it in college."

James nodded, resolute. "Then that's what I'd like to read. I've never read it."

"We don't have that one in the library," she said. "It's about a man condemned to death. Someone probably decided that's not good for inmates."

James rested his elbows on his knees. "I wouldn't want you to get in any kind of trouble. I'm just saying, if a copy were to find its way into this cell, I would be sure to hide it nice and good."

Cynthia turned and headed back for her desk. "You're not worth my job."

"I didn't think so," James said, the words echoing in the empty hallway behind her like a taunt.

CYNTHIA RAN DOWN the hallway, cursing Doug. He took the car and didn't fill up the tank and she had to stop at the gas station and now she'd be the last one to the briefing room.

There were ten guards to a shift and nine seats in the briefing room. It's not that she minded standing. She was more worried that Williams was working today, and that he'd have gotten a seat first.

Cynthia rounded the corner into the room and her heart sank. All the seats were filled.

"Hey, Marks," Williams said, smirking, spilling out his chair, pointing to the wide expanse of his lap. Something about the light in this room made his bald spot shine so much brighter, his pale skin so much waxier. "Plenty of room right here. Pay no mind to my nightstick if it pops up, okay?"

Cap shook his head. "Williams. One more time, I'm writing you up."

Cynthia was keeping count. It was the seventeenth time Cap made that exact same threat. And Williams responded the same way he always did.

"All in good fun," he said, looking at Cap. Then he shot a look at Cynthia. A shadow passed over his face and his voice grew stern. "Right?"

"Yes, sir." Cynthia nodded to Williams and then Cap. "All in good fun."

"Exactly right," said Williams. "You just have to know how to laugh. Marks knows how to laugh."

Cynthia forced a smile. "Good one," she said.

Williams nodded, looking around the room to make sure everyone realized his joke had gotten the sign-off.

Cap launched into his daily spiel and Cynthia was already far off, planning out the route that would take her through the infirmary and up two flights of stairs to the death row cells. Where instead of being catcalled, she would hear something nice from a nice-looking man. She reached back and patted her rear, double-checking she had that copy of *The Stranger* tucked into her pocket.

"**D**O YOU KNOW the origin of the last meal request for death row inmates?"

Cynthia looked up and down the narrow hall. The walk back to her desk was taking longer every time she did it.

She stepped a tiny bit closer to the cell, peering into the dim space. James was standing underneath the showerhead, leaning against the wall. Like he'd been waiting for her.

"Tell me," Cynthia said.

"It was a superstitious act," James said. "By accepting food, the prisoner was making peace with the jury and the executioner. This was so the person didn't come back as a revenant."

"What's a revenant?"

"A ghost."

Cynthia smiled. "Why not just say 'ghost'?"

"It makes me sound smarter."

A small laugh shot out of Cynthia, like air whistling from a balloon. She closed her mouth quickly and took a step back.

"Do you know what I would request for my last meal?" James asked.

"You're not going to get it, so what does it matter?"

"But aren't you curious?"

"No," Cynthia said, lying.

"C'mon." James curled up the right side of his mouth. "Smart girl like you. You're curious. You like knowing things. You're just waiting for an opportunity to use the word 'revenant' in conversation. Tell me I'm wrong."

The hallway was still empty. The crucifix on one end, her desk on the other.

"What would you order?" Cynthia asked.

"A slice of pizza from M&C in Brooklyn. Down in Bensonhurst."

Cynthia took a half-step forward. She looked down at her boots on the scuffed concrete floor, up at James again. Wondering if it looked demure. Wondering if she should be trying to look demure.

"You can get pizza everywhere," she said. "What makes that place special?"

"Well," Jason said. "You can get pizza anywhere, but you can only get good pizza in New York. Some people say it's the dough. Other people say it's the water. Like the mineral content. I think it's the place. Place matters just as much as anything. Do you know what alchemy is?"

"It's the combination of different elements into a new element," she said. "Like magic."

He nodded. "Like magic. What the hell are you doing working in a place like this, smart girl like you?"

The way he said "smart girl" made her smile.

She didn't hide her face. She let him see it, allowed the moment to hang.

"What's so great about this pizza?" she asked.

"It's just...perfect. I can't explain it. If you ate it, you would understand. You never look at a slice of pizza from around here the same way again."

Off in the distance, Cynthia heard a metal clank. A door opening and closing. One of the guards on rotation. She turned and walked back toward her desk.

"It's not fair, you know," James called after her. "What they're doing here is inhuman."

CAP HAD BEEN holding a stack of papers in his hand. When Cynthia was done with her practiced monologue, he whipped it down onto the desk with a crack.

"Are you kidding me with this?" he asked.

"I know it's…" Cynthia started.

"No, you don't know."

He heaved himself down into the beaten black roller chair. Everything in the office except the chair was white. The fluorescent light. His starched uniform shirt and bushy hair. The stacks of papers that framed him and the painted brick walls surrounding them.

Cap looked up, his eye twitching, a sign that he was really and truly annoyed. More so than his general state of agitation. He stared at Cynthia in a way that made her feel like she was getting smaller.

"Cap, look…" she said.

"You know the governor just shut this program down. All requests have to be fulfilled by family, or come from within five square miles of the prison. If I file this, they're not going to just ignore it. They're going to take it like we don't respect them. I'm going to get a phone call."

"The only thing within five square miles of here is an Arby's."

"Then he's got to eat Arby's," Cap said, leaning back, looking up at the ceiling. "That new Angus steak sandwich they got ain't too bad."

Cynthia goes diving for words. Something that will win him over. A cogent argument that'll get him to see the light. Instead, all she sees is light disappearing as she sinks deeper and deeper, drowning.

"Why do you even need to do this?" he asked, his face twisting into a sneer.

"Because it's kind."

"After what that son of a bitch did. All those girls."

She meant to say it with confidence but it came out like a little peep: "Allegedly."

Cap slammed his hand against the desk. It was an intimidation tactic, and it worked. Cynthia jumped, then cursed herself for it.

"He was convicted by a jury of his peers," Cap said. "I'm sorry that we're no longer fulfilling unreasonable demands of murderers and rapists. I'm sorry that offends your delicate sensibilities."

"It's not about that."

Cap sighed, leaning back again. Looking at the ceiling again.

"Do you remember that one guy, wanted that sandwich from the place in Atlantic City?" he asked. "One sandwich. The state has to pick up airfare and overtime and travel expenses. Do you remember that? Probably never been a sandwich that expensive. For a guy who murdered his wife and two children because he didn't want to have to go through the trouble of a divorce. That's actually what he said when they caught him. I remember that. I'm going to remember that for the rest of my life. That he did that hateful thing and then we had to spend thousands of dollars to get him a goddamn sandwich."

Cynthia took a deep breath, exhaled slowly.

"I know women are hard-wired for sympathy but this is a little ridiculous," Cap said.

His face was hard as steel. There was nothing she could say that was going to change his mind and she knew that.

So she went for the last resort.

"I have vacation time due to me," she said.

Cap just frowned and shook his head. At a loss for words.

Cynthia tried not to think too hard about how that made her feel.

"YOU CAN'T USE a microwave," said James. He was standing within arm's reach of the bars. "Do you have a toaster oven? Like in the break room?"

"We do." Cynthia, too, arm's reach from the bars, on the other side.

"Heat up the slices on the 'toast' setting, but carefully. Watch it close. As soon as you start to smell it, pull it out. You don't want to go through all of this and burn them."

Cynthia nodded. "Should I get any kind of topping?"

James laughed. "M&C doesn't need toppings. And...I need to ask you one other favor. And this is an important one"

He looked around and took a tentative step forward. Cynthia stayed where she was, even though she wanted to take a step toward him, but then he would be within arm's reach of her, and she wasn't there yet. She was saving that for when she got back.

"I want you to get two," he said. "And I want you to have it with me. I want you to have your first M&C slice and I want to see your reaction when you eat it. It's not as good as fresh, but it heats up pretty damn well."

Cynthia smiled. "Why is that important to you?"

James shrugged, suddenly taking on the gait and manner of a little boy. "Because I want to see how that pretty face lights up."

Cynthia's cheeks caught fire.

"Deal," she said.

"Good," James said.

"NOW BOARDING ALL zones. All zones may board now."

Cynthia held her ticket in a tight, sweaty fist. She was in the last zone, nearly maxing out the credit card Doug didn't know about to get there. She watched the stream of people dragging suitcases and bags onto the plane. Bleary-eyed, frowning, some of them still even wearing pajamas. Outside the floor-to-ceiling windows, the sun was just peeking over the horizon.

She stood there for a long time, watching the line dwindle. Wondering what it would take to get a refund at this point. Whether that was even possible.

She poked around the Internet the night before but couldn't find a good resource for how many people were exonerated after they were executed. Municipal governments don't want to spend money collecting data on things like that. But there were examples of it happening. Evidence or a witness or a new technology that made a dead man innocent too late.

For the death penalty to be just, it has to operate under a standard of absolutes.

And clearly, it doesn't.

But what if she was wrong? Cynthia couldn't know, truly know, if James was being honest. But she wanted to believe him. She wanted to believe that someone with eyes that kind couldn't do something so bad.

She wanted to believe that people were good.

She wanted to believe this, in spite of the fact that when Doug found out she spent money on this, he was going to hit her. That her co-workers would lose even that last tiny bit of respect they had for her. That Cap would give her that look, like a parent who's failed a child.

For what? James would be dead in the ground, that pizza maybe not even fully digested.

A young Asian woman in a smart navy blazer looked at Cynthia clutching her ticket, the last person standing in front of the gaping door leading to the airplane, and asked, "Ma'am? Are you ready to board?"

THE JAGGED SKYLINE of New York City jutted into the air. She got dizzy trying to count the buildings. Cynthia watched it recede, replaced by long stretches of suburbia, until they were up through the clouds and all she could see was blue sky and a carpet of white.

She tried to watch television, settling on a show about two families renovating their homes in a competition to see who can renovate their home better. The pizza sat in an insulated lunch bag on her lap.

She watched the color and light that flashed in front of her and tried to imagine what was going to happen. She and James would eat their pizza. James would die the next day. She would go home to Doug because she was unable to escape the gravity of their crumbling bungalow. She would come into work and stare at the Statue of Liberty and dream of seeing it up close.

Her stomach felt like an empty pit.

Her first trip to New York, and all those things she wanted to do besides see the statue—ride the Staten Island Ferry, see the Empire State Building, catch a Broadway show—right there at her fingertips. The opportunity disappearing behind her.

And in that moment, she made herself a promise.

She would go back.

Once she saw this through, once she'd proven she could do a difficult thing, she would leave. Doug, the job, everything. She was strong enough. She was proving she was strong enough just by being on the plane.

Cynthia had flown to New York City for a slice of pizza.

She could do anything.

She put her hand on the bag, warm in her lap, and smiled.

"HEY, IS THAT pizza?"

Williams lumbered into the break room and cut a line over to the nook with the toaster oven. He peeked in, his shoulder pressing against Cynthia. She shrank away from him.

"Is that a square slice?" he asked. "I didn't know you could get square slices."

Cynthia nudged him aside and pulled the two slices out, scorching her fingertips as she dragged them onto a thick stack of paper plates. The slices were thick and doughy, and it looked like the cheese was underneath the sauce. There was a snowfield of Parmesan cheese on top and the edges were slightly blackened, but that was okay because they came like that.

Williams reached out a meaty hand. "Let me get one of those."

Cynthia held the plate close to her body and twisted away. "No."

"C'mon, you have two. You could stand to watch your figure a little…"

Cynthia felt the rush of every joke, every comment, every leering glance, and now, coupled with the invasion into her space, something brittle and worn inside her finally snapped. She put the plate down on the counter, out of his reach, and threw her elbow into his gut.

He took a few steps back as he doubled over, face red, gasping for breath. The shock of it froze Cynthia in place, and then the mandatory twelve hours a year of personal defense training took over. She put her entire body into pushing him.

For a second she thought he wasn't going to budge. It was like pushing a fridge. And then he tipped back and crashed into the haphazard arrangement of chairs, going down with enough force, she swore she felt the floor rattle.

He was crying out, yelling something at her, but she wasn't

listening. She left the kitchen, cutting a path through the infirmary and up two flights of stairs to death row. Delicately balancing the paper plate holding the two slices of pizza.

Cynthia stopped at her desk. Wondered how she looked. She wished she had time to stop in the bathroom, maybe put on a little foundation or some mascara, but Williams was surely reporting her to Cap, and someone was going to come looking for her.

When they did come for her, she'd hand over her gear and walk right out. She wouldn't even go home. She'd get another plane ticket. She'd figure out how to pay for it. Go back to New York.

No more Doug. No more prison. She'd go and stand on a corner until something magic happened.

When she reached James's cell, he was sitting on his bed, legs drawn up, reading *The Stranger*. He looked at her and his eyes went wide. He put the book aside, stood, took a few steps forward. Even with the bars in the way, Cynthia felt vulnerable, but not in a scared way, in an open way. His voice was quiet, filled with awe. "I can't believe you actually did it."

She held up the plate with the two slices.

"Like you asked," she said.

He stepped forward until he was at the bars, pressing his forehead against them so he could get a good look. His eyes went glassy, bordering on the verge of crying. "I can remember my first M&C slice with my dad. And now this is the last." He took a deep breath, got lost in the maze of a memory. Finally, he looked up at Cynthia, a tear cutting a path from his eye and disappearing into his beard. "Do you know what that feels like, to know that?"

Cynthia didn't, but she teared up, because the emotion was so thick it was spilling off James and filling her up, too.

She took a step closer to where he could just barely reach her. The closest they had ever been. She wished she could open the cell, sit with him. Not touch, not that, but just sit next to him on that slab. Feel the warmth and weight of him next to her as they shared his final meal.

"I'm not an idiot," Cynthia said. "I just want to thank…"

"I did it."

It was like a punch to the chest, the air getting pushed from her lungs.

She tried to breathe and found that she'd forgotten how.

"What?" she asked.

"I need to be honest," James said, tears streaming down his face. "I feel like I owe you that. I did it. I killed those girls. I need to say it out loud. But I think you knew that. And it speaks to your character that even someone as damned as I am, that you would do a thing like this."

He reached his hand though the bars, nearly brushing the paper plate.

Cynthia took a big step back.

Those soft green eyes suddenly didn't look so soft. That smile looked so much more sinister. She thought of those girls. The sour taste of bile tickling the back of her tongue.

She let one of the slices fall.

It tumbled in the air until it splat, top side down, on the filthy concrete floor.

James fell to his knees, reaching for it, his mouth hanging open.

She wanted to rage at him. To open the cell and beat him to death. She wanted to inject the pentobarbital herself. She wanted to scream and cry. She wanted the world to open up and swallow her. She wanted a time machine to bring her back to that moment she stood at her desk and wondered what kindness was worth.

She couldn't do any of those things.

So instead, Cynthia picked up the other slice and took a bite.

She fought to swallow it, her throat thick and hot. James's face twisted, like someone was dragging a knife across his gut.

She stepped back, coming to a stop against the far wall, and she slid down it until she was sitting. She kept eating, holding eye contact with James as he wailed like an animal, thrashing on the floor, arm stretched through the bars, trying to reach it with the desperation of a drowning man reaching for a life preserver.

The ruined slice just a few inches from his fingertips.

As the metal door at the far end of the hall groaned open, Cynthia took the last bite of her slice. She put the plate down and wiped her mouth and locked eyes with James, who had stopped struggling. He was sobbing, his arm still stretched out.

"You were right," she said. "You were right."

TAKE-OUT

HAROLD WAS DOZING, his head resting against the tiled wall behind his chair, when Mr. Mo placed the brown paper bag in front of him. The bag was nested inside a milky-white plastic shopping bag, through which Harold could make out plastic utensils, packets of soy sauce, napkins, and a folded-up menu. Stapled to the top was a slip with an address on Mott Street.

"Crispy skin fish rolls," Mr. Mo said, his high voice cracking like a whip.

The man's face was flat and unreadable. His blue polo shirt stained with splotches of cooking grease, his slight potbelly and narrow limbs not really fitting into the shirt right. He could have been thirty or fifty. He only ever spoke English when he gave Harold a delivery.

He spoke English one other time, on Harold's first night.

Harold had sat down and pulled an electronic poker game up on his phone. Mr. Mo took the phone out of his hand, turned it off, and smacked it on the table. He placed a Chinese-language newspaper over the phone.

"No play," he said. "Read."

"But I can't read this," Harold protested.

"Read," Mr. Mo said, tapping his finger against the newsprint.

It had been three weeks, and Harold's Chinese hadn't gotten any better, so he looked at the pictures or dozed off until it was time to work.

Harold picked up the latest delivery and exited Happy Dumpling. The evening air was the kind of humid that made it hard to breathe. It was late, probably getting close to midnight, which meant this would, with any luck, be his last trip for the evening.

He hefted the bag, trying to guess at the contents. Then he pulled out his phone and punched in the address. It was close—just below Grand. He walked north, cut down Hester, and made a right. Found an apartment building with a nail salon on the first floor. The number 4 was circled on the receipt, so Harold hit 4 on the ancient buzzer.

After a few moments, the door screamed at him and he pushed it open, climbed the narrow staircase, where he found himself in front of a door painted glossy black, chipped in spots, gunmetal gray underneath. There was a peephole set at eye level.

The door was ajar, and it opened as soon as Harold stepped in front of it. A frail Chinese man in a wrinkled dress shirt and slacks, his white hair thinning, peered out from inside the darkened apartment.

Harold opened the bag, first undoing the staple that held it closed, then reaching in for the white take-out container.

He hated this part. The anticipation.

Sometimes he had to bring something back to Mr. Mo. Sometimes he didn't. He wasn't always sure which. Mr. Mo wasn't big on instructions. This was the first time he'd gotten an order for crispy skin fish rolls and he wasn't sure what that meant.

Harold placed the bag on the ground and opened up the take-out container, his hands shaking a little. Inside was a single pear. He looked at it for a moment, then took it out and offered it to the man, who breathed in sharply and put his hand to his mouth. Tears cut down his cheeks and he began to shake.

Harold pushed the pear forward into the space between them but the man refused to take it. Instead, he took a step back. Harold got the sense he wouldn't be bringing anything back to Mr. Mo tonight, so he put the pear on the floor in front of the door and left.

As he climbed down the stairs, he thought he heard the man weeping.

"**P**EARS ARE TABOO in Chinese culture," said Wen, putting his pint glass on the bar top, missing the coaster by a wide margin because he was looking at the TV mounted in the corner, currently displaying a Yankees game.

He wiped the sleeve of his MTA-issue baby blue dress shirt across his mouth. "The Chinese word for 'pear' sounds like the Chinese word for 'parting'. If I had to guess, it was a warning or threat. Mr. Mo is going to take something from him."

"Not like...his life or something?" Harold asked, his voice low, glancing around the mostly-empty bar to make sure no one else was listening. The only person even close to earshot was the bartender, a pretty college girl in a halter top and a cowboy hat. She was down at the other end of the bar and seemed more interested in something on her phone.

"Probably not," Wen said, undoing his ponytail, then doing it back up. After a moment, he repeated himself. "Probably not."

"Weird," Harold said, taking a small pull of his beer. "Something is unlucky just because it sounds like something else that's not good."

"We're a superstitious people," Wen said. "In China, the number four is *sì*. It sounds like *sǐ*, the word for death. So four is a very unlucky number. In buildings in China, there's no fourth floor, or fourteenth, or twenty-fourth."

"Why so superstitious?" Harold asked. "I thought Chinese people were supposed to be, like…smart?"

"First, that's offensive," Wen said. "There are plenty of superstitious people in the world. Race has nothing to do with it. Second, it's just a cultural thing. But I'm second generation. I don't actually understand any of this stuff. Mostly just what I remember from my grandparents."

Harold exhaled. Contemplated his half-empty beer. It was already warm, but he couldn't afford another. So he'd have to make this last a little while longer, because it felt good to be out. To pretend like Wen was a real friend, and not just another sad-sack he shared bar space with.

"At least I didn't have to deliver anything more than fruit," Harold said. "Just, you know, I was a little worried when I started this. The kind of stuff he might want me to do."

"Mr. Mo doesn't make his delivery boys do any real dirty work," said Wen. "He has Triad goons for the real hardcore stuff."

"I can't wait until this is over," Harold said. "It's hell on my nerves."

The Yankees batter knocked in a home run, putting the team up by two. Wen pumped his first. Probably had money on the game. "You made your bed," he said. "Now it's time to curl up and get some sleep."

"You're the one who got me wrapped up in this."

Wen shook his head, threw Harold a side-eye glance. "I got you in the door. You lost big and ran a tab on the house. I told you that was a bad idea. That's on you."

As much as Harold wanted to protest, Wen was right.

He had no one to blame but himself.

As per usual.

HAROLD PUSHED THROUGH the door of Happy Dumpling. It was just before the dinner rush but the restaurant still had more full tables than empty tables.

He walked to the back and the man at the register didn't acknowledge him as he ducked past the curtain separating the kitchen from the seating area. Harold's glasses fogged up from steam coming off the dishwashing station. He took them off to rub dry on his shirt and waved to Bai, who was hunched over a wok, swirling something around with a large metal spatula.

Bai looked up, smiled and nodded, sweat dripping down his bald head.

Harold was glad Bai was working. The line cook would occasionally come out and offer him plates of food. Dishes he recognized—beef chow fun or pork fried rice—but sometimes things he wasn't used to, like crispy chicken feet, or a meat he couldn't identify in a chili bean sauce. All of it absurdly delicious.

That, at least, was something to look forward to.

Harold cut a hard left into a narrow stairwell. At the top of the stairs was a red door. He knocked and waited until an older woman wearing a green accountant's visor opened it. She looked at him like he was a stray dog.

"*Gweilo*," she said under her breath.

Which meant "white devil."

They sure knew how to make him feel welcome.

Harold stepped into the main room, crowded with elderly Chinese immigrants, mostly from the Fuijan province, according to Wen. They were huddled around flimsy poker tables, playing pai gow and mah jong, the tiles clacking like insects. Nearly everyone was smoking, and with the windows boarded up, the smoke didn't have much to do but collect into a heavy cloud that hung in the air.

Harold crossed the room, turning sideways to slide through the thin pathways between chairs, and stepped into the back room, where the blackjack and poker tables were empty. They wouldn't fill up for another few hours, at least.

Mr. Mo was sitting at the small desk in the corner, a cigarette dangling from his lip, counting out a thick stack of money. Harold looked at the stack and his breath caught in his chest. They were high-denomination bills. A lot of them. He ran the math in his head. Just a quick guess, based on the thickness and the speed at which Mr. Mo was counting. There had to be at least ten grand there, maybe more.

That was two months rent, his phone bill, and a few child support payments.

It was enough to make the next few months of his life very comfortable.

He thought about how easy it would be to pick up something heavy, lay it hard over Mr. Mo's head. The man was often surrounded by young guys with ornate tattoos and cement faces. The Triad goons. None of them were here today. There was no one to defend him, just senior citizens who couldn't be budged from their pai gow for anything short of a nuclear strike.

Mr. Mo stopped counting and looked up.

Did he know what Harold was considering? Harold felt dread bubbling in his stomach, threatening to escape his mouth and heave onto the floor.

After what seemed like a full minute, Mr. Mo shrugged, as if to ask, *What?*

"I'm on tonight?" Harold asked.

Harold came in every day to ask, and Mr. Mo would tell him to work or not. Presumably, one day he would tell him he was done, but Harold had no idea how long the terms of the assignment were for. With a debt to the house of $25,000, he didn't expect it would be anytime soon.

Still, he held his breath. Prayed Mr. Mo would shoo him away, tell him never to return. Harold would give anything for that.

But Mr. Mo nodded. That meant Harold was on duty.

He crossed back through the smoke-filled room. Down the stairs and through the kitchen to the front of the restaurant, the smell of cigarettes clinging to his clothes. He sat at the small table in the corner by the register that no one else ever sat at, next to the fish tank filled with silver and orange fish floating through murky water. He opened the Chinese newspaper that was waiting and flipped through slowly, looking at the pictures.

"**C**LAMS IN CHICKEN soup," Mr. Mo said, placing a bag down in front of Harold.

Clams in chicken soup. This one he remembered. It was a collection. The Chinese food container would be empty, and he would have to wait for something to be placed inside, then bring it back.

Usually, the addresses he delivered to were within a ten-block

133

radius of the restaurant, but this one was different. On Eighth Avenue, up in the 20s. It would take about forty minutes to walk there. That was too much. Though Harold was generally in favor of wasting time, he didn't feel comfortable taking that long, so he headed for the F train, which would get him most of the way there.

He was happy to see there weren't any cops down in the station. No one in the token booth, either. He stood by the gate for five minutes before a mother pushing a stroller came through. He reached over to hold it for her as she maneuvered the stroller out, and he ducked in before it closed.

Seeing the stroller made his chest ache. Cindy was older now, six or seven by his best guess. He only ever remembered her as small enough to push around in a carriage. Back before Marguerite changed the locks and left a packed suitcase outside the apartment door for him to find one morning, when he finally mustered the courage to stumble home.

As he waited for the train, the ache in Harold's chest grew bigger. He promised himself that when this gig with Mr. Mo was done, he would make the changes he needed to make.

Get treatment for his addiction.

Find a steady job.

Take those tiny little baby steps that, once accumulated, would maybe allow him to see his daughter again. He knew things would never be the same, knew he could never make up for it entirely. But he was sure he could at least make things better than this.

ANOTHER NARROW STAIRWAY, another red door. This one had a small security camera mounted to the ceiling above it. Harold looked into the bulbous eye before knocking on the sign that said "Red Spa 22" on a white sign in red lettering.

Red was a color of good luck. This is also why Chinese take-out containers had red script on them, even though they were an American invention. More trivia, courtesy of Wen.

The door opened and a petite woman peeked out. She was barefoot, wearing a slinky black dress, her hair pulled back into a tight bun. Older, odd strands of hair gone gray, but she had the energy and smile of a young woman. She reached for Harold's hand, pulled him inside.

There was a main room with a desk, and, to Harold's left, a long hallway with six doors. The lighting was dim and soft music played from hidden speakers. He was pretty sure it was DeBussy's *Clair de lun*, the delicate piano notes falling around them like raindrops. The woman smiled and snapped her fingers. Another door opened, this time to the right, and three girls came out. All of them much younger. All smiling and done up for a night on the town, also barefoot.

"You choose favorite," the woman said.

Harold shook his head. "No, no. Delivery."

He held up the bag, tried to hide how nervous he was, because the women were pretty and it had been a long time since he'd been around a pretty woman, let alone several.

"Mr. Mo," he said.

The woman's smile disappeared. She snapped her fingers again and the women disappeared, too. She took the bag from Harold and walked to the desk. Took out the Chinese food container and filled it with rolled-up wads of cash.

When she was done she could barely close it, but she managed to get the flaps down and placed it back in the bag and handed it to Harold. She was robotic now, all business. She quickly moved around him and opened the door. Harold stepped into the hallway and she closed it. The deadbolt scratched as it slid into place.

Harold made it down to the sidewalk and stood under the awning of the fried chicken restaurant on the first floor of the building. It was starting to rain, fat drops smacking the pavement. He clutched the bag to his chest.

Thought about the money.

Not as much as Mr. Mo had earlier in the day, but still, it looked like a lot.

Maybe enough?

Harold took out his cell and dialed Wen. He'd never called Wen before, only texted, so when Wen answered, his "What's up?" was weighted with surprise and concern.

"Just had a question I needed to run by you," Harold said. "Some advice."

"Okay. Shoot."

"Mr. Mo. How dangerous is he, exactly?"

"Ah." Wen laughed. "Let me guess. You're running some money for him right now? And you're thinking of taking off?"

"Can you blame me?"

Pause. "Listen, just do the job like you're supposed to."

"How would he even find me?"

"Jeez, Harold. You don't want to mess with this guy. I know it's tempting, but look, I know you're trying to make good right now. This isn't the way to do it. Besides, I wouldn't be surprised if he has someone keeping an eye on you right now. So get the hell off the phone and get back to the restaurant."

Harold's heart skipped around in his chest. He surveyed the street. It was late, and most passersby were young people, stumbling home or headed to the next bar. But across the street was a man leaning against a parking meter, smoking a cigarette, wearing a gray hoodie, the hood pulled up over his head so his face was cast in shadow.

He wasn't looking at Harold but he was looking in Harold's direction.

"Okay," Harold said. "Thanks, Wen."

"You'll be fine. Remember, I had to do this once, too. It'll all be over soon. Maybe I can talk to him. See if we can speed things along."

Relief washed over Harold. "Thank you. I would really appreciate it."

"Hey, what are friends for?" Wen asked.

Harold hung up. Looked across the street and saw the man was still there, still looking in his direction. Harold stepped to the curb and hailed a cab. He didn't want to spend the money, but thought it would be better for his overall health to hurry back.

AS SOON AS Harold walked in the door, Mr. Mo handed him another bag.

"Crispy skin fish rolls," he said.

Another pear, then. A little depressing, but easy enough.

This address was close. The rain had picked up on the cab ride over. Harold walked closer to the buildings, ducking under awnings to stay out of it, not doing a great job. By the time he got to the address, he was nearly soaked.

There was a Chinese grocery on the first floor. It reeked of fish. An older couple sprayed down the empty display cases out front, foamy water running into the street.

Harold found the door propped open and climbed to the second floor, his shoes squeaking and squishing on the steps. He knocked on the green-painted metal door. It flung open and a young Chinese man with spiked hair and black plastic glasses looked at him with confusion and, upon seeing the bag, rolled his eyes.

The man tore the bag from Harold's hands, opened it, and took out the container, letting the bag fall to the floor. He opened the container and took out the pear, took a deep breath, and threw it at Harold's chest as he yelled something in Chinese.

The pear thumped hard enough to make Harold wince. He took a step back and put up his hands. "I'm sorry, I don't understand…"

The man threw out his fist. Harold moved to the side and it glanced off his head, knocking his glasses to the floor. He stumbled over his own feet and fell to the ground as the man drove his foot into Harold's head. Harold put his arms up, tried to protect himself as the man threw his foot into him, again and again.

After a dozen or so kicks, the man spat and went inside the apartment, slamming the door. Harold searched for his glasses, and was happy to find they were still intact. Waves of pain pummeled his body and he was content to lie on the linoleum tile for a few minutes until the worst of it subsided, but he changed his mind when he saw a fat, shiny roach scuttling toward him.

MR. MO SAT at his desk, cigarette dangling from lip, as Harold told him what happened. After Harold finished, Mr. Mo continued to stare at him, like there was more story to tell. Harold shrugged and let his arms flop down to his sides.

Mr. Mo took the cigarette out of his mouth, tapped the end of it into the overflowing ashtray on the desk, and nodded. Harold wondered if Mr. Mo even understood half of what he said. It never seemed like he did.

Harold went back downstairs. Stopped in the dingy bathroom to survey the wreckage of his face, found there was a cut on his hairline, a thin stream of blood trickling down to his eyebrow. A fat bruise blooming under his left eye.

He wet some paper towels, cleaned himself up the best he could, and went back out to his table and chair. It wasn't long before Bai came out and put down a plate of steamed dumplings with a dark brown dipping sauce.

Bai looked at Harold's face and placed his hand on Harold's shoulder.

"I'm sorry," he said.

Harold was a little surprised to find the man spoke English. They'd never exchanged words before, outside of a passing introduction on Harold's first day.

"Not your fault," Harold said. "Thank you for the food. I appreciate it."

"It's not usually like this," Bai said. "It shouldn't be for too much longer."

"My friend Wen said he's going to help me," Harold said.

Bai made a face, and Harold got very nervous. Like maybe he shouldn't have said that. The man worked for Mr. Mo. Maybe it would have been better to just keep his mouth shut.

But Bai looked around. The man at the register was on the phone and the restaurant was mostly empty. After confirming there was no one close to them, Bai said, "Your friend Wen is the reason you're here."

Harold felt his stomach twist. "What does that mean?"

The curtain behind them parted and Mr. Mo peeked out. Bai smiled, said something in Chinese, and ducked back into the kitchen.

AFTER MR. MO dismissed him for the night, Harold wasn't sure what to do. He wanted to go home, to sleep, because his body ached and his head hurt and he thought one of his teeth might be loose.

But he couldn't shake what Bai had said.

So he walked toward Dizzy's, where he and Wen would often wind up. He wondered if Wen would be there, or if tonight he was working, driving the M23 bus back and forth across midtown Manhattan.

Harold thought back to the night they met. They had both been tossed out of a late-night poker spot in the basement of a West Village bar on the corner of Sullivan. Harold for running a debt, Wen for arguing with the owner over the jacked-up price of the beer.

Before that night, they'd been familiar to each other. Two addicts orbiting each other in the darkness of the city's less-than-legal gambling dens. As they stood on the curb, Harold smoking a cigarette he bummed off a friendly bartender, he wondered if Wen might be a kindred spirit. Someone to grab a drink and commiserate with. Harold asked Wen if he wanted to hit a nearby bar he knew served cheap beers and didn't get too busy on weeknights.

Wen responded with an offer to bring him to a gambling den on Mulberry Street.

Harold was nervous from the get. He heard about the spots in Chinatown, and he was curious about them. Without someone to show him the way, he had no idea how to find them. But he didn't know the customs. He figured language would be an issue. It was a very different, intimidating universe.

At that moment, all he wanted was a beer. To quit while he was ahead, or at least not any further down, and for a gambler that was a major personal victory.

But Wen had the kind of easy smile and warm personality that made you want to say yes when he asked you for something. He insisted the place on Mulberry Street had good food and friendly dealers. The language barrier wouldn't be an issue. Anyway, the regular spots in the West Village were getting too expensive, too full of young kids who watched the World Series of Poker on ESPN and suddenly decided they were experts.

Plus, they had beer on Mulberry Street.

Why not, Harold thought.

Maybe this was the moment his luck would finally turn.

WEN WAS SITTING at the bar, nursing an amber beer, watching the Yankees game on the television mounted in the corner. Harold sat down next to him.

The pretty bartender in the cowboy hat didn't wait for him to order, just filled a pint glass with the cheapest beer they had and placed it onto a coaster in front of him. Harold dug a couple of singles out of his pocket and placed them on the bar.

Wen looked at Harold's face and said, "Jeez, man, what happened to you?"

"You did."

"What do you mean?"

"Why did you bring me to Happy Dumpling?" Harold asked. "That night we first hung out. Why did you bring me there?"

Wen exhaled. Undid and redid his ponytail. It didn't take a gambler to see it was a tell. After a few moments, Wen said, "C'mon, man. I was just looking to help a fellow player out. You looked like you were still up for some action."

Harold took a sip of his beer. "You said you worked for Mr. Mo."

"I did."

"When?"

"Before."

"How long did you have to do it for?"

Wen pursed his lips, his words taking on a tone of aggravation. "One day he told me I was done. He sent me home."

Harold twisted the stool around until he was looking at Wen. "Why did you bring me there?"

"Look, man, what happened, happened," Wen said. "You should have kept yourself in check. You didn't. I told you to be careful. But I've been thinking about what you said. About…"

Wen arched his back, looked around the bar. The bartender was down at the other end. No one was sitting close. He leaned in to Harold's ear. "I've been thinking of what you said. You're getting pretty used to the routine now. Mr. Mo is comfortable with you. Maybe we can work together. Give something a try."

"Something what?"

Wen smiled. "You know how much money goes through that place?"

"You mean knock him off?" Harold asked. "You told me he was dangerous."

"Where did you say your wife and daughter moved to?" Wen asked.

"Iowa."

"One big score. You up and leave to Iowa. Get closer to them. Never come back to this nightmare town again. I'm not saying we have to do it right now, but keep your eyes open. If you see there's something we can exploit, let's sit down and have a conversation about it, you know?"

Harold thought about his daughter, and the ache in his chest.

Wen held up his pint glass and smiled. Harold picked up his own glass and clinked it against Wen's.

"Partners," Wen said.

"Sure," Harold said.

Finally, he saw his way out.

HAROLD WASN'T SURE if it was Wen's plan all along, to get him into position and plant the seeds of a heist. Maybe he came up with the plan on the spot, to derail Harold's train of thought.

It didn't matter. Either way, Harold was pretty sure he'd been a sacrificial lamb. That Wen was stuck doing deliveries for Mr. Mo and realized the only way out was to push some *gweilo* into the job. He almost didn't blame Wen. Harold briefly wondered if he could pull off the same. Find some desperate gambler looking for a fix, willing to run up a stupid debt.

Then he just got angry.

That anger festered in his gut, making him feel sick. He thought they were friends. And after years of reneging on loans and breaking promises, Wen seemed to be the only friend he had left.

A long time ago, so long he couldn't even remember when, Harold decided the life of wearing a suit and tie and sitting in a gray box to make some rich person richer was not the life he wanted for himself.

Gambling was a natural fit. He was good with numbers. Gutsy enough to make bold moves but cautious enough to sit on a mediocre hand. For a while, he made some nice money. And it was fun. But as the bills stacked up, he got desperate.

Made bolder moves. Sat on hands less.

When Marguerite left and the alimony payments piled up, it got worse.

Maybe he could exploit some weakness in Mr. Mo's operation. Maybe he and Wen could come up with a plan that would score them some quick cash, and Harold could get on a plane. Mr. Mo seemed to have juice, but probably not out in Iowa. Even if he couldn't get back in his with family, at least he'd be well away from here.

But how long would it last?

What if they came out of the job with a couple of grand each? It would float him for a little bit, but he'd end up in the same spot. The spot that got him into this situation in the first place.

So he chose not to end up there.

And as he explained Wen's idea to Mr. Mo, he felt something approaching serenity. That he was finally making a decision to better himself. Because it was the smart decision. Smarter than a heist. Smarter than maybe getting himself shot or beaten to death by vengeful Triads.

He got himself into this mess. He would ride it out, finish it, and move on.

No more gambling.

He was making his own luck.

Mr. Mo listened silently, that cigarette dangling from his lip. Harold thought at the end maybe he should barter for early release, but thought it best to just let the truth percolate. Mr. Mo was harsh, but didn't seem unreasonable.

After finishing the story, Harold thought he saw a hint of a smile on Mr. Mo's face. Like something flitting on the edge of his vision, but when he looked, found there was nothing there.

Mr. Mo raised his hand and waved him off. Harold went downstairs and smiled at Bai and sat at his chair. It wasn't long before Mr. Mo placed a bag down in front of Harold.

"Last delivery," he said. "Braised frog. After, you go home."

That was a new one. He hadn't delivered braised frog before. Harold picked up the bag and Mr. Mo grabbed his wrist.

"After, you go home," he said, drawing out the words. "You don't come back. Ever."

Harold nodded. He thought about thanking Mr. Mo, but decided against it. It felt perverse to thank him. The only thing he was thankful for was the fact that he'd never see this man again.

The address was for a street Harold didn't recognize. He stepped out of the restaurant and typed it into his phone. It came up in Coney Island. That meant more than an hour round-trip. But Harold didn't mind. It would be worth it, just to be done.

He walked to the N stop at Canal, sat on the train with the bag nestled in his lap, thinking about what he would do with the rest of his day. No beers with Wen, that was for sure. Another person he hoped to never see again.

As the train made its way down the above-ground tracks of Brooklyn, Harold pulled out his cell phone and tapped Marguerite's name on his contact list. Maybe he'd catch her in a good mood and she'd put him on the phone with Cindy.

A gruff voice answered. "Hello?"

"Hi, I'm looking for Marguerite?"

"She changed her number," the voice said. "Number got reassigned."

"I'm sorry. Listen, did she leave a forwarding number?"

The man clicked off.

Harold closed the phone and looked at it. Put it back in his pocket. Felt the ache in his chest grow bigger. Marguerite probably forgot to tell him. Maybe she e-mailed it to him. He hadn't checked his e-mail in days.

He brushed it off. It was nothing. A mistake. He'd get word to her somehow. Chances are she wouldn't believe him because he'd given her this song and dance before. But this time, he would follow it up with action.

That, he promised himself.

When the doors opened at Stillwell, he could smell the salt heavy in the air that came off the ocean. He followed the exit signs down to the sidewalk and checked his phone, found the address was a couple of blocks away.

On the walk back, he would hit Nathan's. Get a hot dog. Maybe some cheese fries if he could afford it. He was all the way down here, maybe not ever coming back to New York. One last hot dog at Nathan's seemed like a proper sendoff.

He walked the long stretches of suburban sidewalks to the little pulsing blue dot on his phone, finally finding it, but the number on the front didn't match the number on the ticket. He looked at it again, and realized there was a second mailbox with the correct number. Must be a side apartment.

Harold walked down the empty driveway to the door with an awning and a single step. He stood in the shadow cast by the house next door and rang the bell before placing the bag on the step, opening it up, and pulling out the Chinese take-out container inside. His heart racing, head spinning, so pleased to almost be done.

The take-out container felt heavier than normal. He pried open the cardboard flaps as the door opened. Harold looked up from the container to see Wen in a tank top and boxers, bleary-eyed and hair unkempt, peering out from inside of the darkened apartment.

They stared at each other in confusion.

Then Wen saw the container and his lips parted a little.

Harold looked down into the white folds and found a small, compact handgun.

"Please tell me that's just a pear," Wen said as Harold contemplated the ache in his chest.

SWIPE LEFT

OPHELIA SLAMMED INTO the exposed brick wall. She tucked her chin to her chest and slapped her hands against the wall as she made contact to disperse the impact.

Breakfall. P1 stuff. Easy.

What wasn't easy: five men and two women weaving their way through the grid of tables and chairs in the dim restaurant, advancing on her from all sides.

The furthest she'd gotten in her training was P2. She hadn't tested for multiple attackers yet. That was top level, probably. P5. Maybe even G-level.

She wasn't prepared for this. Not even a bit.

"I'm going to make you pay for that, you half-breed bitch," Roger said, wiping his mouth and checking his hand. He had blood on his teeth. Good. Ophelia knew the first blow had landed square. She could still feel it on her knuckles.

However it went down, she'd get in a few more before this was over.

Roger pushed a chair aside, creating space in the middle of the hardwood floor. Savoring the moment. Moving with purpose, like a dance. The others stopped, giving him room to perform.

He stepped into the little clearing he created and held up her phone. Made sure she got a good look, then dropped it to the floor. It landed with a sharp crack. The kind where you don't even need to pick it up to know the screen fractured. He brought his knee up high and drove his foot down, the heel of his boot landing hard on the glass and plastic enclosure.

He maintained eye contact with her, the phone making a crunching-gravel sound.

"We're going to make an example of you," Roger said, pushing a large table across the floor, the legs screeching and squealing, the flame of the candle atop jerking. "And there'll be some hemming and hawing in the liberal media." He put his fists to his eyes and twisted them. Mock crying. "Wah-wah, another beautiful flower in our rich tapestry of a country plucked from the earth." He laughed. "But the people who matter, the people who are ready to take this country back, they'll see it for what it is: a call to arms."

"You talk too much, asshole," Ophelia said. "You want to fight, let's fight."

Roger froze. Spine rigid like a bolt of electricity shot through it. The words landed harder than her fist.

He was not the kind of man who could handle a woman talking back to him.

He was the kind of man who thought the world owed him an unearned debt.

The kind of man who wasn't really a man, who picked fights if he had a posse behind him.

Roger looked at her over his shoulder. Like she wasn't worth turning completely around for. The twist of his face so sharp she couldn't believe how it held such a warm smile only moments ago.

"Everyone," he said, raising his voice. "Let's party."

The group moved again, closing in on her. Ophelia breathed in through her mouth. Felt air expand in her chest. Breathed out slow through her nose.

Then she moved her feet into fighting stance.

As they got closer, she started building a plan. Who to attack first. Which fist to throw. But then she stopped. Remembered the words of her instructors. One of the downsides of fight training was it could lock you into routines. You freeze until the angles or distances get right, which they might never be, because real-life fighting was a dirty, crazy, unpredictable thing.

Her Krav Maga tutelage took this into account, with variations and stress drills, but the best thing she could do was trust her training, keep her hands up, not let anyone circle behind her, and, most of all, improvise.

So when the woman with red hair in a tight ponytail launched an attack, Ophelia was surprised at the force with which she drove a vertical elbow into the woman's eye socket. The impact shot through Ophelia's arm so hard she felt numbness in her fingertips. The woman's head snapped back and she nearly left her feet on the way to the floor.

It made Ophelia think she had a chance.

But as the screaming-nerve feel of the blow faded, she realized there were still six people left to go.

THE ROOM FILLED with the sound of slaps and grunts, the gray mats slick with sweat. Ophelia stood still and closed her eyes. A hand snaked across her neck, a forearm coming to rest against her carotid artery. Blood choke. Put enough pressure on the carotid for long enough, you could make a person pass out.

But the arm wrapped around her neck was barely touching her, like she was a thing easily broken.

"C'mon, I'm not made of glass," she said, throwing her elbow back, catching Ethan in the gut. "Do it like you mean it."

The arm tightened. Carefully at first, but growing tighter, until Ophelia could feel her pulse beating in her head like a drum. She breathed in through her mouth. Felt air expand in her chest. Breathed out slowly through her nose.

Then she threw her hands back, at Ethan's face, to claw at his eyes. She felt his ear because he had turned his head to the side. Safety in training.

After a few strategic swipes, she grabbed his arm, her elbow sticking out in front of her, creating a lever. She slammed her free hand down on the elbow. Once, twice. The third time, she dislodged Ethan's grip. Then she twisted around, sliding under his arm until she was behind him, and launched her foot between her legs, her bare toes tapping the hard plastic of his cup.

As she finished the technique, glowing at how smoothly it had gone, she felt a little jab in her lower back. Turned and found the instructor, Jason, holding a black plastic training knife against her.

"Good work, Ophelia. But remember, when you're done, search and scan. Get out. Don't drop your guard."

"Got it, thanks," she said, blushing a little, at both the compliment and the embarrassment of losing track of her surroundings.

Jason nodded and bounded across the mat, looking for another pair to help. Ethan turned, readjusted his black fuzzy headband, which had gotten jostled. He rolled his neck, thick muscles bulging.

"You okay?" she asked.

"Yeah," he said. "Sorry about that. I just, you know, didn't want to hurt you."

"It's fine," Ophelia said. "The reason I'm taking this class is so I can defend myself against someone your size. I'm not going to learn anything if you take it easy on me."

"That's fair," he said. "I know we're supposed to ping-pong, but I feel pretty good about rear chokes. Want me to just keep working on you?"

Ophelia smiled. "Then however are you going to learn to defend yourself against a woman my size?"

Ethan laughed. "Fine. See if you can even reach."

He turned and closed his eyes. Ethan was nearly two heads taller than her—too tall, she liked to tell him—so she hopped up and reached her arm around his throat, not getting all the way around, but far enough to put him in an armbar choke, and pulled back hard, bringing them both crashing to the mats.

A few people stopped to watch, wondering whether it had been an accident, if anyone had been hurt, but the two of them were laughing hard enough that, within moments, the class was back at it. Pairs of students placing each other in chokes, slipping out of them, sliding across the mats.

"One line!"

The action stopped, pairs breaking up, everyone moving to the edge of the mat, lining up alongside the wall. Jason took his place at the front of the room.

Jason was Ophelia's favorite instructor. He was slight, almost her size, but his roundhouse kick was like a wrecking ball. More than that, he carried with him an air of quiet confidence. He could dismantle anybody in the room—too-tall Ethan included—but you'd never know it.

Every Wednesday night, she felt like the worst student in class and told herself she'd never return. Every Wednesday morning, she packed her gym bag because Jason made her believe in herself.

"Good work today, everyone," he said. "Any injuries I need to know about?"

No one said anything.

"Lots of good work today." He glanced at Ophelia and flashed a little grin. "Just remember, always end your technique by searching and scanning. That's the kind of thing you get failed for during testing." He returned his attention to the rest of class. "Stretch out when you get home. As you cool down, your muscles can tighten up. Now, everyone like me…"

Jason put his feet together, brought his fists out and level with his waist, and bowed.

"Kida."

The row of students did the same. Feet together, fists up. Repeating "kida," the Hebrew word for "bow."

Jason clapped. "Good work, everyone."

The line disintegrated, people slapping hands, clapping each other on the back. A moment of shared victory after a night of hard work.

Ophelia loved this moment. Wednesday night existed in a universe separate from the rest of her life. No one shared this with her—not her family or friends or co-workers. Just these people, most of whom she didn't know by any other name than the techniques they'd worked on together: Stick Defense Guy. Push Kick Girl.

She knew Ethan because she liked to work with him. Even though Jason encouraged people to pair up with people who were roughly the same size, she wanted the challenge, and Ethan, who'd already made it to G-level, was happy to oblige.

That basement, with its white painted walls, the guts of the ceiling exposed through missing tiles, was an oasis. And tonight, of all nights, she really needed that rush of adrenaline.

O PHELIA STEPPED INTO the bracing cold, so dry it stung her sinus cavity. She reached into her jacket for her gloves.

"You're really going through with this?"

Ethan was standing against the exterior wall of the gym, freshly-showered, bundled in a heavy black coat and bright red wool cap.

"How do you know I'm going through with it?" she asked.

"You're wearing makeup."

Ophelia laughed at herself. She'd thrown on a little eyeliner and foundation as a matter of habit; she didn't need to look good for Roger Spector.

She knew it was him, soon as she saw his headshot. Even shrunken down the way it was. He'd been doing television interviews non-stop. Been profiled in two newspapers and three magazines. Ever since some pasty goons with tiki torches tried to protest the removal of some racist statues.

There was Spector, at the center of it all, smiling that jagged smile. His hair buzzed tight on the sides, but long and pushed back on top, in that Hitler Youth style that'd gotten so popular lately with pale white men. Especially the kind of pale white men who liked to shout phrases like "blood and soil" and "you won't replace us."

And here he was, a proud emissary of hatred, on a dating app. Looking for love.

She thought about swiping left. She nearly did, her finger hovering over the screen, muscle twitching.

She swiped right. Just to see what would happen.

It was not difficult to discern she was a woman of color. Her exact origins may have been a little hard to peg—her father was Ethiopian, her mother Puerto Rican—but still, she would never be mistaken for pure White Power stock.

Two hours later, she opened the app, having completely forgotten about her swipe, and was shocked to find that she'd been matched with Spector. Not only that, he'd sent her a polite message asking if she'd like to get dinner.

It was so absurd. The very idea of it. Sharing a meal with the country's most visible and virulent white nationalist.

But the more she thought about it, the less it sounded like a joke and the more it seemed like an opportunity. Hatred like that didn't grow in a vacuum. It was a seed that needed to be planted, watered, and nurtured. Maybe this was a chance to, if not talk some sense into him, at least show him a small bit of kindness, in the hopes it might plant a different kind of seed.

Or, maybe he had a thing for colored girls and she could expose him as being completely full of shit.

Seemed like a win-win.

"You know the rule," Ethan said. "We punch Nazis. We don't make friends with them."

Ophelia breathed in through her mouth. Felt air expand in her chest. Breathed out slow through her nose. "I'm not saying you're wrong. I'm not just here to learn how to fight. I thought taking these classes might give me the confidence to become more... socially emboldened. Does that make sense?"

"I thought you were just doing it for the cardio."

"Stop it. Every time I open Twitter and I see people linking to stories about him, I'm just like, why," she said. "Why him? I want to look this asshole in the eye and ask him how he could hate me without even knowing me. Maybe someone needs to just get through to him. Maybe breaking bread with him…I don't know…"

"I will give you this," Ethan said. "You are a kinder person than I am."

"Well, that's the point," she said. "Being kind. It's like, right now, the country feels like a pot that's about to boil over. I don't know that the answer is to turn up the heat." She turned, watched cars rolling down Chambers Street. "I don't know what the answer is. But I'm tired of sitting around and waiting for it to fall in my lap. And I don't want to live in the world where the answer is always violence. That just begets more violence. Doesn't that mean we're no better than them?"

Ethan zipped his jacket to his throat. "It's too cold for a debate and I expect I'm not going to win anyway. Please be careful. And call me? I live nearby. My husband and I can be there in a few minutes."

"If anything bad happens, I'll call," she said. "We're meeting in a restaurant. In New York City. In public. It's sweet of you to worry but I'm sure it'll be fine."

THE RESTAURANT WAS on an empty block in a pool of shadow, the blinds on the windows down so she couldn't see inside. She thought it might actually be closed, until she caught yellow light peeking through the cracks.

She'd checked out the menu online. At least the food looked good. They had a cod dish that would be high in protein and low in carbs and fat, the perfect post-workout meal, and if things really went bad, she'd get it to go.

As soon as she entered the restaurant and the warm air enveloped her, she got a feeling in her stomach like she'd eaten something too heavy for her digestive system to handle. Like a brick pressing down on her insides.

The place was bigger than she would have guessed from the street. Narrow but deep. A thin wooden bar along one side, a rainbow of liquor bottles glittering behind it. The space gridded by small wood tables—the kind where it's a struggle to fit all the plates that come with dinner.

Candles on the tables. Exposed brick walls. Edison bulbs. It was a handsome space.

There was a bartender and a few other diners and Spector, seated in the corner, smiling and waving, like he'd been watching the door, waiting for her to arrive. She was three minutes early.

Socially-emboldened, she reminded herself as her stomach flopped.

Ophelia strode across the restaurant and removed her coat, dropping it, along with her gym bag, onto an empty chair at an unoccupied table next to them.

Spector stood as she approached, bowing a little at the waist, not taking his eyes off her.

"Ophelia," he said. "I'm glad you made it."

It was hard to square what she'd seen in the media with the man standing in front of her. He was dressed well, as was his trademark: slacks, white dress shirt, argyle sweater over it, bow tie, hair perfectly in place.

His voice was soft. His eyes, too. They weren't doing that hundred-yard-stare thing he did in all those magazine profile photos. More than that, his smile wasn't the smile of a monster. There was no smoke, no brimstone. Just a smile. The kind of smile that makes you want to smile back.

156

And yet, it made her think of a bad patch job on a blank wall.

He stuck out his hand. "I'm Roger."

She reached forward and took it. She hadn't meant to take it, but it was a reflex. Someone offers you a hand and the polite thing to do is shake it. She cursed inwardly, then reminded herself this was the start. Treat him with dignity. Show him the meaning of the word.

He gripped her hand tight, maybe almost too tight, or it could just have been his handshake was firm. His palm was a little sweaty, like he'd been holding it over the candle.

They sat, the air heavy between them. She placed her phone on the table, face up. Normally, she'd put it facedown—she thought it was rude when the screen lit up with a text or an e-mail notification, because it invariably drew her attention away—but she had Ethan's number queued up.

Just in case.

Spector looked around the restaurant, then patted his knee and laughed. "I imagine this must be surprising."

"A little. I mean, you are a celebrity, after all." She put a little mark of disdain on the word celebrity. It had the intended effect, and his smile flickered.

He nodded. "I know what people think of me. I'm not perfect." He shrugged. "The way things are right now, people need a villain. I'll tell you what, a lot of what people claim I've said has been taken out of context. Too many journalists these days are just aspiring fiction writers who thought j-school was a way to earn a paycheck."

"So you're saying people are wrong about you?"

Spector's lip curled. "I have some strong opinions. But they aren't as vicious as they're made out to be."

"They seem pretty vicious to me. You've said that the number of dead reported from the Holocaust is grossly exaggerated. Was that taken out of context?"

"We haven't even ordered our drinks yet," he said, throwing up an eyebrow. Then he shrugged. "The simple fact is, there's no official record of the number of people who died. How many Jews died, would you say?"

"I believe the accepted number is six million."

"Whose number is that? Who reported that?"

"I don't...I don't know exactly."

He held up his hand to punctuate his point.

"See?" he asked. "Exactly what I mean."

"Wait, no. That's not how it works. You can't demand sourcing on every little thing and if a person can't give it to you, pretend like it's not a real fact."

"Why not?" he asked, sitting back in his chair. "People say things about me that aren't true. Why should I believe anything that anyone says?"

"See, this is the problem," Ophelia said. "You can't back anything up except to play mind games with people. You win through obfuscation. Which really doesn't count as winning."

He took a sip of his water. Ophelia wished a waiter would show up. Some kind of distraction. She looked around, didn't see one. She did notice each table included a basket of rolls, a mix of beige white bread and dark brown rye. She wished there was a bread basket on this table. Something to do with her hands.

Where was that damn waiter?

Roger put his glass back down on the table, brought his eyes to her without taking his hand off the glass. "I've seen the kinds of things you post on Twitter and Facebook. Just a little recon. Obviously, you did the same on me. You seemed pretty excited to share that video of me getting decked."

Ophelia's breath caught in her chest. She had forgotten about that.

It had happened at a rally, months ago. Spector was giving an interview and some person—who Ophelia referred to in her post as a "hero"—leapt out of the crowd and planted a haymaker across Spector's jaw, knocking him to the ground.

"It was a sucker-punch," he said, bringing his fingers up to his chin. "Pretty low, if you ask me. Hit a guy when he's not looking."

"The way you rile people up…"

"I don't rile people up," he said, his voice frosting over. "I tell the truth, and people are afraid to hear it."

The conversation was off the rails. The two of them stared at each other. Ophelia's mouth ran dry. This was a mistake. She never should have come. She picked up her glass, took a small sip. Formulated some kind of plan for a graceful exit, then wondered why she owed him even an ounce of grace.

Spector nodded toward her bag. "Just come from the gym?"

"Krav Maga."

"Ah." He nodded, like he was impressed, which made Ophelia feel a touch stronger. *Hell yes I train in one of the world's deadliest martial arts. What now?*

"You know the origins of Krav Maga, surely," Spector said.

"Of course."

"Founded by Imi Lichtenfield," he said, as if she said she hadn't. "As the Nazi party rose to power in Bratislava, he sought to train his fellow Jews, so that they could defend themselves. Eventually, he went on to train the IDF."

"As I said, I'm aware of the history."

"What did you think?" he asked, leaning forward. "That you'd show up here tonight, maybe show me a little of what you'd learned?"

"Not at all," she said. "I showed up tonight because I thought it would be possible to have a rational and human conversation with you. But I'm starting to get the sense I was wrong."

"Very wrong," he said. "Very, very wrong."

His smile changed. The warmth vanished. It took on that jagged edge she recognized in all the photos, peaks and valleys like a broken beer bottle. That heavy feeling returned to Ophelia's stomach. She realized the restaurant was too quiet. No music playing.

Still, nobody had came over to take their order.

Even to ask if they wanted drinks.

She turned to look around.

There were four men and two women.

All of them were silent, staring.

She turned back to Spector.

"What is this?" she asked.

"When you were matched with me, I wasn't planning to respond," he said. "I figured you chose me as a joke. Then I thought maybe you wanted to play some kind of trick. Which I can see now is true. I can play games, too. The owner of this restaurant is a good friend of mine. He's a true believer. A patriot. And he...lent us the place for the night. And after I saw you shared that video of me..."

His hand flashed out and he slapped her across the cheek.

She saw the hand, too late to block it, but it sparked the fight-mode section of her brain. She rolled with the blow, leaned forward, and threw a jab into his mouth. She felt his teeth on her knuckles, then pushed away from the table, but he was fast. He knocked the table aside and pushed her hard into the exposed brick wall behind them.

She should have left.

Should have listened to Ethan.

Should have done a lot of things, as the other "diners" got up from their seats and advanced on her.

160

USE YOUR ENVIRONMENT, Jason would say. Pick something up.

As the redhead writhed on the floor in the aftermath of her elbow, Ophelia reached for a candle, whipped it into the face of the bartender. It caught him in the eye and he yelped. The second woman in the crew veered off course to check the bartender, who was on his knees, gripping his face, bawling.

The other two men pushed around them. Ophelia kicked a chair into their path. It caught one of them in the legs and he went down hard, his chin slamming into the table in front of him. It made a sharp crack. The kind of crack where you don't need to check to know he'd just broken some teeth.

She threw a glance at Spector, who was standing off to the side, watching. Happy to let his minions do the work.

The other guy managed to make it around. He was a little taller than Ophelia. Solid. Swimmer body. Shaved head. Gleam in his eyes. Red shoelaces in black boots. He swung, arc wild. She bladed her left forearm to block the blow, and simultaneously drove her right fist into his face.

The trachea was a beer can. About as much force as it took to crush the aluminum, you could crush a windpipe. It would probably be enough to kill him. Still, she aimed high. Went for the nose. Something to make his eyes tear up. She wasn't ready to cross that line. Not yet.

The skinhead absorbed the blow and drove himself into her, pushing her toward the wall. He was trying to grab her around the waist. She leapt forward, throwing her hips back, pressing down on his shoulders. It served the dual purpose of creating distance, preventing him from getting a good grip on her, while using his own momentum to drive him into the floor.

She landed on him hard, rolled off, then tried to stand but

bumped into the underside of a table, lost her footing.

She tried to breathe. Found she couldn't.

Too much was happening.

As she got to her feet, an arm wrapped around her neck. Rear armbar. At least that one was fresh. She scratched at the face of her attacker, felt something give under her fingertips. Eyeball? Then she gripped his arm, made her elbow a lever. Hit it once. Twice. Nothing happened. His grip was too strong. Damn it, Ethan. She balled up her fist and snapped it back into her attacker's groin. He exhaled hard, and that gave her the window she needed. She yanked herself out of the man's grip, threw her foot between his legs, felt his balls give under the point of her toe, then pushed him hard into the wall.

That's when the chair hit her.

As pain screamed through her body, as she fell to the floor, she thought: didn't search and scan.

She hit the floor hard, oxygen knocked out of her lungs, but before she could draw another breath, a boot pressed down on her back.

"Impressive," Spector said. "Pointless   in the end. But impressive. We were going to make it quick. Now...not so much."

Ophelia froze. She was scared, yes, but worse than that, she felt like she'd let so many people down.

Jason. Ethan. Her classmates. Her friends and family.

All because she thought she could reason with a rattlesnake.

She tensed herself, preparing for a moment where she might slip away, counterattack, something, anything to take a chunk out of this asshole before he delivered a debilitating or fatal blow.

Then she heard a yell.

The pressure came off.

She was able to get to a knee.

Ethan had Spector against the wall and was wailing on him.

The restaurant flooded with more people. It took her a second to recognize them. They weren't wearing gym gear and covered in sweat. They weren't lit by the harsh white glare of the Tribeca training studio.

But all the same, they were her classmates.

Stick Defense Guy. Push Kick Girl.

Rounding up the others, holding them down.

Most of Spector's crew didn't have much fight left. The bartender was sobbing, the two women retreated behind the bar. The skinhead tried to launch an attack. But then Jason appeared. So fast she could barely make it out, he put the skinhead in an arm lock. The one he demonstrated for class once, where, if he applied just a little more pressure, he'd rip the guy's arm out of its socket.

The skinhead screamed, then cried, twisting to find a less painful position, finding there was none.

Ophelia stood. Spector was scrambling to get to his feet. Ethan moved in again, fists balled up. Ophelia grabbed his arm, pulled back hard.

He turned, shook his head like he'd just broken out of a trance.

"Mine," Ophelia said.

Ethan nodded. Bowed, and held out his hand, palm up, like a waiter presenting an empty table.

Spector's eyes darted around the restaurant. Shaking. Lip quivering.

"Real tough now that you've got a group of people behind you, huh?" he asked.

It was enough to make Ophelia laugh. She considered giving him some kind of rebuttal. Point out the pot-kettle-blackness of his statement. But he wouldn't get it. And he wasn't worth it.

"Hold on," Ethan said.

Ophelia paused. He took out his cell phone, turned it sideways, and hit the "record" button.

"Okay, go ahead," he said.

Ophelia threw a jab and a hard cross, not bothering to open her palm, which would have been safer. With her fist balled up, even if it meant damaging some of the delicate bones in her hand, it would hurt Spector more.

That was worth it.

She followed it up with a left hook and then a hard elbow. Spector's head snapped back and hit the brick wall. His eyes went vacant and he slid down, collapsing into a heap, like a pile of dirty laundry.

Ophelia breathed in through her mouth. Felt air expand in her chest. Breathed out slow through her nose.

Ethan put his hand on her shoulder.

Asked, "Are you okay?"

She smiled. Jumped up and threw her arms around his neck, nearly pulling him to the ground.

AFTER THE COPS arrived, after arrests were made and statements were taken, Ophelia wandered to a nearby bar, most of her classmates close behind. She ended up at a small, high table with Ethan and Jason, where Ethan explained what happened: he was worried, he mentioned it to a few other students, and word got around until everyone agreed to take a walk over to make sure she was okay.

Ophelia hoisted her glass of wine toward Ethan. "That was some good timing. Gandalf at Helm's Deep in *Two Towers*."

"I don't understand what that means," Ethan said.

"Seriously though," Ophelia said. "If you want to say 'I told you so…'"

Ethan shook his head. "Not the time for that."

Jason leaned into the conversation. "Ethan told me what you said. Your instincts weren't wrong." He took a sip of his beer and put it down, and held his hands out. "The first rule of every martial art is: don't fight. Krav is no different. You should do everything you can to de-escalate. But sometimes." He shrugged. "Sometimes you can't."

"I just feel so…naïve," Ophelia said. "To have thought…"

"Kindness is never a mistake," Ethan said. "Some people, you can't reason with."

Ophelia put her hands on the table, around the base of her wine glass. Jason reached over, put his hand on hers. She looked up, saw he was searching for some kind of sign, for whether this kind of contact was okay. She smiled at him. He smiled back. His hand was warm, and softer than she thought it might be.

"It's never wrong to start with words," he said. "I want you to know I'm damn proud of you. You held your own against multiple attackers long enough to allow help to arrive. I'm half-tempted to talk to Johnny to see if we can bump you up a grade level. I think you earned it."

Ophelia blushed in response.

Ethan arched an eyebrow. Picked up his beer.

Taking the hint.

"I'm going to see who else is around," he said.

"Wait." Ophelia stood up, drained her wine glass. She nodded toward Jason's beer. "Want another?"

Jason knocked it back and put the empty glass on the table. "Sure."

"I'm going to buy a round for everyone," she said. "And there are a few people here, I need to learn their names. And then I'll be back. You'll be here?"

Jason smiled. "Sure."

"Good."

Ophelia made for the bar. As she waited for the bartender to finish up a complicated drink order, flush with the warmth of the alcohol, Ethan slid up alongside her.

"Someone's hot for teacher," he said.

"So what if I am?"

"It would be your first smart dating-related decision of the night."

"Ha-ha," she said. Then she craned her neck to look Ethan in the eye. "I owe you my life."

"Keep me in drinks for a little while and we'll call it even," he said. "Look, I wasn't kidding. I admire you. I admire that you look at the world and you want something…I don't know…more civilized, I guess you could say. But I think we all learned an important lesson tonight. Didn't we?"

Ophelia nodded. "That we did. Swipe left on Nazis."

"No, punch them. Always punch Nazis." He raised his voice. "What do we do with Nazis?"

Everyone in the bar put their fists in the air, and, in unison, shouted, "Always punch Nazis!"

Ophelia smiled. That heavy feeling in her stomach replaced by another warm feeling, of community, and togetherness, and a moment of shared victory after a night of hard work.

THE GIFT OF
THE WISEGUY

ERIC CALABRESE STOOD at the back of The Mysterious Bookshop, surveying the crowd that was nearly spilling out the door and onto the sidewalk. Snow fell in lazy circles outside the tall windows and the space was permeated by the smell of his grandmother's lasagna.

She died years ago, but his sister Christine resurrected the recipe. She made five trays. Eric thought it was a bit much, but that's Italian hospitality: there's not enough food unless there's too much food.

He'd brought Tupperware containers so people could bring home leftovers, a scenario growing less likely every time the heavy doors swung open and a burst of cold air whipped through the store.

He had been warned continuously—by his agent, by his publisher, by his writing pals—that book release parties were exercises in frustration. Especially for a first book. Even more especially during the holidays, with so many people out of town. That he might see a couple of friends, maybe a few stragglers off the street, but that's it.

But then the *New York Times* review hit.

The writer called his book "thoughtful" and "precise" and "heart-rending." Suddenly, it was everywhere. NY1, the *Daily News*, and the *Post* covered it. Buzzfeed shot a short video, in which a writer for the site, who looked like he was playing dress-up as a lumberjack, raved about it. Tomorrow morning, he had to be in Times Square at 6 a.m. for *Good Morning America*.

The plastic cup of red wine in his hand, the first of the night, would also be the last. No sense in being hungover for that.

Someone broke through the crowd and approached the spot Eric had staked out by the coat rack. It was Ian, the lanky bookstore manager.

"You ready to get started?" he asked.

"Sure," Eric said. "What's the plan?"

"I'll do a quick introduction, and then you can have the floor. The owner isn't a big fan of authors reading from their books. Usually, we just do discussion and questions. But with a crowd like this…" He gestured at the packed room. "You can do pretty much whatever you want."

"Could I have a minute?"

"Sure," Ian said. "Just give me a wave."

Eric finished the last of his wine and set the cup on a shelf heavy with Sherlock Holmes books. He ducked into the back room, and then the bathroom, shutting the door and locking it behind him. He put down the toilet seat and sat, running his fingers over the glossy cover of his book.

White Sheep: Growing Up in the Calabrese Crime Family.

There were a hundred more copies in the store—after the *Times* review, Ian said he upped the order. This was one of the first off the press, filled up with sticky notes, marking off passages Eric thought might be good for live readings.

He wasn't thrilled about a discussion. Because there wasn't much about this he wanted to discuss. Everything he wanted to say about his childhood was in black-and-white, between his hands. Writing about it had excised it, and it felt perverse to dwell.

Eric looked at himself on the cover of the book. The photo the designer chose was in color, but faded. He was standing in front of the Wonder Wheel in Coney Island. His mother, short and pear-shaped, with big eyes and a stern smile, had her arm draped over his shoulder. Next to them was his father, holding Christine, wrapped in a swaddling blanket. She was only six months old.

He hated the photo.

He was chubby and his ears stuck out. He was wearing that god-awful *Star Wars* t-shirt, which had been black once, but had stretched and faded to gray. His white tube socks came up to his knobby knees.

Worse than that, his father was in it.

But his publisher, Jason, insisted. The story was about them, and the photo lent it an air of *verisimilitude*. That's the word Jason used.

It meant honesty. Eric was pretty sure Jason was trying to bury the debate under a ten-dollar word. It worked. He handed over the photo and here it was, staring back at him like a bad memory that keeps a person up at night.

When Eric could put aside the weight of it pressing against his chest, when he could separate the memory of his dad disappearing from their lives only a few months after it was taken, he had to acknowledge it did look pretty nice on the cover of the book.

Eric wondered what his father looked like now, twenty years later.

Wondered if he was even alive.

He was a stout man, thick in the shoulders, but in a healthy way. He played football in college and looked like he could still hold his own in a pick-up game. Dark, curly hair that got passed to Christine, whereas Eric inherited his mother's light and fair complexion.

There was a knock at the door. Eric got up and flushed the toilet, so whoever was outside wouldn't wonder why he was just sitting around in the bathroom.

He opened the door and stepped into the back room.

Straight into his father.

Manetto *Calaberese.*

Eric drew in a breath, held it, found he couldn't let it out. He nearly dropped the book, but caught himself.

He knew it immediately. Those pale blue eyes, the dark hair gone gray but still curling in ringlets around his ears. Except, he looked so different. Like a Thanksgiving Day balloon at the end of the route, caving in on itself.

"Hello, Eric," his father said, his voice weak, but still reverberating the way it did, so you could always tell where he was in a room. He was wearing a tan coat, a red scarf, and black leather gloves. His face freshly shaved. Impeccably put together, always, and all these years later.

"Dad?"

His father smiled. The smile stretched his face into something akin to a grimace.

Eric's first instinct was to ball up his fist, throw it into his father's face.

He took a deep breath. Reminded himself that he was not like his father.

"What are you doing here?" he asked, lowering his voice.

"My boy writes a book," he says. "I wanted to wish you well."

Eric felt his temperature and pulse rising in tandem. "So you just show up? You're in witness protection. You can't do that."

"It's too late now, isn't it," he said with another smile, showing a little more strength. "How've you been, kiddo?"

"Don't do that," Eric said, stepping back toward the bathroom door. Wanting there to be space between them, which was difficult in the back room, full of books and shelves that had been pushed off the floor to make room up front. "You missed so much of my life. You missed *mom's funeral.*"

The smile disappeared. "She wouldn't have wanted me there."

"We would have wanted you there. Just some kind of acknowledgement that you even cared."

"I do care," his father said. "I care very much. There are still people in this town who want me dead. You think I do this lightly?"

Eric started to say something, but stopped himself. What was there to say that could sum up twenty years and every conceivable emotion?

Except: "You shouldn't have come."

"C'mon, I know I've made a lot of mistakes," his father said. "And I have to admit, I was a little upset when I first read the book. There's a lot of dirt in there. But it's mostly all correct..."

"You read it already?" Eric asked. "It just came out today."

"I used to run this town, kid. You think I can't get an advanced copy of the book, even all the way out in Arizona?"

The thought of his father in the desert almost made Eric laugh. Before witness protection, his father never left New York. Barely left Brooklyn. "So that's where they put you?"

"Scottsdale," his father said. "All they know about Italian food is Olive Garden. It's tragic. I tried the lasagna up front. I know my mother's lasagna. Did you do that?"

"Christine."

His face lit up. "Is she here?"

"I think you should go."

"I just got here. Let me just see her. See how she turned out."

"She turned out great, no thanks to you," Eric said. "I think we both turned out pretty damn good considering you disappeared. You gave up on this family a long time ago. I'm the one who provided for Mom and Christine."

"Hey," his father said, his voice snapping. "How about a little gratitude, huh? You still found a way to profit off it."

Eric felt himself grow flush. Wondered if he should hold back, but decided he shouldn't. His greatest strength was his words, so he aimed them at his father like a barrage of bullets. "I would trade everything this book has brought me if it meant you stayed. Instead, you ratted out a bunch of guys and ran and hid. Like a coward. You gave us nothing. You left us nothing. All we have is your absence. I figured out a way to make it provide for me and Christine. That's what this book is. You leaving was the only gift you ever gave us."

"Eric," his father said, stepping forward, his eyes misting. "Please. It's Christmas. And I'm trying. Doesn't that mean something?"

Eric turned and looked away, not wanting his father to see him cry. Remembering what happened the last time, when his fourth grade teacher died suddenly; a sharp, disappointed admonishment that it's not what "real men" did.

After a few moments of silence, his father said, "I loved you and your sister and your mother. I want you to know that. For whatever it means to you. Even if it means nothing. The things I did…I did them because I was protecting you. That was always the most important thing."

A pause.

"I love you, Eric. Best of luck with the book, okay?"

Eric heard the sound of footsteps, and the door creaking open.

He turned, and found he was alone in the small space, the door swinging closed.

OFFICER REBECCA BHATI grasped the heavy-duty headphones and pulled them off her ears. They were digging into her head and she needed a little relief. Not that she needed to wear them. She could barely hear over the din coming from inside the bookstore. It sounded like waves crashing into a rocky shore.

But she liked to listen. It was good to be thorough. There wasn't much else to do besides try to find a comfortable position in the ancient office chair, arrived here from points unknown.

The NYPD surveillance van wasn't pleasant. And it didn't smell good. The outside was brandished with the logo of the Fulton Fish Market and she idly wondered if that was a cover, or if that's where the department bought it from. The brackish smell seemed to confirm her suspicion, but that could also be years of accumulated sweat and takeout.

She turned to her right, to Detective Seth Tanner, spilling out of his own office chair, peering at the hodge-podge of monitors, his face cast blue in the flickering light. The setup looked like someone raided a Radio Shack that was going out of business.

She looked up at the mug shot of Manetto "Manny" Calabrese taped to the wall of the van.

"You sure it was him?" she asked Tanner.

"I think so," Tanner said, not looking away from the monitor.

"No one's seen the guy in two decades, but I think it was him. Lost some weight, but same hair. Same gait." Tanner looked down at the keyboard like it was alien technology. "I don't even know where to start with this. Can you play it back?"

Bhati slid her chair across the cramped space to the keyboard, tapped the hotkeys that would rewind and then replay the video. She watched as a hunched figure strode past the camera and turned into the bookstore.

To her eyes, it was a blur.

But Tanner seemed convinced.

Because he was smiling. And Tanner was not a guy who smiled.

"If this is him, it's a pretty big deal, right?" Bhati asked, her breath pluming in front of her.

Tanner reached down and clicked on the space heater by his feet. Within moments, it would smell like a bundle of hair caught fire, but that would be enough to bring the temperature up to a more comfortable level.

"If it's him," Tanner said.

Bhati looked down at the space heater. "Are you sure that thing is safe to be using in here?"

"Not really, no," Tanner said.

Bhati picked up her headphones again, placing them carefully over her ears. Same sounds. Waves crashing. She thought she could pick out a word here or there, but it'd all be useless until the tech people cleaned it up. Which might not even be necessary. She took the headphones off again.

"What do we even do?" Bhati asked. "The Feds have had him in witness protection. There's no active warrant on him. He's just… a guy now. I don't mean to speak out of turn, sir, but why are we here?"

"First," Tanner said. "He's not just a man. He's a monster. Three confirmed kills, and two more suspected. Plus all the lives he ruined. And what, he gets to skate because he dimed somebody out? It's a miscarriage of justice."

"Right, but we're not going after him just to go after him." Bhati looked at Tanner and raised an eyebrow. "Are we?"

The scorched smell from the heater was overwhelming. Tanner noticed, too. He reached down and clicked it off, the red glow of the coils fading.

"He killed my partner," Tanner said.

Bhati paused.

That was a violation not to be taken lightly.

"If you have new evidence..." Bhati started.

Tanner put his hand up. "I'm the detective. You're the officer. Let's do the job and then we can go home, okay?"

Bhati nodded, put the headphones back on her head.

But she couldn't ignore the feeling that was prodding her. Because the more she thought about it, the more she had to question the circumstances that evening. As a member of the intelligence division, she'd done dozens of stakeouts, and all of them included a lot of planning, as well as a good bit of paperwork to sign out the van and the equipment.

Tonight was different.

Tanner approached her at her desk. He asked for her help on a special assignment. The van was parked around the street from the precinct, not in the depot. She went along because Tanner had been on the job since before she was born, and she had no reason to doubt him.

But something wasn't adding up.

"Sir," Bhati asked. "I don't mean to be difficult. But...is this official NYPD business?"

Tanner finally looked away from the screen. Held her gaze. His face was all sharp angles and deep shadows, the way the light from the monitors flickered across it.

When he spoke, he did so in a quiet rumble.

"Do the job," he said. "I can make your life in the department a lot harder. You're free to go, file a complaint about me, whatever. But then you're inviting that upon yourself. Or let's just sit here a little while longer and we can go home. Deal?"

Bhati held his gaze.

She knew that, sometimes, rules needed to be bent in the course of doing the right thing. But only as a last resort. Only as long as the rule would snap back into place, unbroken and intact.

That kind of thing, she could live with.

But this was too much. This was the kind of thing that could result in a major reprimand, if not getting kicked off the force entirely.

She was about to push again when there was a knock on the side of the van.

"Holy…" Tanner said.

"What?" she asked.

"It's him."

She leaned over in her seat and saw Calabrese looking into the pinhole camera next to the door, his features fished-eyed by the lens, making the smile that much more warped.

TANNER RAN HIS hand down his pant leg to make sure his ankle holster was in place. He hated wearing his regular holster on stakeouts, since he spent most of the time hunched over, and it dug into his ribs.

After he confirmed everything was where it should be, he slid the door open.

Most days, the memory burned a small hole in his gut.

But seeing Calabrese standing there, it hit him full-on.

Reggie Sacks bleeding out from a bullet to the throat on a filthy warehouse floor. Trying to speak, but nothing coming out of his mouth but blood and wet gurgles.

Tanner didn't see Calabrese pull the trigger. Didn't even see him at the scene. But they'd been following him for weeks, trying to put together enough evidence for a RICO case that would cripple the Calabrese family.

Instead, Tanner wandered off to take a leak and came back to find the life spilling out of Reggie, whose last word he croaked out before coughing up a river of blood and dying.

"Manny."

Manny Calabrese.

It was all Tanner needed to know.

And here was Calabrese, standing there with a smile on his face. Tanner's hand shook. He wanted more than anything to pull his gun and give Calabrese a taste of what he did to Reggie.

He gripped his knee, fingers digging into the bone until it hurt.

Calabrese was holding two Tupperware containers, flecks of snow layering on the shoulders of his tan coat. He looked over at Bhati, then above her head, at the mugshot. He nodded toward it. "You might be surprised, but that handsome fella up there is me. That photo was taken a long time ago, obviously."

Tanner tried to speak but found he couldn't.

Calabrese nodded to Bhati and said, "Darling, your partner and I have some things to discuss. Why don't you head on inside, huh? Get yourself a slice of lasagna. Probably the best lasagna you'll ever have. The trick is to mix two eggs into the ricotta. Helps the lasagna keep its structural integrity."

Bhati looked at Tanner.

Tanner could see it in her eyes. She was worried that if she left, something bad would happen. And she was right. But he still outranked her, and at this point, it didn't matter.

Best she not be around to see this.

"Go ahead," Tanner said.

"But…"

"Now."

Bhati hung her headphones from the hook next to the monitors. Climbed out of the van, careful to give Calabrese a wide berth, and headed across the street to the bookshop.

Calabrese climbed into the van, pulled the door shut, and put the Tupperware containers on the makeshift desk under the monitors. He eased himself into the battered office chair that Bhati had occupied.

Tanner's heart slammed against the inside of his chest. The last time he saw this man, he was thirty pounds lighter, still had all of his hair, could read small text without squinting. It felt like a lifetime. Calabrese, too, looked so different. Like he was slowly disappearing.

Calabrese slid the chair forward, the wheels creaking and grunting with the exertion, so he could reach past Tanner and turn on the space heater. It crackled and roared to life.

"There, that's better," Calabrese said. "So how are things?"

"Don't you dare…"

"I didn't kill your partner, you know," he said. "Sacks, right? He was a good cop. Believe it or not, I respect cops. You do your job, I do mine. It just so happens they run in conflict with each other. I'd never kill a good cop."

Tanner reached down to his ankle, removed the black Ruger LCR, and placed it in his lap. Not so much as a threat, but to set the tone of the proceedings. Calabrese shook his head.

"I bring you a peace offering," he said. "My mother's lasagna. Best in the world. It's four days before Christmas, no less. And this is how you respond."

"Say your piece," Tanner said. "Because you've got about two minutes before I paint the inside of this van with your brain."

Calabrese sighed. "I get it. I would be angry, too. But you have to understand, what happened that day..."

"He said your name."

"I'm sure he did. I was there."

Tanner gripped the gun.

"Here's how it went down," Calabrese said. "I was at the warehouse following up on a thing. And I run into this guy. You remember Lou Rossi? The man was a thug. An animal. He was cheating on the family, you know what I mean? So I run into him doing something he shouldn't be doing, but he gets the drop on me. He's holding me at gunpoint."

Calabrese extended his index finger, thumb pointed up, imitating a gun.

"And Sacks comes wandering in."

He swung his hand in a wide arc and cocked his thumb.

"And, *bang*. Rossi shoots Sacks in the throat. I don't even think Rossi knew what he was doing. He was just startled, is all."

"And you just left Reggie there to die," Tanner said.

"I heard you coming. You're not exactly light on your feet. Not even then. What was I going to do, besides get blamed for it?"

"Then why did he say your name?" Tanner asked. "It was the last thing he said before he died."

"How should I know?" Calabrese said, shrugging. "Maybe he was saying, 'Manny didn't do it, you meat-head.' All I know is, Rossi's gun killed your partner. Not mine."

"Right. And where's Rossi? Let's see if he can corroborate."

Calebrese shook his head. "That's not going to happen, unless you've got a medium or a Ouija board or something."

Tanner sat back in the chair. It groaned under his weight.

The thought of revenge was the only thing that sustained him. The promise of a period on the end of the sentence that had been running on for the past twenty years. All he had left was an empty apartment in Queens, a few plants, and a futon. The best he could do with the alimony payments, the child support payments. The penalties he paid for a life that became consumed by his hunt for Calabrese.

And now it had been taken from him.

No, it couldn't be true.

Calabrese was trying to save himself. That's all.

"I don't believe you," Tanner said.

"I wish you did. Not that it matters. You want to kill me right now, go ahead. You're only moving up the deadline a bit."

"What do you mean?"

Calabrese sighed. Placed a hand on his stomach.

"Cancer," he said. "I got a few months left, maybe."

The news cast Calabrese in a different light.

His face didn't look thin, it looked sunken.

He didn't look tired, he looked weak.

"What am I supposed to do?" Tanner asked. "Feel sorry for you? Even if what you said is true, you're still a killer. You ruined lives for your own personal gain."

"No, I did it because…" Calabrese stopped. Thought about it. Shook his head. "I'm not here for a philosophical discussion. I was pretty sure this had been eating at you and I wanted to put it to rest. Even if not for you, for me. Now, here…"

Calabrese took the two Tupperware containers off the desk and held them.

"I know we're not pals," he said. "But it's Christmas. Let's put all that hate and regret behind us. Sit here and just enjoy one last meal together. Then you can do whatever the hell you want to me, okay?"

Tanner breathed deep.

Then he reached over and clicked off the transmitter that was recording everything going on in the store, along with the conversation they were having.

Calabrese seemed to get that this was not an insignificant gesture. A look of fear flashed across his face.

"I hate you wiseguys so much," Tanner said. "Stuff like *The Sopranos. The Godfather.* All these movies and television shows that take the horrible stuff you do and glorify it. I bust my hump for going on thirty years trying to make the world a better place, and kids got stars in their eyes for Michael Corleone, like he's a hero or something."

Tanner slid his chair forward until he was closer to Calabrese. Until he could smell the man's wool jacket.

His breath.

"Here's the truth," Tanner said. "Your entire family is a blight. After I'm done with you, I'm coming for your kids. The two of them were raised on the backs of dead men. Right now, your son is in there profiting off your legacy. It's obscene. Pretty soon he's going to find himself in a pair of cuffs. I'll find a way. And once I do that, I am going to take the Son of Sam law and swing it at him like a bat. I will make sure he never sees one more red cent from that book."

Calabrese frowned. "I've done some bad things but I've never threatened a man's family. Never."

"You made your bed."

Calabrese's nostril's flared.

The scorched smell of the space heater filled the small space.

"A threat like that would not have worked out well for you back in the day," Calabrese said. "But times have changed. I'm willing to set all this aside. I will do whatever you want. Just leave my family out of it."

Calabrese's gaze softened.

He added: "Please?"

Tanner shook his head. "No. No, I can't do that." He almost said "I'm sorry" but caught himself before the words left his mouth.

This man didn't deserve his sympathy.

Calabrese looked down in his hands, at the blue Tupperware containers. He considered them for a moment before handing the one in his left hand to Tanner.

"I'll tell you what," he said. "Let's just eat. Pretend for a few seconds like we're two men whose lives haven't been ruined by the mistakes we've made. Then you can do whatever the hell you want to me. Right here, right now. Shoot me in the head, beat me to death, I don't care. My son..." A tear formed in the corner of his eye. "He didn't even want me there. He told me to leave. You can't hurt me by hurting him. Not anymore." His voice dropped and cracked. "I've punished him and his sister enough."

"Fine," Tanner said, snatching the Tupperware container out of Calabrese's hand. "If it'll shut you up."

He popped the cover and picked up a plastic fork sitting on the desk, speared a bite and shoved it in his mouth. Not that he wanted to accept the gift. But there was no sense in letting it go to waste, and anyway, he hadn't eaten since breakfast.

If this was the formality that'd buy them some private time together, so be it.

He could drive the van down to a quiet spot in Brooklyn. Really go to town. Work out all those years of frustration.

He was pretty sure he saw a hammer next to the driver's seat.

The lasagna was delicious. And still warm, too. It exploded in his mouth, a far cry from the cold, congealed pizza and Chinese food that filled his refrigerator lately. Calabrese nodded and opened his own container, produced a plastic fork from his coat, and began to eat.

"Merry Christmas, by the way," Calabrese said, before taking a bite.

"Hmhmmh," Tanner mumbled, his mouth full of food.

They finished at the same time, placing the blue plastic containers on the desk. Calabrese wiped his mouth as Tanner swallowed and went to pick up the gun.

It slipped from his hand and tumbled to the floor.

For a moment he thought his hands were just a little cold, but then realized he couldn't make his fingers curl.

"Well, that's enough of that," Calabrese said, climbing out of his seat and reaching for the door of the van.

Tanner tried to reach for him, but found his arms didn't want to obey him either. They hung from his sides like lumps of dead meat. He tried to speak but only managed to produce a raspy gurgle, as a crooked hand wrapped around his heart and squeezed, hard.

Calabrese opened the door and stepped down to the street.

"For the record," Calabrese said, "I gave you the slice I was going to eat. It includes a very high dose of jimsonweed. Grows all over Arizona. I hope it didn't affect the taste. Figured you'd get your closure and I'd get mine. But then you had to go and threaten my family. That's low. So, here we find ourselves. I know I said I don't kill good cops, but you're not a good cop."

Tanner heaved himself forward and tried to stand, one last desperate attempt to get Calabrese before he died. But his feet buckled under him and he tumbled forward, his face smashing into the floor of the van.

The door slid closed with a *thump* and he watched as the flickering glow of the surveillance monitors faded into blackness.

ERIC EXITED THE bathroom to find Ian standing in the back room.

"Are you okay?" he asked. "I thought we lost you."

The truth was, Eric needed some time for the swelling around his eyes to go down, so it wouldn't be so obvious he was crying, but he didn't want to say that.

He settled on: "I'm sorry, I just needed a few minutes."

"No worries," Ian said. "But we should get going."

Eric followed Ian into the main part of the store, the space filled with people standing shoulder-to-shoulder.

"If I could have your attention, everyone," Ian yelled. Conversations were abandoned as everyone turned. "We're very excited to welcome Eric Calabrese, the author of *White Sheep*. We don't do a lot of memoir here, but it's a great book, and we're happy to have him. Eric is going to talk a little bit about it, and maybe take some questions. Without further ado…"

Ian gestured to Eric as the room erupted in applause.

When it died down, Eric said, "Actually, I want to read a bit."

He thumbed open the book, skipping past the sticky notes to a passage he didn't intend to read, but felt right given the circumstances.

"The truth is, my father…"

"We can't hear you!"

It was his sister, Christine, calling from the front of the store. He smiled, climbed on a chair so he could get a good look at everyone—including Christine, who was throwing a thumbs-up—and began to read again.

"The truth is, my father was a complicated man.

The hands that strangled the life out of Vincent Abruzzo on October 16, 1985, are the same hands that played catch with me in the yard of our home in Gravesend. The hands that beat Michael Moretti to death on June 5, 1987, are the same hands that cradled my sister when she woke up crying in the middle of the night.

I have spent my entire life trying to square this.

It's left me wondering if I'm tainted. If the kind of evil that afflicted my father was genetic, if it could be passed down to us. Or if we had the freedom to make our own choices, to move past it.

I choose to believe the latter, but live in fear of the former.

There is one truth, though, in all of this, and it's that my father did not think of himself as evil. Not good, maybe. I think he was smart enough to know the consequences of his actions, and how they reflected on the world around him. But everything he did was to provide a good life for myself and my sister. And until he disappeared—after testimony in open court twenty years prior to the publication of this book forced him into witness protection—he did.

We never wanted for anything. He never raised a hand to us. If we fell, he picked us up..."

Eric felt his throat growing thick. He paused and looked up.

Standing outside the store, his hand pressed against the glass, was his father.

The words on the page grew blurry, and Eric swallowed, did

his best to recover quickly, lest anyone look back. Because despite the gulf between them, he was afraid someone might see him, and didn't want his presence to get him in trouble.

Eric smiled and nodded and hoped his father noticed.

MANNY WISHED HE could go back into the store, but knew that wasn't an option. He met eyes with his son, who smiled and nodded before going back to reading.

That would have to be enough.

Footsteps crunched in the snow to his left. He turned and saw the pretty young police officer who had been in the van. She was holding a steaming cup of bodega coffee.

"Hi," she said.

"Hi," Manny said back.

"Well, this is awkward," she said with a half-smile.

Manny figured Tanner could use another couple of minutes to stew.

"Listen, Detective Tanner said if I saw you, to ask you to get him a cup of coffee," he said. "I see you've already got one, and I'm sorry if it's an inconvenience..."

A look of relief washed over her face. Like she was happy to be getting away from him. "Oh, I don't mind."

She offered another smile and turned.

"Hey," he called after her.

She looked over her shoulder.

"You seem like a bright kid," he told her. "Tanner is not a nice man. I know, I'm not one to judge. But you should know that, all right?"

She paused like she wanted to say something, then nodded and walked off, rounding the corner.

Manny looked across the street.

There used to be a bar there, the Raccoon Lodge, that had a fireplace in a little alcove in the back. A great spot on a night like this, but the shutter was down. Probably another victim of the real estate market.

He took out his cell phone and dialed the only number programmed into it. It rung three times before a groggy voice answered, "Hello?"

"Agent Wilks?"

"Wait…Manny? Why are you calling? Is everything okay?"

"Not really, no. Listen, you still living in Staten Island?"

"I am, but if there's a problem, I have to contact the local field office in Scottsdale…"

"I'm in Manhattan."

"*What?*"

"It's a long story. Any chance you can come out and meet me? Is McSorley's still open? Or did the rat developers get that one, too?"

"It's still open, but we have to get you back before someone sees you."

"Doesn't matter now," he says. "Only place I'm going at this point is the Tombs. They still got the Tombs here?"

"Manny, what the hell are you talking about?"

"Why don't you meet me at McSorley's? I'm going to have one last drink. I'll order you one. You want light or dark?"

Silence on the other end of the phone.

"I'll be there in twenty minutes."

"Don't rush. Drive safe. I'm not going anywhere."

Manny hung up the phone and stuck it in his pocket. Gave one last look at the bookstore. Eric was still standing on the chair, reading from his book. Manny couldn't make out what he was saying.

His daughter Christine was in there somewhere.

The pair of them, better than he could have hoped.

Better than he deserved.

He turned and headed toward Broadway, where it would be easier to get a cab. The last day hadn't been so pleasant. He'd lost his taste for the cold, between the years living in the desert, and the thing eating him from the inside out.

But as he walked down Warren Street, he found the cold wasn't so bad. The way it is sometimes when it snows and the air is calm, like the flakes are sucking in the chill, pulling it away as they fall to the ground.

It made him think of their last Christmas together. Before he made the hardest decision of his life. The one that weighed on him so heavily he hadn't slept a good night since.

To leave.

That morning, the kids got up early. The Christmas prior to that, they'd set a rule for Eric: no presents until the sun came up The second there was a trace of light in the sky, he had bounded into their room and jumped into their bed.

Manny went to Christine's room and found her awake, contentedly playing with her fingers, like she was waiting for him. He scooped her out of the crib and they made their way down to the tree, where Eric's face lit up like a fireworks display as he tore open the wrapping around his new bike. Christine cooed at the sparkling lights on the tree, not old enough to understand the significance of the holiday. She was so small, and so perfect.

Calabrese stopped. Reached his hand out to the brick wall of an apartment building to steady himself. Turned and took one last look at the van.

At the last gift he would ever give his children.

And he walked on.

DRONE

RICHIE'S HEAD DIPS back and a snore erupts from his throat that sounds like a weed whacker tossed into a pool. I slap him across the back of the head. He jerks forward, nearly falling out of the metal folding chair.

"What the fuck, little brother?" he asks, running his hand over his slick-backed hair, making sure it's still flat and smooth.

I gesture forward and ask, "Have you even been paying attention?"

"Of course I have," Richie says.

I look to Melinda, her arms crossed, looking between the two of us. "He hasn't been paying attention," I tell her. "Can you just start from the top?"

Melinda sighs and walks to the whiteboard. She pulls the sleeve of her black sweater over her palm, clutching it tight with her fingertips, and wipes off the numbers she had scratched out in blue dry-erase ink. Her tight blonde ponytail swings like a pendulum.

Richie goes back to what he was doing before he fell asleep, which is ogling her apple-shaped ass. I kick his leg, tell him, "Pay attention."

"We've heard all this before," he says.

"Tonight is the first test-run delivery," I tell him. "If the client has questions, we need to answer them with some degree of confidence."

"What the fuck is there to know?"

"Just…shut up and listen."

Melinda is tapping her foot, arms crossed over her chest again. One eyebrow furrowed so severely it nearly touches her cheek.

"Are you both done?" she asks.

Richie twirls his hands like a Vegas magician revealing a trick. "Proceed."

Melinda turns to the board, scrawling a string of numbers in tight, neat handwriting. "So again, here are the basics. The drone has an effective range of ten miles. That's five miles out and five miles back. At that range, it can carry up to five pounds. Any more than that is going to impact battery life and make it harder to maneuver."

She's still writing numbers. I don't know how they correspond to what she's saying, but I understand the bullet points.

"Owning and flying a drone is legal," she says, turning back to us. "FAA regulations say you can't fly them over four hundred feet or let them out of your sight. Since we need to fly it over four hundred feet and let it out of our sight, the trick is not getting caught. That's why we'll be flying these exclusively at night, when they'll be harder to spot."

Richie raises his hand.

Melinda points to him with the marker. "Yes, Richie?"

"What if the client needs the package during the day?"

"Then ask the client how much they would like going to prison for a very long time. If law enforcement sees the drone, they're going to follow it to the destination."

I raise my hand.

"Why are you raising your hand, Billy? Just ask your question."

"Sorry." I tuck my right hand into my left armpit. "Will it be a problem, flying this thing at night?"

"The camera has an infrared lens kit. Won't be an issue."

"And you've tested it?" I ask.

Melinda nods, a smile creeping across her lips. "Perfect every time."

"Can we see it?" I ask. "The drone."

"Yeah," Richie says. "Let's see this thing."

Melinda places the dry-erase marker on the lip running along the bottom of the board, and walks to the door at the back of her office.

The next room is cramped and smells like motor oil. Industrial metal shelves line the walls. They're stacked with odd bits of metal, things with wires sticking out that look like they were torn out of larger things. In the center of the room is a table, on top of which is something draped with a white sheet, creating a landscape of peaks and depressions.

Melinda pulls the sheet aside to reveal a matte-black dome, the size of a medicine ball cut in half. Jutting out from four corners are posts that point up, with miniature helicopter wings attached. Underneath, there's a small compartment, which the whole thing rests on like a pedestal.

Richie reaches out to touch it and Melinda smacks his hand.

He pulls it back and rubs it. He's smiling now, probably because he thinks she's flirting with him.

From the look on her face, she is clearly not flirting with him.

"So what if the cops do manage to grab this thing?" I ask. "Can they trace it back?"

"It's a custom job. All the parts were purchased from different distributors, and all the serial numbers have been filed off. Everything was paid for through Bitcoin. I'm not saying they can't definitely trace it back to me, but it would take so much time and effort they'd probably give up halfway though."

"At that rate, playing it safe, how many of these things can you build?" I ask.

"Two a month. Maybe quicker as we get more money through the door."

"I thought it would be shiny," Richie says. "Like a racecar or something."

Melinda shakes her head. "We don't want it to reflect the light."

"But wouldn't it look cooler?" he asks, putting his arm around Melinda and clasping her shoulder. She tenses up like there's a roach on her arm, and steps away with enough force to knock back Richie's arm.

"First, don't touch me like that," she says. "That is not fucking okay. And if you're not going to take this seriously…"

Richie goes from wannabe-suave to alpha-predator like a switch has been flipped. "Don't forget, you came to us about this, okay, bitch?"

I get between the two of them. "Both of you, stop. Let's agree on something." I point to Richie. "We don't have the knowledge or the tools to do this, and we need Melinda. So be nice. It doesn't take any effort to be nice."

I turn to Melinda, who has a smug smile wrapped around her

face. "And you." The smile disappears. "You can handle delivery but you can't get the product. This is a mutually beneficial relationship. It has the potential to be very beneficial, because if this takes off, we'll have the market cornered. So let's all just chill, okay?"

Melinda nods. I turn to Richie. He nods, not taking his eyes off Melinda.

"Great," I tell them. "Richie, go get the thing."

He lingers for a moment, huffs out his nostrils, then dashes out of the room. He comes back and slaps a package wrapped in brown paper, the size and shape of a brick, down onto the table in front of the drone.

Melinda pulls out a small scale and places the package on top, lets the weight register. She says, "One kilo. Two point two pounds on the dot. Perfect."

She's very clearly speaking to me and ignoring Richie now. Which, fine, whatever.

"What are we getting for this again?" Melinda asks.

"A grand per run, at least five runs per week," I tell her. "That's to start. It's a non-exclusive agreement. We can take on more clients if we want, as long as they aren't direct competitors to the first guy."

Her blue eyes light up. "Holy fucktown."

Richie smiles. "Yeah. Holy fucktown is right."

Melinda gives him a forced, tight smile.

THE CITY IS quiet, frozen in that moment between last call and the breakfast rush, when it's just empty cabs and bread trucks. I quicken my pace, glance back to make sure Richie is keeping up. He's still groggy, hands jammed in his pockets, head down.

Richie yawns wide and says, "We need a name."

"For what?"

"The business."

"What are we going to do, take out ads? We don't need a name."

Richie jogs a little to keep pace and come even with me. "We should call the company Speed."

"Like the movie?"

"What movie?"

"Are you kidding? What movie? Keanu Reeves. Sandy Bullock. *Speed.*"

"Never heard of it. Is it one of those goofy fucking indie films you like so much?"

"It was one of the biggest action movies ever. With the bomb, on the bus?"

"I got nothing," Richie says. "Anyway, I still think we should name the company Speed. Get it? 'Cause we're delivering drugs." He puts up his hands and does air quotes with his fingers. "Speed."

We stop at a corner to let a cab barrel past us. "That's a little silly," I tell him.

"I'm not done. Also, we're delivering them fast, right? With speed. It's slick. Kinda modern, right?"

"What we have isn't a company, dumbass. It's a clandestine drug delivery service. The absolute last thing we want in the world is to advertise what we're doing."

"Well, fuck you. I'm calling the company Speed. People will call us up and say, 'I have the need for Speed'. Like in *Top Gun*. Now that's a movie."

"Okay, Richie."

We walk in silence for a bit, trudging up the avenue until we get to the street we're looking for, and hang a left.

Richie says, "I think Melinda wants to fuck me."

"No, she doesn't," I say.

"Jealous?"

"Not jealous. Just living on planet earth. Anyway, she doesn't seem like your type. She's cute but she looks like a mouse. You like women with a few more miles on them."

"She looks like a hot fucking mouse I'd like to see naked. Maybe after we get all the pieces in place on this, we can talk about going out for drinks."

We stop in front of our destination, a blank brick walk-up hidden away in Hell's Kitchen. We stand and wait. I think the camera set into the corner of the doorway refocuses, but I'm not positive. I tell Richie, "No mixing business and pleasure. We stand to make a lot of money if this takes off. Let's not fuck it up. Just this one time, let's not fuck something up."

"What, you think I can't handle my shit?"

"No, I *know* you can't handle your shit."

The door buzzes and we push through and climb the darkened stairwell toward the roof. "You don't even know what you're talking about," he says.

"Richie, if you could handle your shit, you wouldn't ask my opinion so much, and we both know if you didn't ask my opinion so much, you'd be dead or in jail for a very long time now."

"Whatever. Shut up."

We make it to the doorway leading to the roof and I reach up to knock, but before my fist can land, the door swings open.

The guy who opened the door is dressed in denim jeans, a black t-shirt, and a denim coat. The guy flanking him is wearing the exact same outfit. They're both thick in the arms and generally unpleasant to look at for too long. They step to the side and let us pass. We step out into the cool air to see a young Latino guy in basketball shorts, a tank top, and a neon windbreaker perched on a stool.

The guy on the stool looks at us and says, "So you two dummies are the runners. You know it's way too early for this shit, right?"

This is the first time we're meeting in person, instead of through intermediaries. He doesn't introduce himself. He knows he doesn't need to. I don't know his real name, but people in this neighborhood call him T. Rex. The implication is clear.

"I can explain that," I tell him.

"My favorite coffee place wasn't even open," T. Rex says. "I had to get a Red Bull. Red Bull tastes like asshole dipped in cotton candy."

"Just…hold on. The timing is part of the presentation."

"You have a fucking presentation? Did you bring a PowerPoint? Do I need to set up a projector?"

"Hear me out?"

He nods, pulls a pack of Newports out of his shorts. He gets one between his lips, lights it from a crumbled book of matches, and puts his hand up. Says, "Go on with your presentation, then. I want to see this thing work and then I want to go back to sleep."

Richie looks at me and begins to say something, so I hold up my hand. I stand in front of T. Rex and check my watch, reach toward my pocket, and the two guys in denim flinch. I slow down a little, pull out my phone, and dial the number I've got queued up.

Melinda picks up and I tell her, "Launch it now."

I stick the phone back in my pocket.

"You know how hard it is to move product around the city," I tell T. Rex.

He drags, blows out the smoke, and stares at me with slate eyes.

"Especially since 9/11," I continue. "You can't carry through the subways because there are searches. Taxis and gypsy cabs are a workable solution, but they're not foolproof. A little traffic and you get jammed up, or a dispatcher sends the driver to a different neighborhood and they're out of rotation. Bikes are okay but they're slow, and anyway, drivers don't care much for people on bikes. Accidents happen. That can be dangerous with the product they're carrying. And the ice cream trucks…"

T. Rex puts his hand up. "I don't fuck with the ice cream trucks. They got their own thing going. You don't need to convince me of this. I know it makes sense. What I need to know is if this is going to work."

"It'll work," I tell him. "We fly them at night, and as time goes on and we develop more of these, we can ship more than keys. We can send out product that's already been cut and bagged. We might be able to ship other items, too."

"Like what?"

"Anything under five pounds you don't want to get caught carrying."

"Like a gun?"

"Maybe. Do guns weigh less than five pounds?"

"How the fuck should I know?"

Richie wants to say something smart to that so I put my hand up again. Deals go best when he stays quiet. "We can figure all that out. We're open to testing anything once the system is in place."

"And exactly how long does this system take?" T. Rex asks.

The soft whirring tips me off, and thankfully it fits the drama of the timing. I step back and the drone floats softly to the ground and sets onto the gray tarpaper between me and T. Rex. He tilts his head and smiles as the rotors come to a stop.

"That was launched from two miles away," I tell him. "You tell me if that's fast enough."

T. Rex gets up and tosses his cigarette behind him, sending up a spray of sparks as it taps off one of the thugs in the denim, who doesn't budge.

"That's fucking tight," he says. "Let's go to a diner and get some eggs and sort out logistics. I'm not even tired anymore. Now I want to work. Give me the key."

I drop to my knee and reach for the knob on the compartment on the bottom of the drone, and find that the door is hanging open.

My heart twists into a knot so hard it nearly tears. I reach inside and feel the empty space and I must whimper or gasp because everyone is suddenly staring at me.

"What's wrong?" T. Rex asks.

"Nothing, I just…"

Suddenly, his body is eclipsing the speck of sun on the horizon, and now I see exactly where the nickname comes from. "Don't fucking tell me my key isn't in there. Don't you fucking tell me that."

"It's just…hold on…"

Hands grab at me from behind and I'm thrown into the brick wall housing the roof access door, the air snatched from my lungs. One of the denim soldiers is holding me, and without much effort. The other is holding Richie in a double nelson, and T. Rex is pressing the blade of a knife against my throat.

"What the fuck is this?" he asks. "You trying to rip me off?"

"It's not like that…let me just call our girl. Find out what happened."

T. Rex stares at me for so long that I think he's decided to kill me and is just imagining it before he does it. Then he pulls the knife back from my throat, nods to his goon, who lets me go, and I stumble away, pulling out my cell.

I take a few paces when Richie yells out. The guy holding him is squeezing and T. Rex is holding the knife and shaking his head. I step back toward them and Melinda answers.

"Yeah?" she asks.

"Did you, like, forget to put the key into the drone?"

"What do you mean?"

"I mean there's no key in the drone."

"What do you mean there's no key in the drone?"

"I mean exactly that, Mel. Exactly the thing I just said."

Silence on the other end. T. Rex's knife catches the light of the rising sun.

Mel says, "The latch. The fucking latch might have come undone. There was a bird, and I had to bank hard around a building. It might have fallen out."

"You...no. No."

"Look," she says. "It's still early. I'll send you a map of the flight path. Maybe it's still there. If you leave now...just go. I'll send it to your phone."

I close my phone and look at T. Rex.

He must have gotten the idea, because once again I'm against the wall, the knife back to my throat. He's so close that when he speaks, flecks of spit slap me on the face.

"Forty thousand dollars," he says. "That's what that key is worth."

"We can get it," I tell him. "It might still be there..."

He presses the blade harder into my neck. I feel something hot that might be blood.

A trickle running down my skin.

Yes, that would be blood.

"She thinks she knows where it happened," I say.

T. Rex stares at me a little more and I think I feel an increase of pressure on the blade. Wonder how much it hurts when someone cuts your throat. Death looks quick in the movies, but those are just movies.

Then he backs away.

"Go," he says. "Your brother stays until you get back."

Richie looks at me with pleading eyes. There are few guarantees in this world, but I know if I agree to this, Richie is dead. Because even if T. Rex has the best of intentions right now, which I doubt he does, Richie has an incredible talent for taking good intentions and turning them the other way.

"I need him. We're better working together."

T. Rex sighs. "Fine. Take him. But you take Miguel, too. I'm not even going to threaten you. It's not worth the energy. You know you're dead if you don't turn up with it."

The denim-clad thug holding Richie, presumably Miguel, smiles and lets go. His teeth look sharp, but that might just be the fear fucking with my vision.

THE SUN IS nearly up now, the clouds washed orange and yellow. I pull out my phone and open up the map app. There's a pulsing red dot right near where we're standing. This is where Melinda said the drone banked.

In front of us is a very tall building. One of those new buildings with no character that seem to be springing up everywhere now, just flat blue glass and steel. It's shaped like an L, with a foot sticking out that can't be more than two stories. At the base of the building there's a fenced-in courtyard full of playground equipment.

At the end of the block there's a steady stream of parents dropping off toddlers. Through the floor-to-ceiling windows of the building's little foot, we can see kids' toys, bright pastel paint, crude finger-paint drawings pinned to the walls.

"Dios mío," says Miguel.

Richie asks, "What?"

"It's a preschool or something," I tell him.

"You mean these kids got our coke?"

"Keep your voice down, Richie."

"So what's the plan?" he asks.

Okay. If the key fell here, it's either in the courtyard, somewhere around the building, or up on the roof of the school. It can't be on top of the main building; Melinda said she had to bank around it.

"We need to canvass the area, and we need to get up on that roof," I tell them, pointing to the lower portion of the building. "We can check it out and it'll give us a view down into the courtyard."

"And how do you suggest we do that?" Richie asks. "We all look like we shouldn't be allowed near kids."

I turn to Miguel. "Any ideas?"

He shrugs. "No lo sé."

"Do you even speak English?" Richie asks.

"Vete a la mierda," Miguel says.

"That means 'fuck you,'" I say. "So I guess the answer is no."

Miguel nods.

I point up at the roof. "Miguel, can you go up there? Richie and I will search around the building."

Miguel shakes his head.

Which is what I figured. No way is he leaving us both alone together. And he's right, because I was planning on the two of us running away, very fast, as soon as he was out of sight.

"Fine," I tell him. "You and Richie search around the building. Then see if there's a way you can get onto the roof from the outside. I'll try to go in through the front through the school."

"Why do you get the school?" Richie asks.

"Because I look less like a child molester."

"Fuck you. I don't look like a child molester."

"You *just said* you look like you shouldn't be around kids."

"I didn't mean it like that, you sick fuck."

I press my face into my hands to keep from screaming. More

kids are showing up. We're running out of time. I am keenly aware of the raw, hot feeling of the slight wound on my throat, which T. Rex wants to make into a bigger wound. I head toward the school and call out, "Just get moving."

GIVEN THE LIFE I've chosen, this is not the first time I've found myself trying to get into a place I shouldn't be. There's a trick to it, and it's easy: act like you belong there. Don't ask for permission. Don't come up with an excuse. Put your head down. Walk in like you've got a destination in mind. Smile, but not directly at people, because that's creepy.

Most times, people will just assume you know where you're going and let you pass.

Most times.

Three feet inside the lobby, as I'm giving my neck one last wipe with my thumb to make sure there's no more blood, a plump black woman steps in front of me. She has flat blue-black doll hair, her fingers tipped with long, blood-red nails that look like talons. The nametag pinned to her pink button-down shirt says "Dina". She's a foot and a half shorter than me so she's stretching her neck to look up at me.

Her voice booms. "Can I help you?"

Another helpful thing for getting into places you're not supposed to be: keep a script in your back pocket, just in case.

"Yeah," I tell her. "I'm with the city. Just have to take a quick look at the electric. There's was a surge in this neighborhood, so what happens is sometimes that can throw some circuits in a big building like this. Chances are it's nothing. If there's a cause for concern, I come back with a crew and we fix it. Should take five minutes."

None of this makes any actual sense, but I'm betting she's not an electrician. Utility guys are wallpaper. They come in and out of buildings all the time.

It's never not worked.

The woman smiles. "I got you. Show me some ID and then you can head on back."

"Oh, well…"

She purses her lips. "You don't have ID?"

"Well, I mean…"

"You really think I'm going to let some sketchy-looking motherfucker walk into a place that's full of kids with no proof of who he is?"

"I didn't mean to…"

She sticks a finger into my face. The talon on the end of her finger is so long that if she jammed it in my eye, it would surely pierce my brain. "You have exactly until I am done talking to get the fuck out of here, or I'm going to call the police and then beat the shit out of you while we wait for them. If you can come back with some ID, then we'll be settled."

"Jesus, I'm sorry…"

"And don't take the motherfucking Lord's name in vain. There are children here."

In this moment, I legitimately do not know who to be more afraid of: T. Rex or Dina.

STOP RUNNING WHEN I'm sure I'm out of Dina's line of sight, and I find that Richie and Miguel had better luck than me, the two of them poking around up on the roof.

Richie seems me on the sidewalk and shrugs.

It is a shrug of desperation.

Miguel, though, is looking down into the courtyard, where the kids are now outside playing. The way he's looking makes me think something is up, so I walk up to the fence and peer in.

The kids are tearing around the playground, bouncing off objects like rubber balls. Their eyes are wide like they're gripped by madness, their mouths rimmed in white powder.

No.

Oh fuck no.

Richie is looking now, too. He calls down to me but I can't hear him, so he takes out his phone. He fiddles with it and then mine rings. I answer and he says, "Dude, I think those kids have our coke."

The kids are playing some elaborate game that involves jumping over each other while they screech like dinosaurs. One little Asian boy gets close and he looks like Al Pacino at the end of *Scarface* after he stuck his face into the mountain on his desk. He squeals at me like a pterodactyl before he runs off.

Richie is still talking, the words bouncing off me and tumbling to the ground. After a moment I ask him to repeat himself.

"We have to get the fuck out of here," he says.

"No way, man," I tell him. "We have to tell someone."

"Fuck that. Fuck those kids. Let's get the fuck out of here."

"We're not monsters, Richie."

The phone disconnects. I look up and can't see Richie or Miguel.

I look back at the kids, their faces turning red from exertion as they blast around the playground like they've got rockets strapped to them.

I've done a lot of bad in my life and I've lived with it, but this, I can't let go. They're kids. And anyway, T. Rex is probably going to kill me soon. I may as well do a little good before that happens.

DINA LISTENS TO my frantic explanation, that I think the kids have ingested cocaine and she needs to call an ambulance and we should probably get them some water or something, and maybe stop them from running around, I guess? I don't know anything about kids and their tolerance level for drugs.

Dina laughs. "You are some whacked-out motherfucker, you know that?"

"This isn't a joke!"

I scream it at her. So loud that she flinches, and now people are stopping and staring. There are a few parents here now, some of them pushing their children behind them. A few of the dads make their way over to get Dina's back.

"Look," I put my hands up, drop my voice, try to turn on the friendly. "We need to help these kids. I promise, call the cops and they can take me away, I don't care. Just call 9-1-1 and get an ambulance…"

There is now a very large, very angry group of people lined up behind Dina.

"The only thing these kids are hopped up on is the powered donuts," she says. "It's donut day. Now, why don't you just stay there, nice and calm, and we're going to call the cops and sort this out."

"That white powder is…donuts."

"Where are a bunch of kids going to get cocaine, mother…" Dina notices a kid has gotten close. "…jibjab."

"Umm." Shit. "I think there's been a misunderstanding here."

As soon as the words are out of my mouth, two of the dads lunge and grab at my arms. I step back and shake them off and now people are screaming and yelling, so I throw an elbow and catch someone in the head and run outside and around the building, where I slam hard into Richie.

We tangle and fall to the ground.

As we're getting to our feet, I realize someone took a bucket of blood and splashed it across his front.

"Where the fuck is Miguel?" I ask.

A group of parents come around the side of the building, headed right for us, wielding colorful plastic toys as makeshift weapons.

"I think we should be running right now," Richie says.

"Agreed."

SIX BLOCKS LATER and we think we're safe enough that we can duck into the alcove of a delivery bay. The block is quiet; there's a bottled water delivery truck parked at the curb and no one in sight. I bend over and put my hands on my knees. Richie sprawls out onto the ground, huffing and puffing.

When I can breathe enough to talk, I ask, "Seriously, where is Miguel?"

"Yeah, so, T. Rex called him for an update and things didn't sound too good so I figured it was best to make a pre-emptive strike."

"Is he dead?"

"Possibly."

Okay. That's not good.

But it's a problem that could be less severe if we can solve the bigger problem. Maybe T. Rex will go easy on us if we show up with the drugs. We can come up with an excuse for Miguel. Fuck, we can say that Miguel suggested we all make a run for it with the key.

There's an answer here. I can find one.

First, we have to solve the case of the missing coke.

I call Melinda again and she answers, says, "You didn't find it, did you?"

"No. We're in a lot of trouble, Mel."

"Is Richie there?"

"Yes, why?"

"Put the call on speaker. I want him to hear this."

I pull the phone away from my ear, fuck with the screen trying to figure it out. Richie asks, "What are you doing?"

"Melinda wants to talk to you."

He smiles. "I told you she wanted to fuck me."

"Shut up, shut up, SHUT UP."

I find the right button and click it, ask, "Mel?"

"I hear you." Her voice is high and tinny. "Are you both there?"

"We are," I tell her. "What is it that both of us need to hear?"

"Okay, so, Billy, I want you to know I feel a little bad about this, because you seem like an okay guy, but at the same time, your brother is a fucking scumbag, so at the end of the day, I don't feel *that* bad…"

"Hey," Richie says. "I'm not a scumbag."

"Yes, you are," Mel says. "You grabbed my ass three times. Once is bad enough. Twice more after I told you to stop? You know how not-fucking-cool that is? You can't just do that. So consider this a lesson. I never put the kilo in the drone. I'm going to sell it to another buyer. And I'm already out of the state and it should go without saying you won't be able to find me, so, I guess this is goodbye."

"Mel, wait…" I plead.

"Sorry, Billy. Fuck you, Richie."

The line goes dead.

"So…what now?" Richie asks.

"We go. Right now. Don't even go home first. We have to

fucking go, Richie."

Richie climbs to his feet, drops his thin jacket to the ground, and pulls off his gray t-shirt, flipping it inside out to hide the blood. "That fucking bitch…"

"Maybe if you'd didn't act like such a dick all the time, she wouldn't have fucked us."

"Get real, little brother," he says, pulling the shirt back over his head. "She played us. She knew exactly what she was doing. You think me making a grab at her was the deciding factor? She had a plan from the beginning."

"Bullshit."

"Yeah? She has another buyer? How the fuck is some nerd bitch going to line up a buyer for a key of fucking coke unless she did a little legwork? If she had that kind of reach, she wouldn't have needed us in the first place."

That's not an unfair point.

It's also not the important thing right now.

Richie puts his jacket on and buttons it and the blood isn't even visible anymore, save a splash on his chin. I point to it and he wipes at it with the dark sleeve of his jacket. Not great, but better than nothing.

"Let's revisit this," I tell him. "Right now, we have to get gone."

On this much, we're simpatico.

We turn the corner, stumbling in the light of day.

"You know what the worst part is?"

"What, Richie?" I ask. "What's the worst part?"

"This was a good fucking idea. Six months and everyone's going to be doing this. Speed would have been the first."

"You and that fucking name."

"It's a good name."

"No, it's not. And when we're settled, in whatever bumfuck

burg is safe enough that maybe T. Rex won't find us and kill us, we're going to rent *Speed*, because I can't believe you haven't seen it."

But Richie isn't walking next to me anymore.

I stop and turn, and he's frozen a few steps behind, his eyes are wide and set, staring at something off in the distance.

Down the block, there's a flash of denim.

BUTCHER'S BLOCK

NOVA WOKE IN a chair. Groans and shuffling and scraping on either side of her. She tried to lift her hands and found they were clamped down. Her heart rate went up a few ticks.

It took effort, like she was forcing out a sneeze, to remember the last thing that happened before the dark.

The show.

She'd gone to the taping for the show, where she was placed in a room and made to sign a waiver probably a hundred pages long before she met with the casting director. He was tall and had hazel eyes and a sharp nose and the look of someone who was not being fed. He asked her a series of questions related to her health.

Allergies, especially to medications or chemicals (none).

Phobias, and be as specific as possible (geese...long story).

Any kind of injuries or chronic conditions (tightness in her lower back, nothing major).

After the man left, she took out her phone. She wanted to check her e-mail. Make sure the team at her restaurant had things covered while she was gone. She hated being gone. Two years since opening and she hadn't missed a day. But money was tight and cooking competition shows were a good way to get publicity. That's even if she didn't win the grand prize—$25,000. If she *did* win, it meant a new walk-in and updating the restrooms. Maybe she'd go totally nuts and take a vacation.

They kept saying that over the phone: it was a brand-new, never-before-done concept. This would be the pilot and to say more would spoil the fun, said the casting director.

Never-before-done. That hadn't concerned Nova. She expected some cutesy bullshit like that show where you make a meal out of random ingredients in a basket, or the one where you bid on items to sabotage your opponents.

Sitting in the dark, she wished she'd been more concerned.

She wished she'd actually read the agreement, rather than skimming in before ultimately giving up a third of the way through.

"What the hell is going on?" Male voice, hushed, to the left.

"Dunno, brah." Male voice, to the right.

"...some bullshit." Male voice, left, different from the other two.

Nova coughed. "Anyone else rather be at work today?"

No one laughed.

"Good. You're all awake."

The voice rattled and cracked in the darkness.

A blaring white rectangle filled Nova's field of vision and she squinted against it, the brightness searing her retinas. After a moment she could bear it and she watched as the screen flickered and a man appeared in a featureless mask. Like the face of a person with all the definition sandblasted off.

"I am The Butcher," he said. "And welcome..." he raised his hands with a grand sense of theater, really putting his back into it, "...to Butcher's Block!"

"...the fuck?"

Nova turned and could see the voice belonged to a tall black man with a shaved head, fists like hocks of ham, straining against the metal pneumatic cuffs keeping him restrained. His arms bulged inside the black, skin-tight chef's coat with the logo of a bloody knife on the breast. The same coat they all wore.

Next to him was a surfer-dude who was drug-habit thin, with sloppy dreadlocks tied together in a bunch at the back of his head. Slim arms and neck covered in tattoos. Nova sighed. White guy with dreads—never a good sign.

To her right was just a guy. Plain as a high school baseball player. Decent haircut, square jaw. Also the least flustered of the bunch. He caught Nova's look and gave a little smile and shrug, like, *can you believe this?* Like being restrained in chairs was a frustrating but otherwise normal inconvenience.

"What's the deal, brah?" asked White Dreadlocks. "Uh, you can't do this to us?"

The figure on the screen titled his head. He spoke in a quiet voice, less theatrical, less formal. "The release you signed says I can. Did you read the release?" He looked at the four in turn. "Did any of you read the release?"

Silence.

"That's what I thought. Now, the name of the game is spontaneity. I'll introduce each of you in turn, and we'll go over the premise for the viewing audience, and then, game on!"

"Wait..."

"Waiting is over."

A spotlight shone on White Dreadlocks. His head darted

around like he'd been caught with a joint. Probably a sensation he was used to, Nova thought.

"Our first contestant is...Chef Cedar! Hailing from Portland, Oregon, known for his combination of rustic Pacific Northwest tableau with Thai and Japanese influences. Cedar has a very interesting story about how he came to cooking, and we'll get into that a little later."

The spotlight clicked off, and then appeared on the man to Nova's left. "And welcome...Chef Axel! The owner and operator of the famous Nana's Kitchen in Harlem, Axel is known for bringing refinery to comfort food classics! And from what I hear, he's quite the ladies' man."

The light appeared around Nova. She squinted in the glare. "And...Chef Nova! Coming to us from Miami, she brings classic French training to the fast-casual dining scene. She's known for her strong sense of loyalty to her cook staff."

When the light clicked off, Nova was relieved, but she took a little offense at the fast-casual designation. She preferred to think of what she did as simple but thoughtful meals in a café-like setting. And that bit about loyalty. What was that?

The light clicked on to her right. "And finally...Chef Stuart! A native of Connecticut, he's traveled the world and worked under some of the greatest chefs of our time. And he's proven he'll do anything—and I mean *anything*—to make a buck in the world of cooking."

The room filled with dim light, inching away the dark. They were in some sort of dilapidated cafeteria. And from the look of the dirt on the floor, the grime on the windows, the scattered and broke furniture, it likely hadn't functioned as a cafeteria for a very long time. The screen on which The Butcher appeared was suspended from the ceiling and the chairs they sat on were bolted to the floor in the middle of the room.

"Here's how the game is played," The Butcher said. "There will be one round and one round only. At the end of the round, there will be one winner. Unless there's not. I will assign you a dish and you must prepare it to perfection. You will be judged on both taste and presentation. Scattered throughout this building you will find everything you need, from cooking stations to ingredients. The timer is set for one hour. You must be back here with one completed and composed plate when the hour ends. And remember, there is one rule…"

The Butcher leaned forward, his gleaming mask filling the screen.

"There are no rules. You may stall and sabotage your opponents however you wish. Now, I would like you to prepare…a perfect French omelet!"

"…the fuck is happening right now?" Chef Axel asked.

"Now, if you would so kindly." The Butcher raised his hands again.

As he did, the restraints hissed and popped open. Nova rubbed her wrists, trying to focus on the sensation, on the feeling of her skin, the pressure of her touch, because her head was spinning so fast it was hard to concentrate on anything else. She glanced to either side and found her opponents were free, too.

"Now…would you kindly slice and dice!"

Axel was the first to stand, followed by Nova, then Stuart. Cedar remained seated. Nova looked at the three of them and tried to imagine a worse position to be in, but she couldn't. No rules and three men. She slid her hand to the coin pocket of her jeans, where she kept her knife. The blade was only two inches long but sharp enough to slice through sheet metal.

It was gone. Of course it was gone.

"Yo, I didn't sign up for this," Cedar said, still sitting.

"I think we all signed up for it," Stuart said, raising an eyebrow. He looked around. "I'll tell you what though, this is the last time I skip on reading the fine print."

"...this is some *Hunger Games* shit," said Axel.

Cedar paused, then laughed. "Double meaning. I get it."

"If it's like that, it's like that," Axel said. "I'm getting my twenty-five large."

He took off at a jog. Nova looked at Cedar, who seemed lost, and then to Stuart, who shrugged and said, "What else are we going to do? If we sit around and do nothing, we lose."

Nova followed Stuart, who was following Axel, while Cedar called from the back, "I don't think I'm comfortable with this."

Stuart slowed his pace to fall alongside Nova and spoke out of the side of his mouth. "What do you think?"

"I think you're right. We play. What else are we going to do?"

"And this 'no rules' thing?"

"I don't know," Nova said. "I don't know what that means."

It was a lie. She knew. Men barely followed rules as it was, and when there were *no* rules? Fuck. But she pretended like there wasn't a threat lingering in the air. Like maybe if she didn't acknowledge it, she wouldn't give it form.

"What do you make of the other two?" Stuart asked.

"Cedar has probably been high for the past ten years," she said. "But that doesn't mean anything. My best sous chef can't function unless he's high. I'm worried about Axel."

"So you've been to Nana's, too?"

"Guy knows how to cook."

Nova scanned the surroundings. There were little black domes—cameras—everywhere. The place was covered from every angle. So this must be an immersive type of show, like *Big Brother*.

Didn't matter. Nothing mattered in that moment except the omelet. A French omelet being the opposite of the American diner omelet. It was egg, only egg, chives and butter to finish unless you were some kind of fucking animal. Not some pile of shit thrown onto a flattop and cooked until brown. No, a French omelet was rolled out and folded onto itself, a perfectly smooth cylinder of egg, pale yellow, still just a touch runny in the middle.

Nova knew why The Butcher had picked it. Eggs were the way to test new cooks. Tell them to cook an egg dish and you'd see what kind of chef they were, because you could make a million dishes with eggs, and they were easy to screw up.

At the edge of the room, Nova and Stuart found an open doorway, the sound of clanging pots beyond, and when they entered, they found a huge kitchen that could easily fit a team of twenty. Axel was hunched down in front of a cabinet, pulling out pans, inspecting them, tossing them over his shoulder. Nova didn't need an explanation. They were scratched, nicked, dented. A good omelet took a non-stick pan, or at least well-seasoned carbon steel. Anything else, the egg wouldn't lift off clean.

"...not like there are any ingredients," Axel said, without looking up.

It was easy enough to confirm. A soft glow emanated from the stoves, where the pilots were lit, but most of the cupboards and the refrigerator were open. The place was picked clean.

"So what now?" Stuart asked.

"All I know is an omelet takes five minutes to cook, we have a little less than an hour, and I have to pee," Nova said. "If you'll excuse me..."

She stepped out of the room, left Stuart and Axel to figure it out. She didn't have to pee. But it was pretty obvious what they needed wasn't in that room. Maybe they had to bring ingredients back. Maybe not. But nothing was getting done standing around.

Nova jogged to the other side of the cafeteria and ducked down a hallway. Paused and listened. Empty rooms. They were in a school. The windows were blacked out. She didn't know how long she had been unconscious. If it was night or day. Didn't matter. The only thing that mattered was the omelet. Having a goal distracted from the sheer absurdity of the situation.

She jogged down the first floor hallway, and then most of the second, when she came to a locked door. That made her pause. Everything else was wide open. Which made it the first anomaly, which meant it might mean something.

"Now," The Butcher said, again, clear as day, like he was standing next to her. "You all might be interested to know a little more about our chefs. Let's start with Chef Axel. We know Nana's Kitchen is one of the hottest restaurants in New York. That's what he called his grandmother, who inspired him to become a chef. Which is very kind and honorable, but also a little odd, considering his last girlfriend took out a restraining order against him. I wonder what that was about?"

Nova paused. Even better. It wasn't enough to pit them against each other, now he was going to pit the audience against them? Worse, what would happen when it was her turn?

She pushed it out of her head. Knelt down and focused on the lock. She couldn't pick it, didn't know how, but she knew how to kick a door open. Kick near the knob. She learned that when her niece locked herself in the bathroom with the tub running.

She leaned back and threw her foot into it. Didn't budge. Tried again. Nothing. With every crack of her foot she winced at the sound, because it might be enough to attract the other contestants.

One more kick. Nothing. Sweat trickled down her back. She looked around, found a fire extinguisher hanging from the wall.

Better. She slammed it on the knob. Once, twice, and on the third swing the knob broke and clattered to the floor.

Inside was an office, no window, no light, but she could hear a faint humming sound. She could feel the vibrations. She stepped inside, leaving the door open a crack so there'd be light, and found a mini-fridge underneath the desk. Inside: three eggs, salt, butter, a ramekin with freshly-chopped chives, and white pepper. Her heart skipped and sighed.

Next to the fridge was an induction plate. She looked for a pan. Nothing. No plate, either. The omelet had to come out of the pan as soon as it was done, or the residual heat would cause it to overcook.

Nova leaned against the desk. Surveyed the room. She needed to find a pan, to start. Should she bring the ingredients with her? The eggs were fragile. She couldn't carry everything plus the induction plate. She went for a half-measure, opened one of the drawers in the desk, put everything inside, slid the induction plate underneath the desk where it couldn't be seen.

She stood up, checked her work. It would be easy enough to miss. She turned and stepped into the hallway, smacking into Axel, which was like bouncing off a brick wall.

The two of them stared at each other. Nova felt her face do something, betraying emotions she'd rather keep to herself. Axel frowned. "Don't think that. It was a misunderstanding."

"I wasn't…"

"…sure." He shrugged.

She nodded her head toward the office. "Nothing in there."

Axel stared at her, then through her. She didn't like it. She could see the equation playing out in his eyes.

No rules.

He stepped around her and gave the room a cursory look.

Nova hoped he would mistake the fridge for a filing cabinet. He didn't, walked over and opened it.

"Empty," Nova said.

Axel stuck his hand inside. "still cold though."

He stood up, full height, which was a full head over her. Took a few steps toward her and asked, "...You holding out on me?"

"Hey!"

Nova turned to find Stuart. He spoke to Nova but looked at Axel. "All good here?"

"Nothing I can't handle," Nova said.

"Well," Stuart said, still looking at Axel. "I get it, we all want to win, but let's not lose our cool, you know what I mean?"

Axel arched an eyebrow in response, gave one last look at Nova, his eyes patting her down, to see if she was hiding anything, and pushed past her, into the hall.

"You okay?" Stuart asked.

Nova took a deep breath. Willed her heart to slow down. "Doesn't mean I'm going to take it easy on you."

Stuart smiled. It was a nice smile. "Wouldn't expect you to. Find anything?"

"Not yet," Nova said, trying to keep her voice honest.

Stuart nodded. She wasn't convinced he believed her but it also didn't matter. She stepped past him, into the hall, and Stuart called, "Hey."

Nova turned.

"Axel is the strongest competition. We trip him up, we're on an even playing field."

"You proposing a team-up?"

"Just something to think about."

"Okay," Nova said, not really sure what that okay, meant, just that she wanted the conversation to be over so she could get back to work. She jogged down the hallway, in the opposite direction of Axel, climbed to the third floor, gave a cursory run-through—no more locked doors. A chime echoed throughout the corridors.

"Fifteen minutes have elapsed," said The Butcher. "You have forty-five minutes left. You boys might want to keep up with Chef Nova. So far, I think she may be the one to beat…unless someone else is up to the challenge."

"Oh, you motherfucker," Nova muttered.

She picked up her pace. Heard footsteps coming from the other end of the corridor, so she stepped into the stairwell and went the only direction she could: down, which brought her back to the first floor. The stairs led down another level still, into a pool of pitch black. She didn't even have her phone to light the way.

Then something caught her, made her stop. Sitting upright in the middle of the top step leading down to the basement was an object the size of her forearm. She reached for it and felt the cool metal of a flashlight.

She looked around to make sure she was alone, then clicked it on and went down the stairs, following the narrow beam of light.

She didn't like the dark. It seemed to press on her, making her muscles tight. It got worse when The Butcher spoke, like he was whispering in her ear. "Chef Stuart is quite the hero, stepping in to make sure poor Chef Nova was safe."

Poor Chef Nova? she thought. *Die in a fire, asshole.*

"But would it change your opinion of Chef Stuart to know he's the subject of a class-action lawsuit for improperly withholding tips from employees? Seems he's pocketed more than forty thousand dollars that was supposed to go to his waitstaff."

Nova grimaced. That was a cardinal sin. Restaurant margins were tight, but the waitstaff was the front line, and a happy staff meant a happy restaurant. She hated to know it about him. His face was just nice enough she had thought about asking him out for a drink after.

After. She was looking forward to after, no matter what form it took. No more cooking competitions, though. Next time she wanted publicity, she'd invent a burger topped with mac-and-cheese three different ways. Something for the Instagram crowd.

She sighed. Swung the flashlight back and forth in front of her, occasionally catching a black-domed camera. She imagined someone watching this clip, probably shot in infrared, a ghostly white figure stalking the hallway.

What kind of show was this, really?

At the end of the hallway, she came to a large room. Painted on the floor in front of the door was a smiley-face. She wasn't sure if it was graffiti or a clue, but she stepped in anyway.

There were a number of items in the middle of the room, the flashlight catching glimpses, not revealing the whole picture. She saw rope. To the right, just against the wall, was a soft glow. A light switch, covered in fluorescent paint. She flicked it on and blinked hard against the glare.

In the center of the room, suspended from the ceiling, was a non-stick skillet. Attached by a chain to a rope, which ran through a loop at the ceiling, and led down to the floor. Ten feet in the air, and nothing to stand on to reach it.

Underneath the skillet was a meat cleaver.

Nova inched closer. The rope was thick. She imaged it mooring a battleship. The puzzle seemed simple enough—use the cleaver to hack at the rope but don't let the pan hit the floor. The floor was concrete and, if the pan dented, it would be useless. So she picked up the blade with one hand, gripped the rope with the other, and swung.

The cleaver bounced off. She looked at the edge. It was torn to shit, like someone had spent the afternoon smacking it against the floor. It still had a touch of sharpness toward the handle, so she focused on that, swinging that bare two inches of sharp space again and again at the rope, which began to fray, a strand at a time.

She had worked up a sweat by the time she made it halfway through, glancing over her shoulder every couple of swings to make sure she was still alone.

When there were only a few strands left, she tightened her grip. And when the rope snapped, she held tight, lowered the pan slowly, until she could just reach it. She placed the cleaver down so as not to make any noise, and reached up to claim her prize.

Something slammed into her back, throwing her forward. She went down in a heap, her forehead scraping hard against the floor. She rolled over and found Cedar standing over her, holding the butcher's knife, his fist clenched around it.

At this distance it didn't even need to be sharp.

He was smiling. It was a smile she'd seen twice and never wanted to see again.

"You heard the man about no..."

Before he could finish she brought her foot up and nailed him in the balls. He staggered a bit, then folded into himself, dropping to his knees.

Then she stood and swung the pan at the hand holding the knife. The knife fell to the floor and she swung the pan again, catching him on the chin. As he was falling back, she jetted out of the room, the Butcher's voice coming from everywhere and nowhere: "A half hour remaining. Better get a move-on. And it looks like Chef Cedar learned a hard lesson—don't mess with Chef Nova."

There was enough light in the hallway now she didn't need the flashlight, so she ran for the staircase, checking the pan to make sure she hadn't dented it on Cedar's face. She swiped her hand across her forehead, the scrape burning, her palm covered with blood. She wiped it on her chef's coat and made her way up the two flights to the room where she'd hidden the eggs.

She found Axel sitting on the desk.

His eyes dropped to the pan and he smiled. He hopped off the desk and took a few steps toward Nova. She backed into the hallway, wondering if she should swing at him, too. But given his size, a shot from the pan might just make him angry.

The anger bubbled in Nova's stomach, and she was surprised at what the fight-or-flight response was dredging up. It made her want to fight. Because he was coming closer and reaching for the pan like she had retrieved it just for him.

She raised it to swing, and just as he was about to reach out, there was a garbled yell from the end of the hallway. Cedar was charging at them. Nova stepped back, into an open room, holding the pan like a bat, ready to destroy it if it meant saving herself.

"Now it's getting interesting," The Butcher's voice echoed through the hallway.

Nova expected Cedar to come storming in after her, but there was a massive crash outside the door, and she saw that Axel had engaged him, not knowing he was probably after her and not the pan.

Nova went for her stash of supplies and found they were still there—Axel was smart enough to wait but not smart enough to search. She pulled up the hem of her chef's coat to form a pocket, loaded everything into it, and stepped back into the hallway.

"Chef Cedar does not mess around either, does he?" The Butcher asked. "Maybe you were all too quick to judge him. But like I said, his origin story is interesting. He found his love for cooking in his last place of residence—San Quentin prison, where he spent a decade of his life. Of course cooking would come naturally to someone possessing his…skill with a knife. Maybe someone should ask him."

Nova watched as Cedar swung a discarded two-by-four in wide arcs as Axel kept a safe distance, his hands up, waiting for a moment to dive. Neither of them paid attention to Nova.

She ran for the staircase, and then the kitchen, which she found to be empty. She laid everything out, a rough mis-en-place next to the stove. She put her hands flat on the stainless steel and took three breaths.

Concentrate. Focus. French omelet.

She heard footsteps behind her, turned to find Stuart. He looked at her, then at the supplies on the counter, then at the wound on her forehead. "You okay?" he asked.

She nodded. "Yeah."

A lie. Her head was throbbing. He came around the kitchen island and put down his own stash: nearly identical, but a carbon steel pan with an okay but not great season, and one egg instead of her three.

He laughed. "Won't be much of an omelet with one egg, I guess, but at least it's something."

She knew what he was asking. If he could have one of hers. You could bang out a decent French omelet with two eggs. Three were better.

She thought about it. Asked, "Did you really steal tips?"

"My mother was sick," he said. "Cancer. No insurance. It was a horrible decision but I would do it again if I had to."

He sounded sincere. Enough Nova felt a little tug at her heart. She sighed. Picked up one of the eggs and handed it to him. He shook it in the air. "Thank you."

"Don't even know why I'm helping you," she said.

It was a lie. She did. It was penance. But she didn't want to say it.

The way things were going, The Butcher would say it soon enough.

They got to work, falling into the dance of the chef, practically gliding around the kitchen, movements practiced and precise. She found a discarded pan, in which she could crack and scramble the eggs. Put her cooking pan over a flame, let it get to where she could just hold the back of her finger against the dark surface.

"Five minutes to go," The Butcher said.

Nova tossed a pat of butter into the pan and let it foam. Before it could brown, she dropped a pinch of salt into the beaten eggs and poured the mixture into the pan, giving it a little swirl with a spatula and letting it set, taking the pan on and off the flame to control the heat.

As the edges began to firm, she realized she didn't have a plate.

"Fuck," she said, looking around frantically. She had to get it off the pan.

Stuart appeared with a clean white plate, set it next to her.

"Thank you," she said as she lifted the pan and gave it a tap on the handle to roll over the edge of the omelet.

"Happy to," Stuart said, his back to her, focusing on his own work.

Nova plated, took the butter, and ran it over the top of the omelet, then sprinkled on some more chives, and a touch more salt. She realized she had forgotten the white pepper, but too late for that now. Should have gone into the scramble. She looked at the plate, hated that there wasn't enough egg for her to take a test bite, but it looked as close as she was going to get, given the circumstances.

She glanced at Stuart's plate. His omelet was a little haphazard and he was shaking his head. He caught her eye. "Wasn't the best choice of pan."

"You work with what you got."

"One minute, chefs," The Butcher said. "And I'm hungry."

Nova grabbed her plate, cradling it as she walked toward the cafeteria. She turned to find Stuart advancing on her, that look in his eyes, the *no rules* look, and he froze like he'd been caught. What was he thinking? Knock the plate out of her hands?

Nova walked sidestep, keeping one eye on him, and the other on the cafeteria, where she found the bolted-down seats had been replaced by a large hole in the floor. In front of the hole were four X's marked in red tape. She stood on one and Stuart stood on another, holding their plates. Nova held hers extra tight.

She heard a loud crash, and Cedar and Axel stumbled in. Axel held a plate, smiling. He turned and pushed Cedar onto the floor, then ran to join the others.

A horn blared, so loud Nova's shoulders bunched and she almost dropped her plate. The lighting in the room increased. There was a great whirring sound, and from the hole in the center of the room, a platform rose.

On the platform was a simple wooden table, holding a glass of water, a fork, and a knife. Seated at the table was The Butcher. The casting director. She recognized the underfed frame. How he was wearing a carefully-tailored plum suit, with a tie and shirt that clashed horribly and yet somehow worked together.

And he was still wearing the mask.

She took a breath—at least they'd be done soon.

When the platform was in place, Cedar took his spot on the empty X. But before The Butcher could speak, he said, "That's *my* dish. Axel stole it."

Axel shrugged. "Not true."

The Butcher nodded, then looked at Cedar. "You heard what I said. No rules. You're welcome to stay, in case your opponents made such grave mistakes I decide you're the winner by default."

Cedar took an angry breath and folded his hands behind his back. The Butcher nodded to the others. "You three, bring your dishes forward."

They put their plates down on the table and stepped back on their X's. It seemed silly. Nova considered asking him what he thought he was doing, what kind of show this was, if it had even been picked up by a network yet, but every time she tried, she thought: *walk-in cooler, new bathrooms, vacation.*

The Butcher brought Stuart's plate forward, slid his mask up slightly so he could reach his fork to his mouth. He chewed on the omelet and said, "Presentation is lacking and it cooked a few seconds too long. You needed a better pan and should probably have beaten the eggs a little more, too."

Then Axel's. "Needs more salt. Needs salt, period. And it's completely overcooked."

Finally, Nova's. He took a bite, chewed, swallowed, and went back for a second. Nova's heart swelled. "Now *this* is an omelet. Could have done with some pepper, but certainly the most successful dish of the three."

Nova's face burned. She could feel the other three chefs looking at her. She did not care. This was the only moment that ever mattered: success on the plate.

The Butcher sat back in his chair and looked at the four contestants. "What to do, what to do. The real competition is between Nova and Stuart." He turned to Cedar and Axel. "And as for you two..."

"I made that dish," Cedar said. "At least I finished *something,* even if it wasn't ideal."

"Not true," said Axel.

The Butcher nodded. "Cedar, you cooked a subpar dish. A blind man unfamiliar with the concept of eggs could have produced a better omelet than that. And you..." he said to Axel. "There are cameras everywhere. I see everything. Why are you lying to me? Of course I know who cooked it."

Axel took a deep breath, like he was going to say something, but then he stopped, looked forward. The Butcher nodded, like they were in silent conversation.

"Well," The Butcher finally said. "I have one chef who produced a subpar dish and one chef who tried to claim it as their own. I think we know what this means..."

There was a sharp *thwack*, and Nova turned to see Cedar had laid a hard sucker-punch across Axel's chin. Axel went down hard, the back of his head smacking against the floor. Cedar shook out his fist, grimacing from the impact of the blow.

The Butcher froze.

"You said it yourself." Cedar opened and closed his fingers, looking at his hand, not at anyone else. "No rules."

"I was going to propose a sudden death cook-off between you two, just for fun, but that works, too," The Butcher said.

Axel writhed on the floor, groaning, holding his head. His eyes looked screwy, like he was drunk. Nova figured he probably had a concussion. "Can we get someone to help him?" Nova asked. "He's hurt."

The Butcher waved his hand. "He'll be attended to."

"When?"

"After I make my decision," he said. "Which, now I've got sudden-death stuck in my head, so...I'm not going to declare a winner just yet. Chef Nova, Chef Stuart, you both did very fine jobs given the conditions, so I'm giving you one last chance. As for you…" He turned to Chef Cedar. "Your omelet was horrible and you should be ashamed of yourself. You are eliminated."

Nova rolled her eyes. She wanted to be done with this. She wanted to go home. She was beginning to doubt this was even a serious production. Where was the crew?

"C'mon, can we stop this for a second and help him?" she asked, gesturing to Axel, writhing on the floor.

The Butcher sighed. He dropped the theatrics, muttered to himself. "Don't know why you care. Ruining my goddamn run of show here. But fine, fine, whatever." As he spoke he reached down to the cuff of his pants, fiddled with it a bit, and brought up a small, compact handgun. Boxy and black, it looked almost like a toy.

Nova's heart leapt into her throat and tried to push itself out her mouth.

"What the fuck, man?" Cedar asked.

"Whoa, whoa, whoa," Stuart said, putting his hands up in a *calm down* gesture.

Nova's initial burst of shock and fear quickly transformed into anger and she wanted to refuse again, but the muzzle of the gun was closer to her than it was to the other two, and "not getting shot" ranked pretty high on her list of to-dos.

"Sudden death," The Butcher said. "I want vanilla ice cream. A good vanilla ice cream is like nothing else on this earth." He gestured with the gun, toward another end of the cafeteria. "I would like you to proceed down that hallway. At the end of the hallway, you'll find a set of double doors. There, you'll find everything you need."

"So this round we don't have to go hunting for ingredients?" Nova asked.

"I have something else planned," The Butcher said, which made the hair on Nova's neck raise straight up.

"Now…would you kindly slice and dice!"

Nova and Stuart exchanged nervous glances, then left Cedar and Axel, made their way down the hallway in silence. Nova kept wanting to say something but found there was nothing to say.

The double doors led into a room that, given the way the rest of the day had gone, appeared almost like a mirage.

It was another kitchen, but this one was immaculate. Bowls, a stove, and two heavy-duty restaurant style ice cream machines. Two fridges, and when Stuart walked over and popped one open, it was full of cream and eggs.

"Thank god," he said.

"This is weird though, right?" Nova asked. "If this was supposed to be one round, why did he have this set up? He knew there'd be some element of sudden death."

"What does that mean?" Stuart asked.

"I have no idea, I just wonder what kind of game he's…"

She was cut off by a sharp clicking sound behind them.

They turned to find a brown pitbull with a wide jaw and thick muscles walking toward them across the linoleum floor. Nova hoped the dog might be friendly, but it bared down and let out a low, rumbling growl, the sound of it echoing off the polished surfaces of the kitchen.

Nova and Stuart both froze.

"What do we do?" Stuart asked. "Play dead? Not make eye contact?"

"I read somewhere that you're supposed to stand up tall and yell."

"That's bears. I think?"

The dog barked. Once, twice. Nova's bladder fluttered. Her knees felt weak. The dog looked like a tree stump on legs.

"We could *Jurassic Park* him," Stuart said.

"What?"

"The raptors, in the kitchen. There's a walk-in on the far end of the room."

"We have to get past the dog first."

The dog barked again, inching forward on the floor now.

"You go left," he said. "I go right. First one to the cooler wins."

"Sucks to be runner up."

"Yes, it does," Stuart said. "Now…go!"

Nova lunged to the side, nearly stumbled, found her feet. The dog took off, going for Stuart instead of her. She ran for the walk-in cooler, got the door open. Stuart yelled out. She turned to find him on the floor, left forearm up to protect his face, the dog's jaws clamped hard around it. The dog jerked so hard Stuart was being pulled back and forth across the floor. Nova turned to a shelf, found a stone mortar and pestle. She picked up the pestle and threw it at the dog, hitting it in the side. It loosened its grip enough for Stuart to kick away from it.

Then the dog turned its attention to her.

Another flutter. Heart and bladder and probably some other organs. She inched her way toward the entrance to the cooler, and the dog charged, and she held her breath, forced herself to stand until the last possible second, the dog's nails *click click clicking* on the floor as it ran.

It launched itself into the air and she dropped to the floor.

The dog hit the far end of the cooler and Nova reached up to close the door but the angle was bad and she stumbled, so by the time she got to her feet to close the door, the dog was charging again.

She got the door closed as the dog slammed into it, the door popping out an inch, so she threw her back against it and slid down to the floor. The dog slammed into the door again, pushing Nova a few inches forward on the linoleum.

Stuart appeared over her, blood dripping from his forearm. He threw his shoulder into the door, grabbed the pin lock, dropped it into place, then fell on the floor next to Nova. The dog barked inside the cooler and continued slamming at the door. But now it didn't budge and, for a moment, they could breathe.

"You okay?" Nova asked.

Stuart held up his arm, red welling up out of the holes in his skin. "Not really."

"Any chance we'll get a medic now?"

"Suck it up," The Butcher said over the speakers. "Twenty minutes to go."

Stuart stood, reached his hand down to Nova and pulled her up. She rooted around the kitchen until she found some tea towels, helped Stuart rinse his arm in the sink and wrapped it up. The bites were deep but once it was clean, the whole thing didn't look so bad.

"This can't be legal, no matter what we signed," Nova whispered, glancing at the cameras.

Stuart winced as he cinched the tea towels around his arm, little dots of red appearing on the fabric. "Let's just finish it, okay? No sabotage? Let the best cook win?"

He reached his hand out.

Nova eyed it.

No rules.

She didn't know him. He stole from his staff. Could she trust him?

Who said she had to?

The dog barked again and she thought about the gun so she shook his hand.

"Let's get to work," she said.

They did, picking through the kitchen for ingredients, setting up for prep. Nova's heart sang when she found the Mexican vanilla beans—her favorite—and she made sure to grab the salt in addition to sugar. She even found a bottle of cheap scotch, which, while it wasn't something she'd drink on its own, a dash of it in the ice cream base—not enough to lower the melting point, but enough that you got a whiff of the smoke—would add a great layer.

As she was tempering whisked eggs into a pot of hot cream, The Butcher's voice rang out. "Now, Chef Nova, don't think I forgot about you. Chef Stuart, did you know how Chef Nova wound up here today?"

Nova closed her eyes.

"She was a last minute addition," said The Butcher. "In fact, we rejected her when she first applied. But we didn't reject her business partner, Chef Martiza, who was *supposed* to be here. But Maritza was scalded by a pot of boiling oil that Chef Nova was carrying. Chef Nova, where exactly were you taking that oil?"

The image flashed through Nova's head. The one she kept trying to forget. Martiza's eyes squeezed shut, face twisted in pain. Elbow up, palm out, the olive skin of her forearm turning a furious pink, and then bubbling...

Nova looked up at Stuart, who was staring at her.

"It was an accident," Nova said.

Stuart kept staring so she said it again.

"An accident."

She wasn't sure if he believed her. She wasn't sure if he needed to. She turned her attention to the ice cream base, wondering if this was it, if this was when Stuart would turn on her. If he would take it as permission, because men could find permission in the tiniest of places. If she should try to explain how it was a busy night and there was a lot going on in the kitchen, and no, it had nothing to do with the fact that Martiza had gotten the callback and she hadn't, and it didn't matter that Martiza would have sprung for the cooler and the bathrooms but not the vacation.

It wasn't that.

"Sugar?" Stuart asked.

Nova looked at the containers in front of her. Two plastic containers, both filled with white powder. One red, one blue. She couldn't remember which was which, even though she'd tasted them a few minutes ago. She opened the container with the red top and dipped her pinky in and the salt stung her tongue.

"Yeah," she said, and she pushed the container with the red top toward him.

Without looking, without measuring, he poured some into his base. She watched as he whisked hard in the metal pan over the double-boiler, then brought it to the ice cream machine. She expected him to taste it, to turn and look at her with confusion and fury because they'd just shaken hands, but he didn't.

And that was on him. A good chef tasted as they went.

As he dumped the mixture into the machine, she finished hers, dipped a spoon in and tasted—perfect—and poured it into the machine next to his.

"Just a few minutes to go," The Butcher said. "And I've got one more surprise."

They waited, watched, not wanting the ice cream to churn too long into butter. Nova thought about the last time she went on a vacation. Six years ago. And it was to Detroit, for a wedding. She stayed an extra couple of days to check out some restaurants, but that barely counted.

She wanted a beach. She wanted sun. She wanted to forget this place. Six years. Hadn't she earned it?

The ice cream finished. They dosed it into the bowls they'd chilled in the fridge, to keep the dessert from melting too quickly.

Nova watched as Stuart left a large dollop dangling from the machine. He looked at it like he wanted to try it, but didn't.

He saw her looking at him looking at the ice cream and shrugged. "Lactose intolerant. But I've made this a million times. You ready?"

She nodded, suddenly not feeling so clever. The dog barked as they marched back to the cafeteria. The Butcher's table was now empty. They placed the bowls down and stood on the red X's and waited. There was a sound from the other end of the room, and then footsteps.

The Butcher was holding his gun out in front of him. He was flanked by two people. As they got closer, Nova felt herself sinking into the floor.

Maritza. Wild black hair cascading around her, olive skin dim in the light, the sleeve ripped off her blouse, her arm wrapped in heavy layers of gauze. She was supposed to be in the hospital another week. Next to her was a stout Mexican man with a thick moustache staring bullets at Stuart. Nova turned and saw Stuart's jaw hanging open.

The Butcher stopped in front of the table and gestured for his companions to sit. They did, looking at the gun the same way Nova and Stuart looked at the dog. The Butcher stood behind them and said, "Introductions are in order. Chef Stuart, please meet Chef Maritza, who Chef Nova…" he put his hands in the air and did exaggerated air quotes, "'accidentally' burned in the kitchen. And, Chef Nova, please meet Eduardo, who led the class-action suit against Chef Stuart."

"What the hell is this?" Stuart asked.

"This makes it more fun. For me. Not for you." The Butcher gestured toward the bowls. "I didn't tell you to prepare two, because I wanted to keep this a surprise, so, Eduardo, Martiza, you'll have to share. I know which is which, but I won't tell you. I'm afraid you might be…biased."

The two of them turned to The Butcher, wondering if they should really be eating ice cream right now. The Butcher raised the gun and Eduardo reached forward. He pulled Nova's bowl toward them. He took a spoonful, tasted. Maritza did the same. Nothing on their faces betrayed their reaction.

"What do you think?" The Butcher asked.

Neither of them answered, so he prodded Eduardo in the back with the gun. "Good, good," he said, putting his hands up. "Really good, actually."

"Yeah," Martiza said. "Good."

"Not the most eloquent." He picked up the bowl and slid a spoonful under his mask. "Now this is lovely. A little scotch and salt really complement the Mexican vanilla beans, which I generally find to be a bit much, but not here. Very nice. Next."

Eduardo took the second bowl, stuck the spoon in his mouth and grimaced. Martiza followed. "Tastes like salt," Eduardo said.

The Butcher put his hand on the bowl, then pushed it away. "I'm not even going to try it. I saw what you did, Nova. Very smart."

Stuart took in a sharp breath of air. Nova looked at him. He was shaking his head at her, his eyes wet with tears. "I didn't…I thought…we shook on it."

"It was a mistake," Nova said.

"No, it wasn't," said The Butcher.

Nova's shoulders fell. She bowed her head. Closed her eyes. Stuart let out a huff of air, like: *I should have known better.*

"Sounds about right," Maritza said, her voice sharp. "Though I guess given how things played out, maybe I should thank you. Maybe ask me again when my pain meds wear off."

Nova studied the floor in front of her, the black and white linoleum tiles, the way they were worn down, the way she was worn down, the way she'd fought and clawed her way from dishwasher to line chef to owning her own restaurant, to the things she fought and suffered along the way, and the feeling that she had to do whatever it took to survive, and how maybe, just maybe, that feeling had poisoned her.

She wanted to say this to Maritza, to Stuart, even to The Butcher, but the words got jumbled on the way to her mouth.

"I broke my leg."

Eduardo. He was looking at Stuart.

"I took some construction jobs because I couldn't afford to feed my family," he said. "I fell off a ladder and broke my leg. That happened because you took money out of my pocket."

"My mother…"

"Don't you dare say that again," Eduardo said, his face twisting in rage. He stood from his chair, knocking it back, and advanced on Stuart. Nova turned to The Butcher, like he might stop it, but instead he watched as they slammed into each other, and it almost seemed like he was smiling under the mask.

Then he reached into his pocket and pulled out the meat cleaver Nova had used to free the pan in the basement. He placed it next to Martiza and said, "I bet you have some feelings to work out, too."

"What the hell kind of show is this?" Nova asked.

"Oh, this isn't a show," The Butcher said. "It's more of a personal art project. Basically, I guess you could say I like to play with my food."

Nova's heart paused in her chest but no one else seemed to have heard him. Eduardo and Stuart were grappling on the floor and Maritza was sliding the cleaver off the table, testing the weight and the swing of it.

"Remember," The Butcher said. "There are *no* rules."

HAVE YOU EATEN?

FREDERICK PLACED THE three plastic trays balanced on his arms atop the green cafeteria-style table. He sat, and after three hours of wandering through Chinatown, and another half hour queuing up at three different food stalls, it felt good to sit.

It was just after the dinner rush and most of the other tables in the Hong Lim Food Centre were empty, though some of the seats were occupied by tissue packets or umbrellas. In one particularly bold choice, a pocketbook. It was an unspoken rule of Singapore's food markets—leaving an item behind was a way to call dibs on a seat while you were waiting in line.

A good number of the stalls were closed, their gray metal gates pulled down, but the three he wanted to visit had been open, and Frederick counted himself lucky.

The crowd had whittled to office-workers catching a bite on the way home and a few older folks socializing amidst the closing.

Stall owners sprayed out their cookware, thick streams of opaque water running toward the drains in the concrete floor. A stooped old man in a stained white shirt crept between the tables, pushing a broom across the floor, the sound of it like a metronome: *swish swish swish.*

It was hot for February, or at least, hot for what Frederick thought of February—the sun down and still pushing ninety, humidity somewhere around three thousand percent. He breathed in the smell of fryer oil and fish and spices he didn't know the name for.

He didn't know if he'd ever be back to Singapore, especially not after tonight, and he wanted to remember it.

That feeling of sitting in a slowly boiling pot of soup, and what a way to go.

"Well, well, well."

Frederick looked up and found Mateo, standing on the other side of the table, looming, his black pants wrinkled, white shirt soaked with sweat, the sleeves rolled up past his elbows, showing the hint of a tattoo on his left arm, the colors muddy, the shape vaguely military. The look on Mateo's face he couldn't discern. It was a look that carried a lot of years.

"Have you eaten?" Frederick asked, gesturing to the empty stool across from him.

"That's what you have to say?" Mateo asked, his face narrowing into a sharp smirk. "After all this time?"

"Join me."

Mateo looked around, at the emptying confines of the outdoor food market, then down into the courtyard, where a throng of people moved back and forth. Across the way, golden light spilled out from under a red awning.

"Please," Frederick said, trying to the keep the desperation out of his voice. He didn't want to give Mateo the satisfaction, but he didn't want the food to go to waste, either.

Mateo lowered himself on the stool like it might explode. He placed his forearms on the table, fists clenched, shoulders bunched. Waiting for something.

"It's a standard form of greeting in Singapore," Frederick said.

"What is?"

"Have you eaten."

"Is it now?"

Frederick nodded and picked up a pair of dinged silverware, focused on the traffic-cone-orange tray in front of him, the plate of char kway teow, and tried to get every little piece of the dish into one bite: rice noodles and Chinese sausage and blood cockles. There were crisp cubes of pork lard, too, but he couldn't fit one on his fork, so he vowed to come back. "What do you know about Singapore?"

"Enough."

"They take their food very seriously here." Frederick gestured around the market with his fork. "Years ago, it used to be all street food. Like you'd see in Bangkok. But it was getting to be too much. Traffic, sanitary issues. So the government moved them all into these centers. This is an expensive town, but, man, you come to these hawker markets." He shoved the fork into his mouth, chewed, the fat and salt melting. He swallowed and said, "All this food was less than twenty sing."

Mateo nodded toward the plate. "What is that?"

"Char kway teow. And this…" He gestured to the second tray, bright lime-green, holding a plate with an omelet that looked like it had been dropped on the floor. "Carrot cake. There's no carrot in it. Those white chunks are steamed rice flour and white radish. These are both pretty signature dishes. But this…" He put his hand on the third and final tray, deep regal-blue. "Hainanese chicken rice. Pretty much just boiled chicken, served with a sauce, and then the rice is cooked in ginger and chicken fat." Frederick looked up at Mateo and smiled. "There's a place not too far from here that Bourdain endorsed, so everyone goes to that one, but my sources tell me this is better."

"Boiled chicken?"

"Don't knock it until you've tried it."

"I'll pass."

Frederick tapped the green tray. "Extra set of silverware."

"How do I know it's safe?"

"The food stalls are clean," Frederick said. "They're manic about it."

"You know what I mean."

"Do you think that little of me?"

"Shouldn't I?"

Frederick sighed. He stabbed a chunk of the carrot cake and chewed on it, the salt from the dark soy almost blowing out his palate, so he took a sip of water before he took a slice of chicken, bathed in the brown sauce with a little bit of the rice. He chewed slowly, comparing it in his mind to Tian Tian, Bourdain's pick. He had to concede—Tian Tian was superior. Still, it was a hell of a lot better than lukewarm boiled chicken had any right to be.

"Satisfied?" Frederick asked.

Frederick had hoped the gesture might soften Mateo a little, but the man's face remained cast in concrete.

"After all we've been through, it feels perverse to share a meal with you," Mateo said.

Frederick shrugged, leaned over the char kway teow, went hunting for a cube of lard. "You know why I like food?"

Silence. Frederick didn't look up because he knew exactly the kind of look he was getting, and he didn't want to get it. He speared a chunk of lard and a fat blood cockle, popped them in his mouth, chewed slowly. When he was done, he looked up at Mateo, who was scanning the market again, like he was looking for someone who was running late.

"The reason I like food is because it's the one thing we all have in common."

Mateo raised a reluctant eyebrow. "How is that?"

"Think about it." He took a few chews of carrot cake, followed by another sip of the water. "Every culture has its own cuisine. Every city has its signature dish. You could say Hainanese chicken rice is the signature dish of Singapore and, I don't know...pizza is the signature dish of New York. Or moqueca—that's a fish stew—is the signature dish of Brazil. Those three dishes lined up side-by-side couldn't be more different, right? So what do they have in common?"

Frederick asked, like he was going to get an answer, but all he got was another eyebrow, which filled his stomach with an empty space. Even after all these years, he didn't think the gulf between him and Mateo had grown this wide, but then again, the view was probably different from the other side of the table.

"The thing they all have in common is the passion," he said. "Every New Yorker has their favorite pizza place. Everyone in Singapore has their favorite stall, or their favorite dish that best represents their country. And every country has traditions related to food and hospitality." He scooped a big heap of rice, fragrant with ginger and chicken fat, chewed it quickly. "Every person alive can probably name a dish they ate in their childhood that meant something to them. Something that sparks a memory. Do you get where I'm going?"

The eyebrow was still there, arched over Mateo's eye, but

something in his face cooled. Or maybe it melted in the heat. Mateo risked a look over his shoulder, at the *swish swish swish* sound, saw the man pushing the broom, who worked oblivious to the crowds around him.

"Tell me," Frederick said. "What food was special to you? In your childhood."

Mateo breathed in deeply through his nose, then back out, the sound of it whistling.

"C'mon," Frederick said. "I'm not saying you owe me, but after all this time..." He looked around, felt the condensation of the air on his skin. "This is the end of the road, I imagine. So why not indulge me?"

"My grandmother's pancakes."

Mateo said it quickly, and after the words left his mouth, there was a look of almost-surprise on his face, like he had meant to think it, but it just spilled out.

"And what made them special?" Frederick asked.

Mateo glanced at the food. He was getting hungry. Frederick wanted to nudge the green tray with the carrot cake a little closer, but was afraid a stray movement might scare the man off, like a stray cat that knew it was hungry but didn't know how to trust.

"They were just pancakes," Mateo said. "They came out of a box. But my grandmother put blueberries in them. Fresh ones she picked at this farm near where we grew up." His eyes got softer, his voice trailing. "There was something special about the way she made them. When I visit home, I get the same brand, same blueberries. But they don't taste the same."

Frederick took the opportunity of the nostalgic haze to push the tray a few inches closer to Mateo, who was lost enough in the memory to not really notice.

"I believe strongly in the alchemy of place," Frederick said.

"There are certain foods you really need to eat in their region of birth. It's like how a pizza place will say it ships its water and ingredients from New York. But it's still not the same as New York pizza. You know what I mean?"

Mateo's lip curled a little on the end. "You remember Osaka?"

Frederick nodded. "Great takoyaki. Great okonomiyaki."

"Yeah, I don't get down so much with the foodie stuff," he said. "But one day, I was just really in the mood for a bagel. And I walked by this café, said it had New York style bagels, and my stomach..." He laughed a little under his breath. "My stomach did a flip. I thought, even if it's close, I'll be happy."

"Let me guess," Frederick said. "This story doesn't have a happy ending."

"No, it does not. Thing tasted like Styrofoam."

"They can't all be winners," Frederick said. "Sometimes for fun I'll get something I know isn't a regional specialty, just to see how they fucked it up. This one time...remember London?"

Mateo's face reverted back to concrete. "I remember London."

Frederick cursed himself for erasing his progress. "Sorry. Okay. But...I was at this pub one night, and they had nachos on the menu, and I thought, in the land of boiled food, I wonder what nachos looked like. So I ordered them, and you know what came out?"

Silence.

"Doritos."

That earned a laugh. "No shit?"

"No shit," Frederick said. "There was some salsa and some melted cheese blend thing and then god damn Doritos."

"Did you eat it?"

Frederick laughed, shrugged. "I was raised that it wasn't polite to leave an empty plate. Probably why my cholesterol is so high."

"Yeah, well, join the club."

Mateo looked around one more time, less like he was looking for someone, and more like he was afraid someone might see him. Then he reached toward the green tray and picked up a fork, stabbed a slice of the chicken and popped it in his mouth, avoiding eye contact, chewing quickly, but halfway through paused and looked up at Frederick. He swallowed what was in his mouth and said, "That's pretty good."

"Try it with the rice," Frederick said. "And a little bit of that red sauce. It's spicy."

Mateo went in for a more complete bite and Frederick speared some chunks of carrot cake and enjoyed the moment, fleeting as it was. This wasn't his last meal, not if he didn't want it to be, but almost certainly it was his last meal out in the world, his last one breathing fresh air, his last one where any kind of thought or passion went into the dish, so he made sure to savor each individual chew.

"So how'd you find me?" Frederick asked.

Mateo finished the helping of chicken rice and went for the kway teow, spearing a few rice noodles and a chunk of sausage. "A hunch, mostly."

"C'mon," Frederick said. "Give me a little more than that."

"San Francisco, last year," Mateo said. "We found the apartment you used. We went through the building's trash, found the bag for that unit, and then the wrapper for Huitlacoche."

"That was a damn good burrito," Frederick said. "And I now regret not taking my trash with me when I left town. But that couldn't be it. That's not enough to go on. I paid in cash. They didn't have a camera."

"Dublin, two years ago, you used a burner phone, which we found, and we were able to pull some location data," Mateo said. "Two hits at a pub popular for its full Irish breakfast."

Frederick was fascinated, almost enough to forget his food for a moment. Then he looked down at the plates, at the rapidly dwindling portions, and realized he didn't have much longer. He took some more kway teow.

"Three years ago, Japan," Mateo said, going for a bite of the carrot cake. "Sukiyabashi Jiro. Tough to score reservations."

"I worked three jobs in Tokyo before I was able to get a seat," Frederick said.

"We had a much looser description of you back then," Mateo said. "But we had a witness put someone we thought might be you eating there, the night of."

"And that's how you found me?" Frederick asked. "I mean, in this line of work, you expect to be caught, or worse eventually, but a reservation? A breakfast? A wrapper?"

"Food Ventures."

The bulb went off. Frederick exhaled, bowed his head. A laugh built in the center of his chest and there was no use trying to keep it contained. He let it spill out. "Food Ventures."

Mateo nodded. "I can't even take, credit. We had a few other little pieces, too, other places you ate, so we knew you were a foodie. Got a kid in our office, he's a foodie, too. So I asked him to take a look at all the evidence. Like I said, a hunch. I didn't think anything would come of it. But he put it together. All the places we had you visiting were places recommended by this one website."

Frederick wanted to clap his hands. He wanted to cry. He wanted to scream. He wanted to dance. Undone by a food blog. The blog he visited whenever he was in a new city, because Food Ventures was dogged and reliable in its recommendations.

It was so pedestrian.

"We knew you were doing a job in Singapore," Mateo said. "So we looked up Singapore, found they did a list on the food centers.

We've got men covering a half-dozen more of these. But Hong Lim had the most recommended food stalls, so, again." He shrugged. "A hunch."

"Well," Frederick said. "I'm impressed."

"Are you?"

"Of course I am." He piled together a big spoonful of chicken and rice, saving the best bites for last, so he could end the plate on the highest note possible. "Kind of proud, actually. How long we been at this now?"

"Going on fourteen years. I figure I had another six months before they pulled me off you entirely."

"For what it's worth, I'm glad it was you who caught me."

"That seems like a silly thing to say."

Frederick swallowed. "I'm serious. You think I didn't notice you, a few steps behind me the past couple of years? Look, I get it. We're playing for opposite sides, and if the universe is a just place, which I like to believe it is, you're the one who's going to come out on top. That's how these stories are supposed to end. So…I know this sounds ridiculous. Maybe it is. I never knew how I'd react if I got caught and I guess this is it. I'm just…glad it was you, and glad we got to share a meal before it went down."

Mateo opened his mouth, to say something, to argue or refute, certainly not to agree, but then he closed his mouth, and picked up the fork, and took another bite of the carrot cake.

"This is really good," he said.

"There's this place in Little India, not too far from here, supposed to do an amazing fish head curry," Frederick said. "I'd ask if we could swing by there before you put the cuffs on officially, but I suspect that's not in the cards."

"No, that's not in the cards."

Frederick scooped up the last of the kway teow, his heart going a little wobbly, time slowing down for that bite. Savoring the thick skin of the sausage, the slippery texture of the rice noodles. "So what happens now?"

"That's up to you," he said. "You want to make it easy, we both get to go to bed early tonight. You want to make it hard, you'll be dead before you leave that seat. There are two dozen men surrounding this place and two snipers with their eyes on you. My guys, plus the locals. And you know Singapore. The government put more people to death last year than there were murders in the street. They don't fuck around."

"No, they do not," Frederick said, taking another bite of carrot cake. Two bites left, maybe. Three if he stretched it out.

He considered it. Stretching it out. What that would look like.

A quick death, or a long life in a jail cell. Prison food was Z-grade meat and overcooked grains and no salt. Stale or moldy bread and coffee like it'd been filtered through a sock. Not that death sounded better, but he wasn't excited for it.

If you're creative, though, there was always another option.

And his appeared right on queue.

Swish swish swish.

What Mateo didn't know is that before he took this seat, Frederick stood in an obscured alcove for a few minutes, balancing his trays, waiting for this particular table to free up. Because this particular table was next to a tall metal receptacle, where diners could return their trays when they were done. It was laden with a rainbow of plastic trays, covered in plates and bowls of finished or mostly-finished meals.

"I guess this is it," Frederick said, holding Mateo's attention. "Like I said, I'm glad you caught me and I'm glad we could share a meal together. I may be a bastard, but I do like to adhere to some aspects of social decency."

Mateo's hand snaked behind him. Frederick figured he was going for his cuffs, so slowly, as if it were an afterthought, he reached up and very deliberately scratched the bridge of his nose.

The old man in the stained white shirt skidded on the floor and slammed into the receptacle, sending it to the ground in a deafening crash, plates smashing across the concrete floor, and as soon as Mateo turned to find the source of the commotion, Frederick was off the seat, moving low and fast through the maze of tables.

Mateo and his team made several mistakes.

The first was not filling the seats around Frederick with undercover agents so that he'd be boxed in. But given the high volume of civilians, it was probably deemed too dangerous. Anyway, Mateo seemed like the type who wanted to play cowboy.

The other mistake was not noticing Frederick had stopped to speak to the man with the broom, or noticing the exchange of the money, and the signal, Frederick demonstrating how he'd scratch his nose so that the man would know exactly when to push over the cart. A hundred sing well spent.

Hong Lim was like most of Singapore's Chinatown: a maze of concrete hallways and staircases linked to parking garages and shopping malls, the entire byzantine thing immensely complicated to navigate, which meant maybe, just maybe, he'd find a clear path, especially if he moved up, toward the roof, toward the top of the city, where escape seemed harder and therefore less important to cover.

Frederick didn't want a quick death and he didn't want a slow death in a cell, either. He would take his chances on a violent death, even if there was just a small chance he could avoid it all and make it out of here alive, because there was a great big world out there, and still a great many things he wanted to eat.

Acknowledgments

Thanks to the editors who published these stories: Todd Robinson, Otto Penzler, Ron Earl Phillips, David James Keaton, Joe Clifford, Eric Beetner, Steve Weddle, Ehsan Ehsani, Emily Schultz, and Brian Joseph Davis. Thanks to all the readers and fellow writers who encouraged my pursuit of this theme—far too many to name. As always, thanks to my wife for her eternal patience and support. Thanks to my grandmother and my dad (as well as his fellow members of the FDNY) for instilling in me the value of a good meal. And finally, to my publisher, Jason Pinter, for letting me collect these, and my agent, Josh Getzler, for putting a bow on it.

About the author

Rob Hart is the author of the Ash McKenna series: *New Yorked*, *City of Rose*, *South Village*, *The Woman from Prague*, and *Potter's Field*. He also co-wrote *Scott Free* with James Patterson. His next novel, *The Warehouse*, will be released in 2019 and has been optioned for film by Ron Howard. He lives in New York City with his wife and daughter. Find more at www.robwhart.com and on Twitter at @robwhart.

CPSIA information can be obtained
at www.ICGtesting.com
Printed in the USA
LVHW042118151218
600557LV00003B/3/P

9 781947 993426